MORE MYSTERIES FROM THE
BERKLEY PUBLISHING GROUP ...

THE HERON CARVIC MISS SEETON MYSTERIES: Retired art teacher Miss Seeton steps in where Scotland Yard stumbles. "A most beguiling protagonist!" —*The New York Times*

by Heron Carvic
MISS SEETON SINGS
MISS SEETON DRAWS THE LINE
WITCH MISS SEETON
PICTURE MISS SEETON
ODDS ON MISS SEETON

by Hampton Charles
ADVANTAGE MISS SEETON
MISS SEETON AT THE HELM
MISS SEETON, BY APPOINTMENT

by Hamilton Crane
HANDS UP, MISS SEETON
MISS SEETON CRACKS THE CASE

MISS SEETON PAINTS THE TOWN
MISS SEETON BY MOONLIGHT
MISS SEETON ROCKS THE CRADLE
MISS SEETON GOES TO BAT
MISS SEETON PLANTS SUSPICION
STARRING MISS SEETON
MISS SEETON UNDERCOVER
MISS SEETON RULES
SOLD TO MISS SEETON
SWEET MISS SEETON
BONJOUR, MISS SEETON
MISS SEETON'S FINEST HOUR

KATE SHUGAK MYSTERIES: A former D.A. solves crimes in the far Alaska north ...

by Dana Stabenow
A COLD DAY FOR MURDER
DEAD IN THE WATER
A FATAL THAW
BREAKUP

A COLD-BLOODED BUSINESS
PLAY WITH FIRE
BLOOD WILL TELL
KILLING GROUNDS
HUNTER'S MOON

INSPECTOR BANKS MYSTERIES: Award-winning British detective fiction at its finest ... "Robinson's novels are habit-forming!"
—*West Coast Review of Books*

by Peter Robinson
THE HANGING VALLEY
WEDNESDAY'S CHILD
INNOCENT GRAVES

PAST REASON HATED
FINAL ACCOUNT
GALLOWS VIEW

CASS JAMESON MYSTERIES: Lawyer Cass Jameson seeks justice in the criminal courts of New York City in this highly acclaimed series ... "A witty, gritty heroine." —*New York Post*

by Carolyn Wheat
FRESH KILLS
MEAN STREAK
DEAD MAN'S THOUGHTS

WHERE NOBODY DIES
TROUBLED WATERS
SWORN TO DEFEND

THE SEA
HATH SPOKEN

❧❧

STEPHEN LEWIS

BERKLEY PRIME CRIME, NEW YORK

THE SEA HATH SPOKEN

A Berkley Prime Crime Book / published by arrangement with the author

PRINTING HISTORY
Berkley Prime Crime edition / January 2001

ISBN: 0-425-17802-1

Berkley Prime Crime books are published
by The Berkley Publishing Group,
a division of Penguin Putnam Inc.,
375 Hudson Street, New York, New York 10014.
The name BERKLEY PRIME CRIME and the BERKLEY PRIME CRIME
design are trademarks belonging to Penguin Putnam Inc.

PRINTED IN THE UNITED STATES OF AMERICA

10 9 8 7 6 5 4 3 2 1

ONE

❧❧❧

THE FIRST THING Massaquoit noticed as he approached Newbury harbor was the sound of the gulls. Ordinarily, he would expect to see two or three circling the waters at first light, searching for a school of minnows or other small fish. Perhaps one would give a hoarse cry to scare off a competitor for a crab washed up on the beach. But this morning, their cries rose as though in pitched battle. And as he made the last turn on the path leading to the harbor, he saw two or three dozen of them swooping down and landing in the eddying water where the waves broke against the shore. Wings beating and bills darting, they fought for the best position from which to feed on the body.

He broke into a trot and clapped his hands as he approached. One gull snatched something floating near the body and flew off with it in its mouth. Massaquoit watched the gull work its wings hard, lifting itself against the weight of what it carried in its beak. Massaquoit followed the bird's heavy flight until it dropped what it was carrying and rose into the sky. Several of the remaining gulls looked at Massaquoit and then flew off, but the others cawed at him as though he were just another, oversized bird looking to compete for breakfast. He stooped to pick up a four-foot-long piece of driftwood, which he swung over his head as he reached the water's edge. Two gulls, one on each side of the body, pecked at one another as the others flew away. With a final jab of its beak, one of the fighting gulls discouraged the other, and it took off. The one that remained stared stubbornly at Massaquoit and then at the dead man's flesh. Massaquoit swung the wood at the bird and caught it on the side of the head. It fell off the body and floated a few feet away. Out of the corner of his eye Massaquoit saw something down the beach. He turned in that direction. A figure darted into the water where the gull had dropped its burden, bent down, and then ran off.

Massaquoit knelt and grabbed the feet of the dead man. He pulled him onto dry land. The man was dressed as a sailor. The exposed skin of his face, neck, and hands had been shredded by the gulls' beaks. Massaquoit leaned over him, his cheek above what was left of the man's mouth. He waited until he was sure that there was no breath. The acrid smell of brine, along with the miasma of the decaying reeds in which he had been floating, rose from the corpse. He put his nose closer, and the sweet scent of rum greeted his nose.

He heard the sound of someone running toward

him, and he stood up. The constable, a middle-aged English, approached to within ten feet and stopped. He did not look anxious to come any closer.

"What have you there, Matthew?"

"A dead English," Massaquoit replied.

The constable was sweating more than he should in the mild morning air. He looked past Massaquoit, toward the hulking shape of *The Good Hope*, tied up at the dock.

"That is your mistress's ship," he said. "Do you think he fell in?"

"I do not know," Massaquoit replied. "The gulls were feeding on him when I arrived."

"Indeed, that is peculiar." The constable came close enough to see the mangled flesh of the corpse, brought his hand to his mouth, and turned away. Massaquoit sensed movement coming from the direction of the dock. A man wearing a coat adorned with brass buttons, followed by another whose gray hair and stolid bearing suggested someone used to responsibility, were trotting toward him. Behind them came an ordinary sailor. Massaquoit recognized the man in the coat as Martin Gregory, the master of the ship, which was owned by Catherine Williams. He guessed that the other man must be the ship's mate. The ship had docked several days before, and Massaquoit, sitting in front of his wigwam on a hot afternoon, had seen the captain accompany a young Englishman and Englishwoman to Mistress Williams's door.

Captain Gregory had heard a commotion on deck sometime during the middle of the night. The windows and door to his cabin had been open to capture what little breeze might move through the hot and heavy air. He did not pay particular attention to the voices; two or three sailors seemed to be in a drunken argument. He was a strict taskmaster, ordinarily, but this had been a particularly difficult voyage from England. His ship was better equipped for the coastal trade between Newbury and the Caribbean islands, and he had lost one man to fever when becalmed in midpassage, and another overboard during a violent storm just two days before reaching Newbury harbor. After all that, he was inclined to let the fracas work itself out without his intervention. He tried to get back to sleep, hoping his first mate would deal with the situation. The voices stopped, and he had begun to drift off when he thought he heard one more cry and then a splash. He sat up in his bed and waited. He noted someone walking away, then nothing more. He was very tired, and lay back down. He was not sure that he had not dreamed the episode.

A knock on his door a couple of hours later woke him. His mate stood there, his lined face serious.

"You had better come have a look," the mate said. "One of our men has got himself drowned. There must be a hundred hungry gulls at him."

Now the captain stared down at the man. The face was so badly disfigured that he was not sure who he was looking at.

"That's young Billy Lockhart," the mate said. "Isn't he, Henry?" He looked to the sailor for confirmation. Henry, barely out of his teens and sporting a dark purple bruise beneath one eye, inched toward the body and leaned over it. He nodded his head and then turned away.

"He was a wild one," the mate said, "no doubt about that. I don't wonder if he just fell overboard after drinking a bit too much."

"I heard a noise outside my cabin," Gregory replied. "Sometime during the night." He turned toward Henry. "Tell me, lad, how did you get that bruise?"

"I were not in any fight," Henry replied. "Not with him, anyway." He pointed at the body.

"Well, come then," Gregory insisted.

Henry's lips quivered but he did not speak. The mate leaned toward him, and Henry whispered into his ear.

"The lad is ashamed," the mate said. "It seems he sneaked off the boat, and there was this woman, who was already . . ."

"Enough," Gregory snapped. He looked from the dead man to the young sailor. "You will know better in the future, I trow."

"Aye," Henry replied.

Gregory turned to his mate. "Did you not hear anything?"

"Aye, that I did, too," the mate said. "And when I went to see what the trouble was, a couple of the boys was having a disagreement, but Billy was not there with them. He liked his own company when he had a bottle, he did."

Gregory nodded. "Well, he is very much alone now, isn't he? Without a bottle, facing his God."

The mate lowered his head. "He is that," he said. "As for that, I do not doubt that those Quakers we had on board might have had something to do with this.

They are witches, you know. Could have cast a spell on Billy. Out of envy at the joy he took in his life."

Captain Gregory's frown suggested his desire to distance himself from speculation.

"Does he have kin?" Gregory asked.

"Not that I knows of," the mate replied.

"We have room in our graveyard," the constable interjected, "if he was a good Christian, that is."

"As to that, I cannot attest," Gregory said, "but I trust Mistress Williams would want one of her own properly put to rest."

"As you want, sir," the constable said. "I will see to it."

The captain turned and, followed by the mate, returned to the ship. Henry, though, lingered a few feet away.

"Do you mind waiting with him?" the constable asked Massaquoit, with a nod toward the body.

"No, I don't," Massaquoit said. "I do not feel his spirit anywhere near."

The constable shrugged and walked off. Massaquoit waited until he had disappeared around a turn in the path, and then knelt again to look at the body. Henry approached and looked down at the body.

"Did you not find anything on it?" he asked Massaquoit.

"No."

"He had a leather pouch he wore around his waist. I was thinking there might be something about his family in it."

"I thought he had none."

Henry sneered. "As for that, do you think them officers know about us sailors, or that we tell them what they don't have no business knowing?"

Massaquoit studied the young sailor, his face aging from overexposure to the sun.

"I found nothing," he repeated.

"Aye. I imagine it must be at the bottom of the water," Henry said, then walked toward the ship.

Catherine looked at the door of the meetinghouse as though she could will the latch to lift. Captain Gregory, sitting between Catherine and Magistrate Joseph Woolsey, shifted his angular body on the bench, as though unable to find a comfortable position. Catherine turned toward him and a small smile fought against the tension in her jaws, a tension that had been growing with each moment the door remained closed.

"I do not think they attend meeting as we do," Catherine said.

"My mate thinks they cast a spell on Billy, that poor lad, and that is why he fell into the water and drowned."

Catherine saw no humor in his eyes, but then he was a man who faced life as though it were a series of storms through which he must navigate his ship, leaving no time for levity.

"What think you?" she asked.

"I know that the lad was a favorite of Jane Whitcomb. And that the lad could not control his thirst. It is most like that he was drunk, and in the fog—for there was a mist on the water last night—he stumbled, lost his balance, and fell."

"I fear we may never know more than that,"

Catherine replied, then glanced again at the door.
"Did they dine with you?" she asked.

"Indeed, Roger did, as befits their status. But his
sister had such a terrible voyage, keeping to her cabin
until we had cleared the Canary Islands. I did not lay
eyes on her before we were almost halfway across.
Billy took her meals to her."

"And was her brother prompt to meals?" Woolsey
asked.

"Aye, that he was."

"Then perhaps he has a larger appetite for food
than for hearing God's Holy Word preached as it
should be. People say that at their meetings there is
no preaching."

"No more of that, Joseph Woolsey," Catherine
chided. "Let us judge their actions, not rumors about
their sect."

Captain Gregory stretched against the back of the
bench on which he sat. He seemed ill at ease.

"Perhaps you can sit more at your ease if you do
not have to balance your hat," Woolsey offered.

"Yes, it is a grand hat," Catherine said, thankful for
the distraction. The air in the meetinghouse still carried the rich aroma of the newly worked wood of the
board that now ran along the side walls. Most of the
pegs on the board held hats or an occasional cloak;
Catherine noted a couple of empty ones toward the
very back on the wall nearest where she sat. She
pointed in that direction, and Captain Gregory smiled
his thanks as he rose to his feet, carrying his plumed
tricorner hat. He walked with a wide-legged gait,
more appropriate for the rolling deck of a ship than
for the plank floor he now crossed. He found an

empty hook, and as he turned to regain his seat, the door was flung open. In walked Roger and Jane Whitcomb, the brother and sister whose arrival he and Catherine had been so anxiously awaiting.

Catherine felt herself tense. She had heard about some of the Quakers' strange practices, and she feared an immediate disturbance. The young man was wearing a broad-brimmed, high-crowned hat. Catherine waited for his hands to move toward his head, but they did not. Instead, he took his sister's elbow as they made their way toward Catherine. They arrived just as Captain Gregory did, and there was a moment's confusion as the three stood uncertain who should sit down. Captain Gregory stepped back and gestured toward a space on a bench several rows back.

"Master Whitcomb," he said with a slight nod, "I can hear as well from there."

"That space will suffice for us, thank thee kindly, Captain," Roger said. Catherine's eyes fastened on Roger's hat until he sensed her glance. His face reddened.

"Thou need not worry, Mistress Williams," he said, "whatever thou might have heard about our ways, we know how to show proper respect to God in His House." He lifted his hand to the brim and with a slow, graceful movement, he pulled his hat to his side, revealing thick black hair. As if in sympathy, his sister raised her hand to her head and pulled at the strands of bright red hair that strayed from beneath her bonnet. She offered a quick, tentative smile that brightened her delicate face for a second; then they walked back to the bench Captain Gregory had been looking at and found seats on the end of it close to the wall. The brother located an available peg, and put his hat on it.

Minister Davis had been watching with an expression on his face somewhere between amusement and exasperation as the beginning of his service was delayed by the tardy arrival of the newcomers whom the whole town had been waiting to see.

"Mistress Williams," he said, in his deep, authoritative voice, "I see that your guests have joined us. I trust they are well bestowed and ready to join our service."

Catherine felt caught off guard. Minister Davis did not usually interrupt the beginning of meeting in such a manner as this. The colony was growing, and it was not at all uncommon for new arrivals, either permanent or transient, to attend a Sunday service. In fact, permanent Newbury residents were compelled by law to worship, whether their hearts were involved or not. So, Catherine could only wonder what moved the minister to make a special case out of her guests. A moment's reflection brought his motive to mind, and a second later a comment from behind her confirmed her conclusion.

"They do say," a woman said in tones louder than were necessary to communicate with the woman next to her, "that they are members of that new sect."

"You don't mean. . . . ."

"Verily."

"Quakers in Newbury," the neighbor said. This last was said even louder, and rose above the heads of the congregants to fill the meetinghouse with fear and loathing. All eyes now turned to Roger and Jane, sitting with expressionless faces.

Catherine stood up and looked at the two women, good wives of Newbury, smug beneath caps starched for Sunday.

"They, and I, await you," Catherine said, her gaze aimed hard and bright at the two women although her remark was addressed to the minister.

"Well, then," Minister Davis said, "let us begin."

From his seat at the rear of the meetinghouse, Massaquoit watched with amusement in his mind but a passive expression on his face. He had been living among the English for fifteen years, ever since Catherine Williams had chosen him from all his fellow sachems to live. The others had been dumped into the sea, and he had gone to live as Catherine's servant, although she had never treated him as such. He lived in a wigwam under a tree behind her house. Over the years that he had been there, he had contemplated trying the English style of living in their large wooden structures with many walls and doorways and stairs to higher levels. Catherine had often invited him into her house, but he had refused. It was not that he did not recognize the advantages of such a structure, especially in the middle of a severe New England winter. He might warm his feet better by a fireplace inside Catherine's house, just as he could cook better with an English iron kettle, or cut better with an English steel knife. But the simple and essential fact was that he was not English, and he had no intention of becoming absorbed into that culture, as had his companion sitting to his right.

Wequashcook, too, had noted the disturbance caused by the newcomers' arrival. He nudged Massaquoit with his elbow, but his face remained an impassive mask. He sat next to Massaquoit because the last bench in the meetinghouse was reserved for those Indians who had accepted Christ and had become good enough Christians to attend services, but not quite enough to permit them to mingle with the English Christians sitting in front of them. And on the bench reserved for them, there was just enough room for the dozen or so Indian congregants. Wequashcook and Massaquoit found themselves side by side partly out of choice, in recognition of their long and tangled history, and partly in preference to other men and women whose spirits long ago had been crushed or who had heartily adopted the white people's God. Massaquoit made just enough pretense to such a conversion to maintain his relationship with Catherine, whereas Wequashcook displayed a more aggressive assimilation into the English faith so as to better promote his business interests. Neither was sincere, and neither respected the other's motives, but still, somehow, they felt closer to one another than they did to the other Indians sitting with either blank faces or expressions of exaggerated joy.

Minister Davis looked out over his congregation, his gaze pausing, as it always did, on that last bench where the Indians sat, as though to insist on his policy of inclusion of all those in his meetinghouse. He was preaching today on the question of sanctification, and how it followed justification in turning God's elect away from sin and toward Christ's model of goodness.

"By your acts shall you be known," the minister intoned, "for a natural man can only wallow in his sin, like a hog in the mud, until he is cleansed by God's saving grace."

He paused, as he frequently did, for emphasis, waiting until the words he deemed most portentous had had an opportunity to penetrate the rational functions of his listeners. Like most New England Puritan ministers, he believed that human reason had been corrupted, but not destroyed, by original sin, and that preaching God's word could still have a positive effect, for its light was bright enough to shine through the dismal, sin-induced fog that enshrouded his congregation's minds. He tapped his finger on the open page of the huge Bible on the lectern behind which he stood, and observed the nodding heads and brightening eyes until he was satisfied that his point had been well received and he could go on. Just as he opened his mouth to continue, he became aware of a stirring to his right. There, several rows behind Catherine Williams, Roger Whitcomb stood up.

He was tall, a little over six feet at a time when the average height for a man was something like half a foot less. Now that his large hat was removed, his black hair rose in wild disarray, tumbling over his ears and the nape of his neck. His eyes, which had been gentle in his deference to Captain Gregory, now were bright and intensely focused. He looked down at his sister. She turned aside for a second, and then she nodded. Catherine, whose eyes had followed the minister's gaze, saw that an almost imperceptible shrug preceded the nod of her head.

"Thou art surely mistaken," Roger said, in a voice

every bit as commanding as the minister's. "Thou wouldst mislead these poor lambs to their damnation in hell."

The color rose in Minister Davis's face, moving up from the folds of his neck through his fleshy jowls and then continuing across his cheeks to his forehead, which now bulged with the pressure of the veins that carried the angry blood. Catherine worried that his head might explode, for much as she disagreed with the man of the cloth on many points of doctrine as well as on his approach to pastoral care, which was far too magisterial for her taste, she yet retained a human care for the man beneath the cloth. His fury was reaching a level dangerous to his well-being. He opened his mouth to speak, but no words came out, as though he could not, from the wealth of his erudite vocabulary, select the words of opprobrium sufficient to contend with this brash challenge to his authority.

Roger filled the silence as all in the meetinghouse waited for the minister to gather himself.

"What sayest thou?" the young man demanded. "Art thou not confounded?"

Minister Davis clamped his mouth shut hard, passed his hand across his forehead as though to dispel its confusion, and then found his voice. A young woman on the front bench across from Catherine half rose and glanced from the minister to Roger. Catherine recognized her as Grace Davis, the minister's niece, recently arrived in Newbury. Grace's eyes lingered on Roger, and then she sat down as Minister Davis spoke.

"Surely not. Am I, who stood up before the tyranny of the king's ministers, who could put my head in a noose for preaching the true gospel, now to be confounded by such a pup as you, who do not know how to address your betters?"

"What meanest *thou*?" Roger asked, but the smirk on his face revealed that he full well understood the minister's point.

"Why, that *you* show forth your ignorance even now."

"No, the fault is thine, as thou art surely but one person." Roger moved his arm in a sweeping gesture toward the congregation. "Now surely, *you* are many, and so correctly addressed." He raised his arm to point at Minister Davis. "But he is but one man, although he seems unaware of that simple truth."

Minister Davis's face had resumed its usual authoritative expression, and his skin had almost lost its red glow.

"My young friend," he said, "we need not argue over 'thou' or 'you.' And I will even forgive your impertinent interruption, so that in answering your objection to my opening of the doctrine of sanctification, I can the better show you its truthfulness."

"Sayest thou so?" Roger said.

"I do," Minister Davis replied in a voice informed by the calm of thirty years in the ministry, facing adversaries of every stripe.

Roger made his way to the aisle and strode to the rear of the meetinghouse. He stopped in front of the last bench and pointed at Wequashcook and Massaquoit.

"There is a light in all men," he said, "even these that thou termest savages. They, too, carry the light within them. Is it not so that heat follows from a flame but does not cause the fire?"

"It is," Minister Davis agreed, his voice raised to reach and confront Roger at the back of the building.

"Just so is the light within these savages like the flame. Heat follows the flames, and righteousness follows the light. Stand up, men, and leave this building, for you need it not," Roger declared. He seized Wequashcook by one arm, and Massaquoit by the other, and tried to raise them to their feet. He strained for a few moments, then dropped his arms.

"They have been better instructed," Minister Davis said. "They know they must hear the word of God opened to them by their minister."

"They are the more deceived, then," Roger retorted. He stepped back into the aisle and strode deliberately toward the pulpit. He stopped at a point even with the frontmost bench, and turned to face the congregation. He paused for a moment as his eyes engaged Grace's. His height gave him a commanding presence almost equal to the much shorter minister ensconced behind the massive oaken pulpit. "Rise up, I say, and free yourselves from the slavery of this ministry. Learn to nurture the seed of righteousness that God has placed in your bosoms. It is not so difficult to do, for I have come to show you the way."

Catherine rose to her feet. She felt the blood beneath her cheeks, and she knew her face was red. At that moment she could not have said whether she was more angry or humiliated. Although she found Roger's point more than passingly compatible with her own distrust of a church polity based on a powerful ministry, she could not condone his rudeness. And further, as Roger's hostess, and therefore his sponsor in the community, she would be held responsible for his behavior. The fact that she had first laid eyes on him two days ago would not lessen her responsibility in the eyes of her neighbors.

She wanted very much to reach Roger and silence him, but others had also stood and the congregation was forming itself into an angry human wall between her and Roger, whose head remained visible above everybody else. Catherine turned toward the pulpit, hoping that Minister Davis would find some word to cool the hot anger she felt fill the meetinghouse, but for once the clergyman seemed struck speechless. He stood, face purple, his elbows leaning on the pulpit on either side of the massive Bible open to the page of his text. He glanced down at that page, perhaps hoping to find something there that would defuse a situation that had escaped his grip on the emotions of his congregants. He moved his lips, as though the calming words he sought would thereby form themselves, but he could say nothing.

Roger, on the other hand, glowed with the confidence of those informed by a self-defined sense of righteousness, fueled by a fierce desire to bring the light of truth to the benighted. He raised his eyes toward the ceiling of the meetinghouse and then lifted both arms, as though inviting his hostile audience to embrace his words. However, before he could utter them, an arm reached out from the human wall that was now leaning toward him from the benches immediately in front of him. Catherine saw the lace cuff of a shirt above the hand, which held a leather glove rolled into a ball. She raised herself onto her toes, but

still could not see the body to which the arm belonged. She nudged Woolsey with her elbow.

"Who is it?" she asked.

"Who . . . ," the magistrate repeated, unsure of
what he was being asked.

"The hand," Catherine said.

"I see it," Woolsey replied.

The hand's mate, with another flash of lace cuff,
circled the back of Roger's head and its fingers
grabbed a handful of hair. Roger's expression turned
startled, his mouth agape. The hand holding the glove
shoved it into the opening. Roger pulled his head
back, but the insistent hand followed until the balled
glove all but disappeared down Roger's throat. He
stepped back, gagging. Two more hands, these
rougher and larger, extending from sleeves of coarse,
dark brown wool, appeared from behind Roger's
head and clamped his mouth shut by pressing his jaw
up with one powerful hand while the fingers of the
other pressed down on the crown of his head. Roger
flailed his arms in a windmill motion.

"Let him go!" The voice boomed from the chest
of a man who now stood clearly visible next to
Roger. The other man released his grip on Roger's
head, and Roger fell to his knees. The one who had
issued the command straightened his lace cuffs and
stepped aside, much as he would have done if Roger
had been a steaming clump of manure encountered
in his path. Roger attempted to rise but collapsed to
the floor. The fingers of his right hand seized the tip
of the leather glove and yanked, but the glove was
caught in his throat, which his terror now sent into
spasms. His jaws, perversely, had clamped shut. He

grunted and pressed his left hand against his throat. His right hand pounded the rough planks of the meetinghouse floor.

The man with the powerful hands knelt over Roger. He pried open Roger's mouth and grabbed the end of the glove. As he began to pull it out, Roger's mouth shut again, and his teeth drove into the man's fingers. The man brought his other hand down in a hard slap against Roger's jaw. Roger's mouth opened from the impact and the man removed his hand. The impression of Roger's teeth was clearly visible on the man's index finger. Where the skin had been broken, a thick drop of blood oozed. The man lifted his finger to his nose, as though to smell the blood, and then wiped his finger on his sleeve.

"I do not think you will be wanting that glove back, Master Worthington," the man said.

"I will not miss it," Master Worthington replied.

Roger was now thumping the wooden floor with one hand while clutching his throat with the other. Catherine forced her way through the crowd that now formed a semicircle in the aisle where Roger lay. She saw the telltale blue tint forming beneath his skin. Jane was right behind Catherine and seized the end of the glove. She pulled, but to no effect.

"He cannot breathe," she said.

"He had breath enough for his blasphemy," Master Worthington replied. He addressed Catherine. "You will be better advised to see to George's wound."

George extended his hand toward Catherine. Another droplet of blood had formed on the wound. She brushed the hand aside and got down on her knees next to Roger. His eyes had all but rolled back into his head, and he thrashed about as he felt her cradle his head with her arm. He managed to focus his gaze on her, and he calmed long enough to point to his throat.

"Perhaps it is God's will," Minister Davis said from the edge of the semicircle, where he had stood for the past few moments after descending the pulpit. Grace stood by his side and shook her head.

"Uncle, I do not think it," she said.

Minister Davis turned a withering stare at his niece, and Grace retreated a few steps.

"Govern you tongue," the minister said. Grace reddened.

Massaquoit was on his feet, observing this strange spectacle. He knew he could help, perhaps save the life of the tall English who had caused so much anger. He had to decide whether he wanted to, and he did not hurry, even as he saw the man's life ebbing. The English stood around the fallen man and seemed unable or unwilling to come to his aid as he brought his fists down on the floor with increasing violence. Massaquoit saw the concern in Catherine's face, and felt himself drawn to her aid. He strode toward her, but his way was blocked by the English, who had now formed a full circle several bodies deep around Roger. He pushed against the gap between two young English. They turned toward him, their expressions changing from surprise to contemptuous resistance and finally to acquiescence before the set of Massaquoit's jaw and the determination in his eyes. He did not speak. Long experience had taught him that silence was far better than his words in dealing with the English, who seemed to delight in willfully misunderstanding his intention. For a couple of moments, nobody moved, and then one of the English, a young man no more than sixteen, of slight build and poor complexion, shrugged and stepped aside. His companion, a little older and sturdier, held his ground as Massaquoit stepped past him.

He reached Catherine's side just as Roger began bucking so hard that she could no longer cradle his head. His face was now clearly blue, and his eyes indicated he was staring at death.

"Can you do anything?" Catherine said. "He will die."

"Yes," Massaquoit replied.

He squatted next to Roger and grabbed the young man's arms. Roger flailed in his agony, but Massaquoit was able to raise him to a sitting position with his arms pinned to his sides. Massaquoit lowered his head and buried his shoulder just below Roger's sternum. He threw his arms around Roger and tried to rise. He got halfway up, but then Roger's weight proved too much. Catherine seized one of Roger's elbows, and Jane, who had been standing helplessly by, took the other. The two women looked at each other for a moment, and then, as though at a wordless signal, they lifted. Massaquoit added his effort and managed now to stand with Roger on his shoulder. He dipped his knees, almost lost his balance, and then steadied himself. He stiffened his legs with a sudden movement that lifted Roger off his shoulder by an inch or two. When Roger landed again, his mouth opened and the glove shot out. He gasped and pulled air into his lungs. Massaquoit sat him down on the floor. Roger threw his arms out as though to open his lungs to the air. He cast his eyes upward toward the ceiling of the meetinghouse, and then he brought his glance down so that he could look at each of the by-standers in turn. A gurgling sound crept out of his throat, followed by a large glob of spittle. He jerked his head to one side so that his saliva landed on the floor within a few inches of the buckled leather shoes of Master Worthington. The merchant stared at the small pool and then stepped back.

"What think you of our new arrival?" he said, ad-dressing the question to Governor Peters, whose head was clearly visible above the crowd around Roger.

"Why, that he is rude, in speech and in manner." The governor cast his eyes about until they landed on a stout, middle-aged man.

"Constable Larkins," he said, "be you so kind as to escort Mr. Whitcomb to our jail, there to be held until we can better decide how further to entertain him."

"He is in need of my attention," Catherine said. "I will accompany him, if the governor has no objec-tion."

"I expect nothing less than that you should want to minister to your guest," Governor Peters said. "Stray Indians, dogs, or Quakers—you seem not to distin-guish, Mistress Williams."

"Oh, but I do, Governor Peters. I know well the difference between an Indian, a dog, a Quaker, and even a magistrate."

Governor Peters's face reddened. Catherine braced herself for the rebuke, but it did not come. Instead, the governor felt himself yanked about as Magistrate Woolsey pulled on his elbow.

"Now, we must be about our business," said Woolsey. He looked out over the crowd. The congregation ringed the spot where Roger lay. Many faces were dark with anger, and words passed behind the screen of hands.

Governor Peters nodded. "Your friend and protector is right, Mistress Williams, for he reminds me that I have more important matters to attend to than correcting that wayward tongue of yours, whose bite I have indeed felt these many years."

"For that I must beg your pardon," Catherine said, thankful that Woolsey had once again shielded her. Behind the acquiescent smile of a woman who had been shown her place, she fought to contain her emotions. The foolish young man at her feet had almost been murdered before her eyes for speaking in public words he knew would invite retribution, and now he was to be dragged off to prison, where he would remain until summoned for his punishment. Catherine bowed her head to underscore her submission and knelt to offer Roger her hand. Jane did the same. Roger grasped each woman's hand and struggled to his feet. He looked toward Massaquoit and nodded.

"Thank thee, friend," he said.

Massaquoit held the gaze of this strange young English and then returned the nod with a slight movement of his head.

Constable Larkins stepped forward. "Come along, now," he said, "and don't be about calling me your friend when I never did lay eyes on you before this morning."

"And yet, a friend in Christ, I trust," Roger said.

"I would not know anything about that," the constable said, and took Roger's elbow in his hand.

"There is no need," Roger said. "I will follow thee where thou leadest."

"To the jail, that is where," the constable said. He maintained his grip on Roger as they began to make their way out of the meetinghouse. Roger brought his free hand up to his head and ran his fingers through his hair, stopping at the crown. He looked to Jane, who was walking at his side. She turned down an aisle of benches, now empty, to retrieve Roger's hat from its peg. She trotted back and held it out to him; and he put it on with elaborate care, as though his head were as fragile as an egg that the hat might crush. Constable Larkins yanked on his elbow, but Roger, now seemingly fully recovered, braced himself against the pull until he settled his wide-brimmed hat to his satisfaction. Then he nodded and let himself be led out of the meetinghouse and across the square to the jail, followed by Jane and Catherine.

Massaquoit watched them leave and then walked to the back of the meetinghouse, to the last row of benches where Wequashcook still sat. Wequashcook stood up and stretched the stiffness from his joints.

"The English are sometimes amusing," he said.

"Even in their amusements they are dangerous," Massaquoit replied.

"I think I will follow after," Wequashcook said.

"To see what crumbs might fall from the English table?"

Wequashcook shrugged.

"I have seen enough for one day," Massaquoit

said. He walked out of the meetinghouse, cast a glance at the knot of English gathered outside the jail, and then turned up the road that led from the town square to Catherine's house and his wigwam beneath the huge maple.

TWO

❦

NEWBURY'S JAIL OCCUPIED one side of the town common, directly opposite the meetinghouse and diagonally across from Minister Davis's parsonage. The jail was no more than a small house divided between a living area for Matthew Drake, the jailer, and two rooms in which prisoners were locked up. Drake, a man in his fifties, his face blanketed with gray stubble that grew in patches, here thick and there only a hair or two, stood blinking in the sun. He had slept past meeting, as he often did, and his red eyes and rich breath suggested that he had found more comfort in a pitcher of beer than in Master Davis's sermon.

The town of Newbury had been enjoying a period of civility and observance of its various ordinances for several months, and as a consequence Drake's jail had been empty of prisoners. This circumstance caused the scowl that always lurked beneath the false servility of his yellow-toothed smile to emerge with growing intensity as each law-abiding day passed. It was not, of course, that he sought the company of those who fell afoul of the law, but that he regretted the opportunity to skim a few pence from the money paid by friends or relatives for food or other comforts of the incarcerated. Newbury jail's inmates, as was common at that time, could not expect much more than the barest subsistence, if that, from the towns-people, who had no stomach for feeding sinners. Drake lived rent free in his portion of the jail, and was paid a salary that allowed him to eat about as well as his prisoners. The good people of Newbury were no more generous toward their jailer than toward his charges.

So it was not surprising that on this afternoon, as he stood scratching his belly, in which sloshed only the beer he had been drinking, his face brightened at the sight of the constable leading a well-dressed young man toward the jail. Judging by the young man's appearance, some friend or relative with deep pockets would likely come forward and press a few shiny coins into Drake's hand with the instruction that the money be used to supplement the prisoner's diet. Drake could only lick his lips at such a prospect.

Catherine's nature was to make allowances for all people, believing that only God knew the workings of a person's heart. Drake, though, was the specific instance that sorely tested the general tolerance. She had had numerous dealings with the jailer since he had assumed that post, now more than ten years ago, and in all of these interactions she had found him to be without scruples in promoting his own interest.

Now, as she walked behind Roger and Jane toward the ramshackle prison, she stared hard at Drake's bloodshot eyes squinting in the sun, at the coarse stubble on his cheeks, and at the saliva dribbling out from between the rotted stumps of his lower front teeth. She noted, as well, Drake's nervous habit of rubbing his palms together and then extending first one hand and then the other as though he expected to be offered a gift.

This bottomless greed was the one element in his disreputable character that Catherine had long ago realized she could turn to her advantage whenever the need arose, as it most certainly did at the present moment. She had come prepared for this encounter. She put her hand into the pouch she wore about her waist and moved her fingers about until she felt the smooth metal of the shilling coins. She pulled out two and held them between her thumb and forefinger for just an instant, long enough for Drake's red eyes to focus on the sun glinting off the coins. He nodded. Her intention was to gain entrance to the jail, once the prisoners were ensconced inside, and there to counsel them about the dangers they faced if they continued to provoke Governor Peters and Minister Davis, respectively the secular and spiritual heads of the colony, who in the short history of Newbury had developed a formidable reputation for severity and intolerance.

To this end, Catherine hurried to reach the jailer so that her coins could vouchsafe her intentions, but as she stepped forward, her path was blocked from the side by four fully armed soldiers, pikes at their shoulders, leading the governor, the minister, and Magistrate Woolsey to the jail on a path that cut across the common from the parsonage. Catherine could only marvel at the speed with which this pageant had been organized.

Roger and Jane turned toward the group. Governor Peters began to speak, but hesitated. Catherine knew why he waited, and chastised herself for her slowness in preventing what she now saw as the inevitable confrontation. The constable, who had removed his hat, a shabby affair of coarsely woven flax, nudged Roger, and waved the hat in front of Roger's eyes. Roger nodded, but made no effort to imitate this gesture of subservience to a social superior. A look of disgust darkened the constable's face. He grabbed the broad brim of Roger's hat and pulled it off.

"Show proper respect for your betters," he said.

Roger looked about him as though searching for such a person. "We are all one in Christ, are we not?" he asked.

Minister Davis stepped forward, his expression warm with condescension, as though ready to instruct a child in his sums.

"Verily," he said, "our Lord's spirit touches all His chosen equally. But God has so ordained matters in this corrupt world that there are those who rule and those who are ruled. That is God's order. To deny it is to deny God His judgment."

"My head might be bared by this man's arm," Roger said, indicating the constable, "but even wert thou to force my knee to bend, my heart would not, for thou canst not touch it. Only my God can do that."

Catherine's ears processed this ill-advised speech, but out of the corner of her eye she detected the po-

tential for a more explosive action. Jane, who had
been standing a few feet to the side of her brother,
was now agitated. She shifted her weight from one
foot to the other, she beat the fist of her right hand
into the palm of the left, and the muscles of her face
contracted into a frown so intense that it seemed the
skin might lift from her bones. Her eyes moved from
the governor and magistrate to the hat at their feet in
a furious squint, then snapped wide open, bright and
laden with an idea that Catherine, although she did
not know what it was specifically, recognized would
be like a match to powder. She stepped to the young
woman and took her arm. When Jane did not respond, Catherine tightened her grip. Jane turned to
her, her mouth open, a defiant phrase at her lips, but
she stopped herself when she saw who was holding
her arm. Without a word, she pulled her arm free.
Catherine relented, resigned to what was about to
happen. She could only watch as Jane stepped forward and with great deliberation lifted her foot, revealing her buckled shoe, and brought it down on the
flat crown of her brother's hat.

"Thou wouldst have my brother off his hat for thy
honor," she said. A bright smile now flashed, and for
a moment Catherine believed the young woman was
about to burst into laughter. She stomped on the
crown of the hat several times, using both feet, until
the crown lay flat against the brim. "Now see how thy
honor is beneath my foot," she said—not with a
laugh, as Catherine had anticipated, but with a giggle
that rose from her throat and out of her half-opened
mouth with a restrained hilarity more insulting than
any outright laugh. She moved one foot off and away

from the hat, and raised her hand in front of her mouth, as though to silence herself. She kept her other foot on the hat. Nobody—not the minister, the governor, the constable, nor Catherine—could find voice to respond to her action. In this stunned silence Jane waited, and when it persisted, she again raised her foot to stomp the hat. She was like a performer waiting for an audience to clap, or boo, or hiss; she would not stop until there was some reaction.

However, before she could bring her foot down again, the constable grabbed her by the shoulders while she was balanced on one leg. He spun her around as though she were a child's top. She did not resist. Instead, she seemed to enjoy the motion, and when her momentum no longer carried her, she permitted herself to fall in a heap onto the offending hat. She lay on the ground for a few moments and then pulled herself up to a sitting position, one leg on each side of the hat.

Governor Peters's face turned purple; Minister Davis's expression seemed more red with embarrassment; Magistrate Woolsey contracted his brows in puzzlement.

"On your feet, you impudent hussy!" the governor demanded. When she did not move, he turned to the constable. "Seize her," he said, "and throw both of them in there. He gestured to the prison door, in front of which Drake stood, his mouth agape and his eyes wide open, clear, and focused on the young woman on the ground in front of his jailhouse.

The constable, a burly middle-aged man, bent down, seized Jane's arms, and with one quick motion raised her from the ground and onto her feet. She let her body go limp, so that when the constable released her and stepped back, she started to fall to the ground. He caught her, held her for a moment, until with a nod she indicated she would stand. He again released her, and she stood still for a second or two. Then she swooped down, picked up the hat, and placed it on her brother's head.

"Inside with the both of them," sputtered the governor. This time, the constable grabbed each by an arm and propelled them toward the door. They did not resist being thrust into the jail as Drake opened the door. Drake followed, and closed the door behind him.

Catherine watched, helpless. Any chance she had to intervene on their behalf had been taken from her by Jane's wild and provocative behavior. The governor was overwrought, and one glance at Minister Davis's furrowed brows told her she could expect no forgiveness of youthful folly from that stern guardian of the communal morality. Woolsey, she knew, would do what he could when he could, but the brother and sister had crossed way too far over the line. At a word from the governor, the soldiers reorganized themselves around him and the minister. Peters looked toward Woolsey, but the magistrate indicated he was not yet ready to leave. Peters and Minister Davis walked off between the soldiers, who again held their pikes on their shoulders.

Catherine looked at Woolsey for a moment, and in their exchange of glances she confirmed her sense that he remained on her side, and therefore supportive of Roger and Jane. He would intervene when he might succeed in softening the governor's anger. She nodded to let him know she understood his position, and then watched as he shuffled off, his shoulders bent beneath the weight not only of his age but also of his impotence to remedy the immediate situation. Nothing pleased him more than to help Catherine, the daughter of his oldest friend and his companion on his journey from England to Newbury two decades before.

After a few moments, the door to the jail opened and Drake stood there. He rubbed his palms together, but then shook his head.

"Aye, Mistress, truly would I accommodate your generosity, but now is not the time. The young man and woman are on their knees in prayers and will speak to nobody."

"Do you have them locked up together, then?" Catherine asked. She did not know why that question jumped to her lips, but when it did, she gave it expression.

If the question surprised Drake, he did not show it. Instead, he shrugged.

"That I did, and they are together talking to God in their own peculiar way, with no help from clergy or a poor jailer such as myself."

"I will return," Catherine said, "at a more convenient time." She turned toward home. After a few steps, she was joined by her servant woman, Phyllis, who had been watching from a respectful distance. Phyllis had been with Catherine for more than fifteen years. As a girl of thirteen, she had come to Newbury as the indentured servant of a man who took more pleasure in beating her than in providing her employment. When that man ran into financial difficulties, Catherine had bought the remaining time of the indenture. Over the years, the relationship between the two had evolved from mistress and servant to something a little closer to mother and daughter. In quiet moments, Catherine conceded that Phyllis now occupied a place in her heart left vacant by the death of Abigail, her youngest daughter.

"Are we to leave them here, then?" Phyllis demanded.

"Hush," Catherine replied. "Just walk with me."

"But . . . ," Phyllis insisted, her faced flushed. She looked over her shoulder every step or two.

Instead of offering a response, Catherine accelerated her pace, and Phyllis struggled to keep up. About a hundred yards from the town center, the road narrowed as it reached the summit of the slope and then turned abruptly to the west before resuming its northward direction down the far side of the hill. As Catherine and Phyllis rounded the curve, and thus were out of sight of anybody still in front of the jail, Catherine stopped, her face damp with perspiration and her chest heaving from the climb. Phyllis had so energized herself to the faster pace that her inertia carried her a few steps beyond Catherine. She planted her right foot as a brake and spun half around, breathing hard, confusion written large on her face. To their left was a fallen log beneath a towering old pine and to their right was a field of coneflowers. Catherine motioned toward the log.

"We can rest ourselves here," she said.

A question began to form on Phyllis's lips, but she was so overheated from their walk in the hot sun, and attracted to the cool shadows blanketing the log, that a question seemed less important than seeking shade. She followed Catherine to the log and sat down next to her. After a few moments, Catherine glanced at Phyllis and saw the question beginning to form itself again on her face.

"We are to return to the jail," she said, before Phyllis could give the question voice. "You surely did not think I would leave Roger and Jane to the tender mercies of jailer Drake, did you?"

"Not for a moment," said Phyllis, although that was exactly the form her question was about to take.

Catherine gazed out over the field. The coneflowers were in full bloom, sitting on stalks three to four feet high. The daisylike petals around a deep purple disc remained motionless in the still air.

"They are pretty flowers," Phyllis said.

Catherine walked across the path, knelt down, and snapped off one of the blossoms. "They will be feeling the lash soon enough," she said. "That put me in mind of these flowers. And I wondered if we should not haste us home."

Even though Phyllis had long ago grown accustomed to her mistress's sudden jumps of thought and utterance, she had not been able to train herself sufficiently well to prevent her own confusion from blooming on her wide and honest face.

"But home . . . ," she began.

"Indeed," Catherine replied, "My mind reached home before us, and searched my cupboard, only to find it bare of what we need. That is why I thought to stop in front of this field."

"A poultice," Phyllis said as her color returned to

normal, "for the skin of those two that will open beneath the lash."

Massaquoit, as was his custom when the English were behaving in ways that he found amusing or curious, even after his fifteen years residence among them, had followed the crowd out of the meetinghouse as Roger and Jane were being led away. He noted that they were being taken directly to the jail, and so he trotted in an arc that took him first away from the knot of people trailing the constable and his prisoners, and then to a convenient pair of maples twenty yards to the side of the jail. The two trees, like competitive siblings, grew with roots tangled in common soil and branches jostling each other all the way up their trunks. At their base, however, they were six or eight feet apart, and Massaquoit knelt between them, enjoying the cool of their shade as he watched Jane stomp on her brother's hat. A tug on his shoulder told him that Wequashcook, too, was enjoying the spectacle. Wequashcook's bald pate glistened with perspiration, which he swept with the palm of his hand toward the fringe of white hair. A jagged scar bisected the bald spot.

"Do you think that is a new dance?" Wequashcook asked. "And if it is, what think you is the significance of stomping on a hat?"

Massaquoit ran his fingers over the scar. "I do not know what the English intend with such violence toward a simple hat. When I had anger, as well you know, I sought your flesh."

"Yes, and I wear a beaver hat to hide my shame." Wequashcook looked at the hat in his hands, and then shook his head, as though to dismiss both the thought and the remnants of the shame that had clung to him ever since he led the English troops to the village where Massaquoit's wife and son were killed in the ensuing massacre. "I understand that you cannot forget."

"No, I cannot," Massaquoit replied, "but we have our terms, as you well know."

"Those young English are rich," Wequashcook said. "There might be profit in helping them."

"That is your way," Massaquoit replied.

"As it should be yours."

The jailhouse door creaked open. Its hinges were loose, and the heavy oaken door scraped the ground as it was pushed outward. The burly figure of Constable Larkins emerged. He paused at the doorway and looked back inside. He gestured with his hand, then waved a farewell and turned to face the common. His eyes scanned the trees on its perimeter, pausing when he saw the two Indians. He strode to them, and when he was a few feet away he stopped, his hard, alert eyes on Massaquoit.

"I think we have had business before in front of that very place," he said, pointing toward the jail.

"I think I was drunk," Massaquoit replied.

"Or so you would have me think, so you could gain entrance and free that girl."

"It was even so," Massaquoit said, his voice calm.

Constable Larkins shrugged. "I do not entirely regret it, although you did cause me some shame among my fellows." He studied Massaquoit's face for a moment, and then turned his gaze back to the jail. "I hope you know I am better prepared this time."

"I do not have reason to be concerned about those two young English."

"Aye, but Mistress Williams does."

"He is too much his own man, now," Wequash-cook offered.

"But you . . . ," the constable began.

"I am only a man of business. No more, no less."

"Then I do believe you are the more dangerous," the constable said, and with a nod toward Massaquoit he walked on his way.

Catherine watched as Phyllis made her way on her knees through the field of coneflowers, digging around the stalks of the plants and pulling them up with roots intact. She glanced down at the dirt beneath her broken fingernails, winced as she tried to straighten the arthritic joints of her fingers, and felt the imprint of a large stone on the flesh of her right knee; the guilt she had begun to feel for leaving the task of gathering the plants to Phyllis rapidly dissipated. In any case, it was not so much an egalitarian spirit that had motivated her to crawl besides her servant through the field as her enduring conviction that she would do a better job selecting the plants to gather. Now she comforted herself that Phyllis's judgment, after all, had profited greatly from her years of apprenticeship, and she could be trusted to do an adequate job.

She sensed of a figure coming around the bend before she saw the constable. He looked toward Phyllis and then made his way toward Catherine.

"A good day to you, Constable Larkins," she said.

"And to you, Mistress." He looked back over his shoulder, down the road toward the jail. "But I expect you have seen better."

"That I have."

"Do they not know of the new ordinance?" the constable asked.

"I do not think so," Catherine replied. "They have only just arrived, and I did not wish to trouble them, as they promised they would not call attention to themselves."

"Aye, if only they had kept their word."

"They were provoked."

"Not overmuch," the constable said.

"I must go to them," Catherine said.

"You will find Matthew and William beneath a tree not far from the prison house."

"To what purpose?"

"That I cannot answer. I did hope you could instruct me."

"I am sure I do not know."

"Verily?"

"Indeed."

Constable Larkins bowed and doffed his crude, woolen cap. The sun glinted off the round bald spot fringed by his dark brown hair. Perspiration formed on his bare scalp as he held the gesture for effect.

"Such a simple thing," he said, as he stood up straight and replaced his cap.

"Aye, it is, to you, but for those two, I am afraid, beyond their conscience."

"Better to stretch their conscience than their necks," the constable said. Then he continued on up the road and around another bend. As soon as he was no longer visible, Phyllis was standing next to her mistress.

"What did he want of us?" she asked.

"He came to tell me what I know: that my young charges do not recognize the danger they have placed themselves in by their stubborn refusal to bow themselves to our customs."

"Do they think they are better than we are?" Phyllis asked, with disbelief in her tone.

"I do not think so. Nor do they think they are worse than any."

"I do not understand."

"You needn't, but they must be made to." Catherine glanced at the pile of uprooted plants. "Take those home and begin to prepare a poultice, which I hope is all that we will need to salve the results of their impertinence."

Phyllis frowned.

"Do not worry, child," Catherine said. "I go now to talk with them. Tomorrow, you can accompany me when they are to be punished."

Phyllis brightened. "It is not that I wish to see them hurt," she explained after an embarrassed pause.

"I know that well," Catherine replied, and turned her steps, without a further glance at her servant, toward the prison.

Jailer Drake was squatting in front of his door. He waved a branch that still held a full complement of maple leaves in front of his face to create the semblance of a breeze in the sullen air. Every once in a while, he swatted a fly that landed on his face or buzzed by his ear. His eyes remained focused on the road, and he rose to his feet as soon as he discerned Catherine hurrying toward him.

Catherine glanced toward the trees where the constable, using their English names, had said he had seen Massaquoit and Wequashcook, but they were gone. She then took note of Drake's shape and considered why he would choose to sit in the full sun instead of in the living quarters of the prison. As she got close enough to see his hands moving the maple branch and to recall how those hands had extended palm upward toward her earlier in the day, she realized that he had chosen to endure the discomfort of the middle of the day heat rather than miss an opportunity to be bribed. In her mind's eye, she saw him sitting at the crude table in the front section of the prison, his head resting in a drunken stupor next to the mug of beer, unable to hear or rouse himself when a knock came at his door. She slowed her pace and kept her eyes on his hands, which he strove to keep at his sides, but by the time she was ten paces from him, he gave up the attempt and let first one, and then the other, hand stretch toward her in a gesture both welcoming and solicitous.

"Mistress Williams," he said, "you can be sure that your charges are safely and comfortably accommodated. I cannot vouch for their disposition before the magistrates, but they will be well cared for in my prison." He turned toward the trees where Massaquoit and Wequashcook had been standing.

"Your savage, Matthew, and that other one, were there keeping a kind of vigil, like, and making me somewhat nervous," he said. "I trust you have sent them on their way."

"No, I have not, nor do they need me to tell them their place."

"But once . . . ," he began.

"That was a long time ago," Catherine replied. She reached into her pouch for her coins, and Drake leaned toward her, his hands now clasped behind his back. His shoulders twitched with the tension of keeping them there. Catherine held out the coins. "Some things do not change," she said.

Without a reply, Drake took the coins from her in a gesture so practiced and efficient that a careless on-looker might not have seen it. He bowed low, straightened himself, and then opened the door for her.

"See that they sup well," Catherine said. "I shall have a report from them."

"As you like, Mistress. But, in truth, as I have not been expecting company, my larder is quite bare and it is late to go to market."

"Be sure you manage, nonetheless," she replied, and stepped into the doorway as Drake stepped aside.

"I needs must wait on you. I can bide outside until you are quite done with your little talk," he said. "They are together in the room on the left. It is the one that captures more of the breeze on a hot after-noon."

Catherine breathed in the still and sultry air. "I thank you for them for your consideration," she said.

Catherine ducked through the doorway into the dank living quarters. Her nostrils closed against the fumes of beer and the noxious odor of a piece of

cheese gone rancid that was lying in a corner near the
door. She turned in the direction of the smell in time
to see two mice, one so fat it rolled more than it scurried, and the other lean and agile, dash across the
room and disappear under Drake's unmade bed and
into the wall.

She approached the door on her left, then hesitated, the jailer's odd warning that they would not
speak to anyone still playing in her mind. She could
not settle on a reason for his remark, and because she
could not, she decided not to heed it, even at the risk
of ignoring her usual manners. The door was held
shut by a heavy log, crudely split, laid in a pair of
brackets, one on the adjoining wall and one on the
door itself. She slid the log toward the wall until she
could free the door. The movement of the log created
a low, grating sound, softer than a knock from her
fist. Somehow the noise emboldened her to push the
door open with a sudden shove.

She heard them before she saw them, because the
room, whose one window faced north, was in shadow
even in the middle of the afternoon. By the time her
eyes adjusted to the gloom, she saw them sitting with
their backs against the far wall. They appeared unre-
markable except for a slight glow on Jane's face,
which might well be a flush from the heavy heat in
the room. Roger rose.

"It is so kind of thee to visit us in our durance," he
said.

Catherine took in the smile, a flash of white teeth
in the darkened room, and for a moment she felt herself respond to the charm. But then she righted herself.

"Roger, when I agreed to your father's request to act as your guardian during your stay in Newbury, I was also aware that you were coming here to start over. Yet, now I find you are repeating the same mistakes that caused you to remove from England. I fear that you do not understand that those mistakes in Newbury will have even graver consequences."

Roger clasped his hands around his neck in imitation of a rope. "But I am most certain of the risk I take in the service of God."

His voice was solemn, but a hint of a smile played on his lips. Jane reached up to seize his wrist, and with one swift and strong motion, he aided her to her feet.

"I do not think thou shouldst be scaring us in this manner," she said.

Catherine felt the heat of her anger redden her face. "I do not come here to play. And it is now only the high regard I have for your mother and father that stops me from walking out of this sad place and leaving you to your fate, which it appears you are eager to run toward. If that is what you truly have bent your heart toward, tell me now, so I can save both my breath and my pity."

Catherine waited for an answer. Jane lowered her eyes, her jaws clenched either in shame or in repressed merriment. Roger looked as though he would speak as soon as he found the right words. Before he could, however, there was a loud knock at the door.

"I did not think our jailer would be so courteous as to knock," Roger said.

"He would not," Catherine replied. "I am certain that on the other side of that door now is a kind, old gentleman, who to do me a service would do you one. I am of a mind to send him away."

"That would be unkind," Jane said, "to have him come here to no purpose."

Again, Catherine found herself not quite able to read this quixotic young woman's intent; she seemed always to hide between, or behind, her words. Her actions, though, were clear enough, and now she strode to the door so quickly that Catherine did not have an opportunity to stop her. The door opened out, and Jane gave it a vigorous shove. It swung heavily on its hinges, and when it stopped, there stood Magistrate Woolsey. Jane bowed and beckoned him in. He nodded, his lips drawn into a tight smile, and walked to Catherine. He glanced at Roger's hat, now on the floor near the wall where he had been sitting, and then turned to Catherine.

"I have managed to prevail upon the governor to have these two released to your management and care until their hearing tomorrow."

"I do not know that I should thank you, Joseph," Catherine said.

The magistrate looked stunned. "But . . . surely. . . ."

"Yes," Catherine replied. "It is my sad care to watch over these reckless children. Do not worry, Joseph. In your heart and in your head, you did what you ought, and now so must I."

Jane approached Catherine and kissed her on the cheek. Catherine searched the young woman's eyes for sincerity, thought she saw the hint of it, but could not hold on to the moment's warm feeling. It slipped away from her like the juice of a ripe grape, sweet but transient. Roger embraced her, and she felt the strength of his arm more than the depth of his convictions. Without another word, she walked to the door, where Drake now stood.

"Happy I am to give them to your custody," he said, but his voice betrayed his anxiety.

"You need not worry," Catherine said. "I do not demand my money back. Use it well for yourself, and remember it when I next need you to recall my generosity."

Drake smiled broadly and rubbed his hands together, as though pressing the coins again into the flesh of his palms.

"As you say, Mistress, so shall I do." He led the way to the front door of the prison, opened it, and watched as Catherine went out, followed by Jane, Roger, and Magistrate Woolsey. He closed the door behind him and headed up the path to the Lion's Paw, a newly opened tavern just at the edge of the town common.

Woolsey caught up to Catherine and took her elbow.

"Permit them to walk ahead," he said with a gesture toward Roger and Jane. He waited for the young people to distance themselves, and then leaned toward Catherine and lowered his voice.

"The governor is much overwrought," he said.

"They are scarcely more than children," Catherine said.

"Pshaw!" the magistrate replied. "They are of age, are they not?"

"In years," Catherine said.

"Be that as it may, it is only your care and protection that prevents them from being put on the next ship back to England."

"Well I know it," Catherine answered, "and between now and the morning I must endeavor to instruct them." She bent down to pick up a stone. "Howsoever, I think this would heed me better."

That night, after supper, as Phyllis cleared the table, Catherine turned to her guests. "Well, you know," she said, "that your parents have sent you here to me in Newbury to give you a fresh start." She spread a letter in front of her.

"Yes," Roger agreed with a quick smile, "Alford no longer could abide us."

Catherine frowned, disappointed that her young guest still did not realize the seriousness of the situation. She picked up the letter, squinted, and then held it closer to her eyes.

"It is all here in your father's own words," Catherine said.

Roger's face darkened for a moment, and his jaws quivered as he controlled his anger.

"Indeed, I do know the contents," he said. "Father has made it quite clear that I must abandon the Society of Friends, even though my mother remains dedicated to them."

"That is so," Catherine murmured, "for he does say that his heart is torn." She glanced down at the letter. "Your mother is perhaps a saint, he says, but saints swing at the end of a rope oft times, and he fears for her, and for you."

"He has not seen the light," Roger said, "as our mother has."

"And yet he asks only that you rein in your religious enthusiasm, and he will give you control of his business interests here, which will make you a very rich young man ere long."

"And if not, I am disinherited, and"—he turned to Jane—"my sister left deprived of dowry."

Catherine studied the letter.

"It does say words to that effect, but your father declares that you are to have freedom of conscience as long as you govern your tongue and your behavior." She read on and then turned her eyes to Jane. "Here your father has words especially for Jane. He says he hopes I can tame her passions that seem to rise from her blood into her head."

Jane ran her hand through her thick, red hair, now unrestrained by her bonnet.

"Father has a peculiar fancy that my hair is this color because of the heat of my blood. It is a wonder," she added, her voice rich with irony, "that his is so cold that the Lord's spirit cannot warm it. Mayhap that explains the success that he is."

Tension hovered over the table for a few moments. Phyllis dropped a trencher, and it clattered to the floor. Catherine waited for her to pick it up. Then there was a knock at the door.

"See to that," Catherine said to Phyllis. She turned again to Roger and held his gaze until he looked down.

"If you do not mend your ways, you will find Newbury even less hospitable to you. Quakers are no more welcome here than in Alford."

"'Tis more the pity, then," Jane said.

"The pity will be if I fail your parents," Catherine said.

Phyllis returned, her face bright with excitement. "It is Miriam King," she said. "She bids you come attend to Abigail."

"Tell her I will come by and by," Catherine said.

Phyllis did not immediately respond, and Catherine knew well why not. "Do as I say," she insisted.

Phyllis turned to walk back to the entrance. Catherine watched her broad back until it was lost in the shadows, and then she looked sternly at Roger and Jane.

"I think you know well enough what I intended to say to you. I do not know that I will return before you must go to your hearing tomorrow. You must promise me that you will listen and not provoke the governor's anger further."

"We do," Roger said, "surely we do."

Catherine glanced at Jane, and she nodded her head with unusual vigor.

"I must be content, then," Catherine said.

She found Phyllis waiting at the front door.

"Goody King thanks you and says she left Abigail alone, and so could not stay for you."

"The birthing stool and the butter," Catherine said. "We must haste."

"They say," Phyllis began, then hesitated, as though waiting to be stopped. When Catherine said nothing, she continued, "that Abigail carries the devil's child got in the woods one night when there was no moon and the wolves was roaming and howling about."

"I think not," Catherine said. "I think the babe's fa-

ther has no cleft feet, nor no tail nor horns. And that
the only darkness there is what he hides in."

"Still, I fear what we shall see."

"The stool and the butter, and no more talk of dev-
ils," Catherine replied.

She strode through the door, waited a moment for
her eyes to adjust to the dim light of stars and moon,
and then began to walk down the familiar path from
her house to the road. Once on the road, as her feet
felt the familiar terrain, she gathered speed, heading
northward to the outskirts of Newbury, where the
poorer farms were located. There she knew she
would find a frightened fifteen-year-old servant girl
about to give birth to a baby whose father she had not
yet named, giving rise to the rumors that fed Phyllis's
overactive imagination.

THREE

❦

THE KING HOUSE was a ten-foot-square hut of wattle-and-daub construction, with a door in the front, windows on the side, and a fireplace opening to a wooden chimney at the rear. The mud walls were cracked in several places, and as she approached, Catherine could see dim light oozing through these openings. She pushed open the door. Abigail lay moaning on the pile of straw that served for her bed, perspiration dripping from every pore. Her mother sat on a stool next to her, holding her daughter's hand. A contraction seized the girl. Her moaning rose to a scream that gurgled in her throat, and her fingers tightened so hard around her mother's hand that Miriam's face contorted in pain. She leaned over her daughter, made a cooing sound into her ear, and wiped the girl's brow with a piece of rag.

Catherine placed her palm against the girl's abdomen and exerted a gentle pressure until she could feel the rock-hard uterus beneath. She held her hand there until the contraction eased and the girl settled back into the straw. She motioned to Phyllis to put the birthing stool near.

"I do not think it will be long," she said. She turned to Miriam. "Have you not sent for your gossips to attend?"

Miriam swept her arm in a gesture that pointed to the empty corners of her tiny house. "You see how it is," she said. "I did indeed make inquiries at the houses of Esther Farnworth and Josephine Matthews. The one's husband was abed with the ague and the other's son could not shit. But if you ask me, if you was to go there, you would find Frederick Farnworth fit to dance and young David Matthews sitting down to a meal that would shame many a man."

"Yes," Catherine replied, "it goes hard with you, I well know."

"And what am I to do? There is not bread enough for the two of us, and now this." She swung her head toward her daughter, whose face, relieved now of the pain of the contraction, had formed itself into a sullen scowl.

"First we must attend to the babe, and to Abigail. All else will follow."

"And the Lord will provide," Miriam said, her voice tinged with a dark and despairing irony, "just as He did when my Peter went to sea and got himself drowned like Jonah, only he did not find no friendly whale to swallow him up and spit him back out on the land, a changed man, for he was not much good, if the truth be spoke, when he was alive with his feet on solid ground."

"Has she not told you who the babe's father is?"

"She did a moment before you came. I told her she must. That you needs must ask her, and that she must answer."

Abigail again moaned. Catherine lifted her shift and probed with her fingers.

"I feel the babe's head," she said "Phyllis, the butter."

Phyllis handed her the cloth through which the melting butter oozed. Catherine opened the cloth and covered the fingers of her right hand with the oil. She coated Abigail's perineum. The girl offered a wan smile. Catherine stroked her forehead with her other hand, and then ran her fingers down her cheek.

"Soon, my love," she said. "But you must tell me the name you told your mother."

Abigail nodded. The pain of the contraction tightened her jaws, and her front teeth came down hard enough onto her lower lip to draw blood. She forced her mouth open for a deep breath.

"Jonathan," she said. "Jonathan Peters."

Catherine had heard many childbed professions over her years as a midwife and had trained herself not to respond to even the most shocking revelations, including hearing years ago that the young girl, no more than fourteen, writhing in agony before her had been impregnated by her own brother. Abigail's naming of Governor Peters's young nephew, recently arrived from England and an ordained minister with a special interest in bringing the Gospel to the savages, almost caused her to lose that well-trained composure. She permitted herself only a small nod and then turned to Phyllis.

"Take an arm, if you will, while I lift the other, and we will have her onto the stool. She will not wait much longer."

Almost as soon as Abigail settled on the U-shaped seat of the stool, another contraction began, and tears filled her eyes,

"Mother," she cried out, "I cannot bear it."

Catherine was on her right side, holding her hand, and Phyllis on her left. Miriam leaned over from behind and cradled her chin.

"You can and you must," she said.

"Aye, mother, but cannot you send for Jonathan? He should be here. He. . . ." She tried to continue, but the pain forced her mouth closed, and she shut her eyes against it. Her body tightened as the contraction reached its peak, and then she let herself fall back against her mother.

"Jonathan," she whispered.

"Hush," Miriam said. "You know he will not come, that the governor does not open his door to me, and the lad himself would not greet you if he saw you on the street. So how can you believe that he will come here to see his babe born?"

Abigail sighed, and her face set into an expression of resignation that dulled her eyes at the same time it puffed out her cheeks.

"Then he and the governor care not that this babe be a bastard."

"Perhaps in time," Catherine said. She knelt in front of Abigail and searched between her legs with her fingers. She felt the tuft of coarse hair, and she permitted herself a small smile. "The next one," she said, "push your babe out, for it is halfway through the door."

The contraction came almost immediately, and Abigail threw herself back against Miriam. She planted her feet hard against the floor and pushed. She rose off the stool, and the babe's head was out. A moment later, the babe was in Catherine's arms. She held it upright, and squeezed the nostrils to clear them. The babe opened its mouth, scrunched up its cheeks, and announced his entrance to the world with a loud and prolonged cry.

Abigail straightened herself on the stool and stared at her child. Her eyes showed a mixture of disbelief and pride. Catherine held the babe for her to see.

"A boy," Abigail said, "and his name will be Jonathan, whether his father acknowledge him or not."

Catherine was not listening. Her fingers had probed, and she had felt the warm blood mixing with the butter on the torn perineum.

"Phyllis," she said, "we will need the needle."

The needle was a fish bone with its natural point sharpened to a fine edge. It broadened slightly toward its base, where a hole had been drilled to accommodate the catgut that served as a suture.

"Take her legs," Catherine said.

Phyllis leaned over Catherine, who was kneeling between Abigail's knees, with the fingers of one hand holding the torn flesh together, and the needle poised over the wound in her other hand. Phyllis seized Abigail's thighs with her strong hands.

"Right," she said.

Abigail's eyes started and saliva flecked her lips.

Her nostrils flared with fear like those of a captured animal as she struggled to move her pinioned legs.

"This is nothing like what you just felt," Catherine said, "but I cannot have you moving about, so you must bide a while longer."

As she talked, she pulled the needle through the edge of the wound, and with a few efficient motions closed the tear. She rose stiffly against the resistance of arthritic knees.

"I warrant you will not be walking about much," Phyllis said, "or. . . ."

"Hush," Catherine said.

"Or sitting, for that matter," Phyllis muttered under her breath.

The afterbirth was slow in coming, but Abigail did not lose much more blood when it did. Still, her head lolled and her flesh was white and damp with perspiration.

"Do you fear for her?" Miriam asked.

"As I always do, but I think she is no worse than exhausted, poor girl." Catherine turned to Phyllis. "I fear more for those two under my roof. Phyllis, get you home to them, and see if you can help them ready themselves to stand before the magistrates. I follow as soon as I am content that Abigail is not in danger."

"I do not think they will listen to me," Phyllis said.

"Speak to them, nonetheless, and say your words come from me."

"I do believe. . . ."

"You may be right, but try anyway."

•   •   •

Catherine heard the voice as though from far away, and for a moment she was a young wife again, listening for the sounds of distress from her three-year-old daughter. She began to rise before she realized that the sound was not coming from her memory of that night so many years ago when all of her skill could not save the life of her own Abigail. She looked about, confused for the moment, until she saw Miriam, holding the babe, standing over her daughter, who stirred now on the straw.

"I was dreaming of my daughter," Catherine said

"I trow you will always remember that night."

"Yes," Catherine replied, "but how is your Abby?"

Without waiting for an answer, she leaned down and ran her hand over the girl's cool forehead.

"Well," she said, "very well indeed."

"I thought so, but better it is to have it from your lips."

The babe cried, a soft, needy cry, and Abigail rose to a sitting position and extended her arms.

"My Jonathan," she said, "I must have *my* Jonathan, if I cannot have the other."

Those words rang in Catherine's mind as she paused before the house of her old friend Magistrate Woolsey. The pain and anger, and perhaps something like love, in Abigail's words demanded a response from Catherine beyond her duties as midwife. She turned on her heel, walked to the magistrate's door, and knocked. In a moment, Woolsey's serving girl, Dorothy, opened the door and, without a word, motioned Catherine into the front room. There at his desk, with a shawl about his shoulders in spite of the summer warmth, sat her old friend. He rose a little out of his chair but then sat back down again with a shrug.

"It's the ague," said Dorothy, with the emphasis of one who speaks only with certitude. She bowed and left.

"I must attend the hearing on the morrow," Woolsey said with a frown. "I hope you did not come to sway me to leniency in my illness."

"Not at all," Catherine said. "I would never so presume to anticipate your settled judgment. It is another matter brings me here."

Woolsey groaned.

"Worse and worse, I fear."

"Not so," Catherine said with a grim smile. "Just a little matter of justice for one who has no one else to speak for her."

A look of recognition spread over the magistrate's face.

"Dorothy tells me you have been attending Abigail King."

"I have."

"And you now know the father of her babe."

"I do."

"And you want me force him to acknowledge his responsibility."

"Why, yes," Catherine said. "You see how simple some matters are."

"You have not told me. . . ."

"Ah, but you do admit the principle?"

"I must."

"Then the man you seek is Jonathan Peters."

Woolsey settled farther back into his chair, his shoulders slumped.

"Simple, you say."

"With your authority I will have him fetched to you."

"Do so, and I will do what I can," he murmured.

"I thought you would," Catherine replied. "And I will send Phyllis around with a tea that will relieve your ague."

"I trust it will give me strength," he said.

"It, and the Lord," Catherine answered. She turned to take her leave and, appearing as though on call, Dorothy led her to the front door.

Massaquoit's wigwam, stationed beneath the spreading limbs of a huge maple on a rise behind Catherine's house, had a flap entrance facing south toward Newbury Harbor. Massaquoit had built it with this orientation so that the wind blowing off the water would reach him at his front door. He did so not because he yearned for the ocean, but to remind him that the water just beyond the harbor was where his comrades' bodies rested fathoms beneath the calm, blue surface, victims of the English treachery that had promised life in exchange for an end to war and instead had delivered death to guarantee the peace.

If the south brought sad memories, the east and the rising sun reminded him of life's promise. And so he had cut an opening in the summer reed sheathing on the eastern side of his wigwam so that he could feel the sun's rays as soon as it rose above the horizon each dawn. Even in the winter, except in the harshest weather, when he felt compelled to cover the opening with a deer skin, he kept this window to the dawn un-covered, choosing to suffer the cold air it admitted so as to feel the distant slant of a December morning's sun.

This morning he had been up for some time, roused by the hotter rays of the sun, and he now sat cross-legged at his fire circle, heating a pan of samp, a mixture of cornmeal and maple syrup. He had dipped a spoon into the samp to test its warmth when he heard a concatenation of voices, two sopranos be-longing to females with the occasional baritone of a male. He recognized Phyllis's voice, of course, and he surmised that the others belonged to the English brother and sister. He peered through his window and saw Phyllis's broad back. Her arms were spread out and her voice was raised to something approaching a shout. Her words, which issued in a steady stream, al-ternated between threats and pleas. The other fe-male's voice, much lighter and almost lilting, was like bubbles bouncing above the vehemence of Phyl-lis's language. It seemed that the young English-woman was amused, for she giggled whenever Phyllis paused for breath.

Phyllis stepped aside, and standing in full view was the young Englishwoman with her chest bared to the morning sun, her red hair running down her back to her waist, her hands on her hips, her voice a song of merriment. Some twenty yards away, Catherine's manservant, Edward, was hoeing between the rows of beans. He did not look up.

"But they are staging this farce. I come to them only as a player," she said.

"Even so, you might come covered," Phyllis replied.

"I expect I am to be whipped."

"I cannot say."

"But I am certain, and when I am, will they not bare my back, and in so doing. . . ." She did not complete her sentence. Instead, she thrust her chest out, and turned toward Edward. When he kept his head down, she whistled, a trill like a songbird's. Edward looked up, stared at her for a moment, and then bent back to his hoeing.

Phyllis looked to the brother.

"It would be well to cover thyself, now," he said to his sister. She looked at him with a sly smile, and then nodded. She joined the two ends of her bodice together and pulled the laces through the eyelets, one after the other. Phyllis waited until the lace reached the top of the bodice, and then she seized the ends and tied a firm knot.

"She does as the spirit moves her," the brother said.

"What spirit might that be?" Phyllis asked.

"Why, the spirit of the Lord," he replied.

"In Newbury," Phyllis said, "she would do well to listen to the magistrates who have summoned you both to attend them this morning. It is only the influence of Mistress Williams that gives you the freedom to make your own way. Else the constable would be here to lead you there himself."

Jane grabbed Roger's hand, and with an exaggerated step toward the path leading away from the house, pulled her brother along.

"Why, then, we must not keep them waiting, and

so sully Mistress Williams's good repute. Come along, now, but do not forget thy hat."

Roger smiled and put his hand on the wide brim of his hat.

"I surely would not."

"But you will remove it before the magistrates, will you not?" Phyllis demanded.

"Let us hurry along, then," Roger said.

Massaquoit watched them leave. The young woman was determined, he concluded, to create trouble for herself, for her brother, and therefore for Catherine, and that trouble would sooner or later find itself at his door. For now, though, he chose to make his breakfast and enjoy the sudden quiet, broken only by the *thwack* of Edward's hoe against the sun-hardened earth.

A sense of foreboding weighed on Catherine as she made the last turn and started up the rise toward her house. The sun was already up, and she could see her manservant, Edward, stooped over a row of beans, pulling out weeds one at a time with a deliberate care that sometimes impressed her with its thoroughness, and at others irritated her with its slowness, but this morning served only to indicate that she was too late to accompany Roger and Jane to their hearing before Governor Peters and the magistrates. Edward always breakfasted after everybody else, and since he was now at work, the others must have left for Newbury some time ago, perhaps as much as an hour. She saw the smoke rising from Massaquoit's wigwam. She would get more information from him than from her taciturn manservant, and so she paused before the flap. Long custom had taught her that Massaquoit would sense her presence without her announcing it, and within a few seconds he emerged through the flap.

"They left"—he glanced up at the sun and held his hands about a foot apart—"some time ago. I was making my morning meal."

"How left they?"

"There was an argument. The English girl and Phyllis."

"What about?"

Massaquoit shrugged.

"I cannot be sure. But I believe it may have had to do with her clothing."

Catherine sensed what he was to say next, recoiled from her suspicion, but knew she must ask.

"What exactly can you tell me?"

"Only that she bared her chest, and Phyllis insisted she cover herself."

"I see," Catherine said, and then hesitated.

"How was she when she left?"

"Covered," Massaquoit replied.

Catherine looked toward Edward. "And him?" she asked.

"He hoed," Massaquoit replied.

"I must haste after. Will you attend me? I must talk to you about another matter, and I cannot pause to do it now."

"I am content to hear of other things," Massaquoit replied.

They headed down the path. Edward looked up from his beans for a moment as they hurried by, and then he finished pulling the weed he had in his hand.

• • •

A cart sat in front of the meetinghouse. The ox attached to it rooted in the dry grass at the edge of the town common. A small crowd of Newbury citizens idled nearby, and others strolled toward them.

"Why do they gather to look at an empty cart?" Massaquoit asked.

"Because they know what purpose it will soon serve."

Constable Larkins stood with his arms across his chest before the heavy oaken front door of the meetinghouse.

"The governor and the other magistrates are inside," he said. "He says he has heard how these Quakers sometimes has been known to put on a show at their trials, and he do not want to give them that opportunity here in Newbury."

"How very thoughtful of the governor," Catherine said. She looked over her shoulder at the crowd. "He does not seem to mind putting on a show himself."

Constable Larkins nodded. "But this be his show."

"Those two young people are under my roof and are my responsibility."

"Aye, Governor Peters said you would make that very point, and he instructed me to direct you to enter through the rear of the building." His voice had dropped to a conspiratorial whisper. He motioned them toward the back of the meetinghouse with a quick gesture of his left arm, then resumed his pose, arms crossed in front of his chest. He leaned forward and looked toward Massaquoit. "He did not say nothing about him,"

"He is, of course, with me," Catherine replied, and

stepped onto the narrow dirt path that led around the building.

They slipped into the meetinghouse through the rear door. Roger and Jane were standing before a table, behind which sat Governor Peters, Magistrates Woolsey and Pendleton, and Minister Davis, a gnarled figure with prominent eyebrows beneath his skullcap. The governor was reading from a document in front of him. Roger was holding his large-brimmed hat in his hands, spinning it slowly in what appeared to be a nervous gesture. Catherine noted the dark brown cloth of Jane's bodice drawn tight across her back. The eyes of the men behind the table shifted from brother to sister without especial attention to one or the other, and Catherine felt relieved that the immediate crisis had not occurred. Woolsey looked past the two young people to offer a quick nod to Catherine as she made her way toward the front of the meetinghouse. Massaquoit, as was his wont, sat down on the rearmost bench, the place assigned to him when he attended services to learn to worship the English god he could never accept as long as the memory, now fifteen years old, of his drowned comrades remained vivid in his recollection.

Governor Peters paused in his recitation from the document and fixed his eyes on Catherine. Then he looked toward the prisoners and continued.

"Roger and Jane Whitcomb, you are adjudged to have violated our statute against the promulgation of the doctrines of your pernicious sect, the Quakers, which our learned doctors have declared have no sanction in Scripture and which run counter to our

well-established beliefs." He paused and looked to
Minister Davis as for confirmation.

The minister rose slowly to his feet and adjusted
his skullcap.

"The doctrines of the Quakers are but the opening
of that vast and horrid sink such as makes the land to
stink in the nostrils both of God and man, more than
the frogs that sometimes annoyed Egypt."

Roger's back stiffened, but much to Catherine's
relief he held his tongue. Minister Davis sat down,
and the governor offered a nod to him before turning
his gaze back to the document from which he had
been reading.

"The punishment prescribed by law for your sect's
refusal to observe our customs, most particularly the
showing of disrespect to superiors and the interruption of our services, which together undermine the
authority of the civil government and destroy the authority of our churches, is whipping at the tail of a
cart and banishment." His voice slowed as he uttered
the last words, pausing on each element of the judi-
cial remedy. He lifted his glance to Catherine, who
had remained standing near her accustomed place at
the foremost bench.

"Your arrival is most timely, Mistress Williams,"
he said, "for you have missed the recitation of these
young people's offenses, which could only have
caused you pain, and can now hear how we intend to
deal with them, and that is a matter most close to
you."

Catherine leveled her gaze at the governor, a man
who more often than not was her adversary for reasons that had nothing to do with personal antipathy.

On that basis they neither liked nor disliked one another; rather, they were indifferent. Where they came into conflict was on the broader, impersonal stage of social and religious vision, for there Governor Peters, in alliance with Minister Davis, insisted on a centralization of religious and secular power to produce a theocratic state in which the individual must always bend a knee to the interests of the community. Catherine stubbornly, although mostly silently, insisted that the individual be permitted to listen to his or her own heart. In the present instance, much as she disapproved of the deliberately provocative acts of the two young people about to receive the harsh punishment of the community, she felt she must stand firm against the pervasive and invasive reach of the governor as he sought to impose his vision on them. She did not have many weapons at her disposal, but the one she did possess could be potent, if she did not play her hand too soon, and this she had no intention of doing. Rather, she would show the governor the card and then place it discreetly back into her hand.

"I beg forgiveness for my tardiness," she said in measured tones that insisted her words be attended to with appropriate seriousness, "for I was at Abigail King's childbed." She paused for a reaction from the governor. He, practiced politician that he was, contained the grimace of displeasure that for a moment darkened his features. That was all Catherine needed to see, as she watched the forced smile return to his face. Perhaps she should tap the card on the table, face up, before turning its back. "As is my duty, you well know, I inquired as to the babe's father."

The smile froze on the governor's face and then

metamorphosed into magisterial disdain. "I am sure you understand, Mistress Williams, that is a matter for another day, should it ever reach the attention of the court, which I do not think will happen."

"As you like," she replied, "I meant only to show how faithful a servant I am to the town's laws."

"We know well your service in that way," Magistrate Woolsey said, "and do commend you for it."

"Indeed we do," Magistrate Pendleton echoed, restrained as he always was by his relative youthfulness, being a man of thirty as opposed to the white hair of the others, as well as his status as the newly elected third magistrate in accord with the town's growing population.

Governor Peters looked from Woolsey to Pendleton, then back to Catherine.

"If we might then proceed," he said.

Catherine sat down. "I wait on the court's pleasure," she said.

"The court's pleasure is to decree that Roger Whitcomb and his sister Jane be tied at a cart's tail together, both to be naked to the waist down and severely whipped. The constable shall apply the lash as they walk, thirty stripes to Roger and fifteen to Jane, until they come to Mistress Williams's house, where they will be left to her pleasure."

Roger clenched his hat until his knuckles turned white, then he took a step toward the table.

"Is it not thy law that a gentleman cannot be whipped? I have money in my purse to pay a fine."

Governor Peters fought to repress the smile that formed on his face, but after a few seconds he could not, and his expression had the contented air of a cat with its paw on the trapped mouse. Jane, meanwhile, glanced askance at her brother with the look of one betrayed.

"Indeed, that is our law. But is it not a tenet of your sect to deny such civil distinctions?"

Roger offered only a mute nod.

"I see," the governor continued. "Therefore, as you see no such distinctions as valid, as such would require you to doff your hat to your superiors, and have your inferiors bow before you, it is the judgment of this court that your claim to a gentleman's privilege is forfeit, and you are to be whipped like the commoner before Christ you profess to be."

Jane stepped in front of her brother, her eyes bright. "And am I to be stripped naked like a common whore?"

"Indeed, you are," Minister Davis intoned, "for like the Whore of Babylon you do threaten to corrupt our churches."

The governor waited a respectful second for the minister's point to settle. "If you were only a whore," he said, "we would have you clean up the offal in our streets. But you are a graver threat."

Jane looked from the governor to the minister as though they were two flies buzzing about her head. She threw back her head and shook her long red hair. "Thou saidst thy law requires that thou banish us as well, does it not?" she asked.

"Child," Catherine said, rising to her feet, "you would do well to govern your tongue."

The governor's face hardened. "The law does so state, but"—he paused and nodded toward Catherine—"in view of your youth and in deference to Mistress Williams's interest in your welfare, we have decided to tolerate your stay among us a while longer. After you are whipped, the court places you under the governance of Mistress Williams to see if she can open your minds and mend your ways of walking. Be it so ordered, and let the punishment be executed forthwith."

As though by a prearranged signal, the front door of the meetinghouse swung open, and Constable Larkins entered. He held a short whip in his right hand, and he swung it in a tense arc in front of him as he walked. He was followed by four soldiers wearing corselets and helmets, and carrying pikes on their shoulders. Massaquoit, sitting in the back of the meetinghouse, watched the men enter. He saw how the sun glinted off the blades of the pikes and the steel of their armor, and for just a moment the ancient rage filled his chest. He forced it back with an audible sigh, which went unremarked by everybody else in the building save Catherine, who turned to the sound. She looked from the soldiers to Massaquoit, her eyes sad with the shared memory, and then she turned back to the front of the meetinghouse, where the soldiers had now formed a tight box around Roger and Jane.

Governor Peters and the other magistrates stood while the soldiers led the prisoners out. They joined the small procession, and then Minister Davis, taking his time, rose and followed. His niece Grace walked a couple of steps behind. The sun shone into the meetinghouse through the open door, and so Catherine sensed more than she saw the crowd that had gathered outside, waiting for their entertainment. She heard the drum start to beat, and that was followed by a murmur of excitement rising from the unseen multitude as the prisoners walked out the door and into the sunshine.

Massaquoit waited until he was alone in the building. He understood that the two young people were to be punished because they prayed to the English god in a way that the other English did not approve. Even after living among the English for many years, he still found situations such as this hard to fathom. He had seen warriors tortured to prove their worth as enemies, their skin flayed or burned, their fingers and toes amputated one by one, but this made sense to one who judged the value of his conquest in battle against the measure of his victim's courage and ability to withstand pain. But to whip young people such as these, especially the woman, was to subject them to a humiliation that brought no honor to those wielding the whip.

He rose from his bench and walked slowly to the front of the meetinghouse, drawn by his curiosity although repelled by the concept. As he approached the door, he heard the drums reach a crescendo and then stop. He shielded his eyes from the sun as he reached the doorway just in time to see the constable place his hands on the young woman's shoulders. She recoiled as though touched by something evil, and then clasped her arms in front of her chest. Roger started to come to her aid, but a soldier stopped his motion with the blade of his pike.

Constable Larkins slid his hands from her shoulders down to her wrists and pulled until he had straightened her arms against her sides. He then mo-

tioned to another soldier, who stepped forward. At a
nod from the constable, the soldier seized the girl's
wrists. Larkins then began to unlace her bodice. Jane
threw herself into a paroxysm of resistance, straining
against the hands of the soldiers and jerking her body
from left to right. The constable's face darkened and
he muttered between his teeth. He could not manage
to hold onto the tip of the lace. The crowd's murmuring grew impatient and angry.

Catherine stepped forward.

"Permit me," she said.

Jane looked from the constable to Catherine. The
constable dropped his hands. Catherine motioned to
the soldier, who released his hold on Jane's wrists.
The girl relaxed her body and permitted Catherine to
unlace her bodice, and then pull down her shift, exposing her bare upper torso. The constable motioned
for Catherine to step back. Roger pulled his shirt over
his head. He hesitated and then tossed it high in the
air, over Catherine to Grace. It fell at the young
woman's feet, and she picked it up.

"We would not want it stained with my blood," he
said.

"Give it here, girl," Catherine said, and Grace
handed her the shirt.

Meanwhile, Jane stood with her arms across her
chest for a moment, and then swung them down to
her sides hard. She turned about in a tight circle, a
bright smile fixed on her face, as a murmur arose
from the onlookers.

"Now, have you seen enough?" she said. She
turned to face the constable, who was holding a
length of rope. She held out her hands, and he tied

one end of the rope about her wrists and the other to a ring on the backboard of the cart. A boy who had positioned himself beside the ox swatted it hard on the flank with a stick. The beast looked around to see the source of this attack. The boy yelled, "Giyyup, you," and hit the animal again. It took a step forward, pulling the clumsy cart forward, enough for Jane, now tied to the tail, to be yanked off her feet. She fell to her knees, onto a steaming turd left by the ox minutes before. She got to her feet, her eyes filled more with manic exuberance than with anger.

"Again," she said, "if thou darest."

The boy raised his arm, but a soldier stepped forward and the boy let his arm fall to his side.

"Enough," the constable called, and the boy stepped back, his face sullen. Then he permitted himself to share a knowing smirk with his friends.

The constable tied Roger with quick motions, then picked up the whip he had placed on the ground behind the cart. It was a short, vicious affair of hardened leather with three thongs, on each of which were three nasty-looking knots. He spat on his hands, rolled the whip handle between his palms, and looked to the governor.

"Begin," Governor Peters said.

The drummer, a boy of ten or twelve, raised his sticks and brought both down. Then he struck the drum, first with one stick and then the other, in a slow, rhythmical beat, such as might accompany the condemned to the gallows. The crowd quieted in anticipation. Constable Larkins lifted his whip high over his head and held it there, as though waiting to join the rhythm of the drum. Roger cast a wary eye over his shoulder, and saw the whip poised over his back. He sucked in his breath and stiffened his arms. Jane kept her eyes closed. The whip came down with a *whoosh* and a *thwack* across Roger's back. The crowd let out its collective breath. Roger grunted in pain and fell to one knee. The knotted cords left three parallel lines of torn flesh between his shoulder blades. The welts reddened, but there was no blood. Grace stepped to him, looked down at his back, and then covered her eyes. Minister Davis took his niece's arm and led her away.

Constable Larkins moved a step or two to his left, so as to position himself behind Jane. She still kept her eyes closed. She had flinched just a little as she heard the whip whistle down and strike her brother, but she offered no other response or preparation. The constable lifted his whip above her bare back and brought it down with as much force as he had applied to Roger. Again there was the *whoosh* of air cut by the descending whip and the echoing slap as the corded knots bit into flesh. Jane's eyes started open in the sudden realization of pain, and she staggered to both knees. She began to cry out but bit down on her lips until her teeth drew blood, remaining mute.

"One," the constable called out, and the crowd nodded. The boy who had provoked the ox held up one finger. He walked to the rear of the cart and stopped a few feet away from Jane. He stared at her back and then her breasts. She returned his look, holding his eyes until he turned away. Again, he held up his one finger, and returned to his position near the head of the animal that was once again fruitlessly trying to find something to eat in the barren dirt.

The drum rolled again, and Constable Larkins brought his whip down on Roger's back. Without waiting, as he had before, he brought the whip down again. "Two and three," he called out. As the whip cracked off his back, the drum reached a crescendo. That was a signal to a soldier who climbed into the seat of the cart and snapped a long whip over the ox's back. It did not respond at first, but a couple of lashes encouraged it to move, and it began a ponderous forward motion. The cart lurched ahead, and the two tied to it stumbled behind.

It was a quarter of a mile from Newbury to Catherine's house. With notable judgment, the constable rationed his strokes, two to Roger to every one for Jane, in proportion to their sentences, and all spaced evenly so that he would finish the whipping at the entrance to the path that led to Catherine's house. Each time he raised his arm to bring down the whip, the drummer would roll his sticks on his instrument, and the constable would yell out his count. The governor and magistrates walked behind, their faces stony and their expressions blank. The crowd followed in a ragged semicircle, watching with approval as each stroke hit the bare flesh. The young people now fell each time the lash struck. Tears filled their eyes, and their backs were laid open in bleeding stripes.

As they neared Catherine's house, Constable Larkins grew careless in his strokes, which on several occasions fell on their legs, arms, or neck. The fifteenth and last stroke to Jane glanced off her side, and the hard knots at the end of the cords cut into her breast. She howled in pain, no longer able to stop herself.

Catherine trudged right behind the magistrates, her expression alternating between sorrow and anger as each stroke of the whip gave evidence of the cruel righteousness of her colony's leaders.

Massaquoit, as was his wont, drifted along at the extreme edge of the moving mass of people. As he witnessed this ritual, he shook his head. He applauded the young woman's courage until she could no longer repress the expression of pain. He did not understand how such a savage beating, as he was now witnessing, should be administered to a young man who refused to lift his hat, or to a young woman who was clearly too spirited for her own good.

Catherine glanced over her shoulder at Massaquoit and intuited what he must be thinking. She shrugged to herself, knowing that she would not be able to explain this harshness to him. She grimaced as the whip landed for the last time on Roger's back just as the cart stopped in front of her house. He lay on the ground, his back a mottled mass of torn flesh, blood, and dirt. Jane knelt next to her brother, her back only marginally less torn.

They will be a long time healing, Catherine thought. *I can only hope they will be instructed by this pain and humiliation.*

Although, unlike Massaquoit, she did not question the sentence, recognizing its harshness as both logical and unwarranted, she did question whether she had served the young people well—and their parents, for that matter—by saving them from banishment only to subject their flesh to the tearing of the constable's merciless whip.

• • •

Massaquoit did not see the last blows land. His attention had been drawn away from the cart and the bloody victims tied to it. Just as the constable's whip was about to come down for the last time, out of the corner of his eye, Massaquoit caught a glimpse of a beaver hat. He turned to see the owner of that hat leaning toward both the governor and the minister. The three held an earnest conference for a few seconds, not bothering to look up as the whip snapped one more time against flesh. Then the governor and minister walked to the cart as the constable untied Roger and Jane, while the other blended into the crowd and moved away as the citizens of Newbury, now that the spectacle was over, moved in desultory twos and threes toward their homes.

And just what did Wequashcook have to say to the English? Whatever it was, it surely would be to his advantage, whoever else might be hurt or endangered.

FOUR

❧❧❧

CATHERINE STOOD BETWEEN the two beds in what used to be her oldest sons' room but now served her guests. Instead of looking at John, who shared both his name and his curly brown hair with his father, and Charles, whose straight black hair mirrored Catherine's before age silvered it, she stared at the torn flesh of Roger and Jane. So it had come to this, she thought, so late in her life to witness the sorry spectacle of two young people under her governance so shamefully and painfully subjected to the colony's insistence on conformity. She recalled others who had been expelled from the colony for their divergent views, but had not been so physically assaulted. She felt the anger rise in her, directed for the most part at the magistrates and minister, but not a little leavened by her recognition of the provocation offered by her two young guests.

They both knelt rather than lay on their beds, in a

kind of vertical fetal position, their heads down between their arms, their elbows supporting their upper
torsos. They attempted to remain absolutely still—
even the slightest motion racked them with sharp
pain—but they must breathe. They inhaled with the
gentlest of motions, but still grimaced as their di-
aphragms expanded. Then they held the air in their
lungs before ever so slowly releasing it. In spite of
their best efforts, they could not draw breath without
an accompanying moan.

Phyllis continued her work on Roger's back, ap-
plying the coneflower poultice with the softest touch
she could manage, yet the young man winced as the
cloth even approached his skin. Catherine examined
her own work on Jane, and concluded she could do
no more. Massaquoit stood at a respectful distance in
the entrance to the room. Even from where he was,
some twelve feet from the two beds in a room only
half lit by the late afternoon sun coming through one
clouded glass window, he could see enough of the
crusted blood and lacerated skin to conclude that
these two young people would not have a night's
sleep for a very long time. He recalled a similar spectacle when he was a young warrior after a successful
raid against the Narragansetts. He and his companions had returned with two captive braves, and he had
watched as their skin was peeled from their backs,
layer by layer, their faces set against the pain until
first one and then the other collapsed in silent and un-
expressed agony. The intention was to wait for them
to revive so their torture could resume, but somehow,
during the night, they roused, overpowered the un-
suspecting guard, and made their way into the woods.

They left a trail of fresh blood as they crawled through the underbrush, and thus were easily pursued and recaptured. As they were surrounded, they tried to lift their arms to strike their tormentors, and to rise to their feet to offer a fatal charge that would result in their quicker deaths. But their wounds so pained them that they were struck immobile, and could only sneer as once again ropes were looped around their necks.

They were returned to the camp, the torture resumed the next day, and they died in silence. Looking at the backs of Roger and Jane, Massaquoit again saw those two young warriors from long ago, and he could only shake his head and let out an explosive sigh. Jane lifted her head at the sound. She struggled to raise herself a few more inches so she could turn her head more fully toward him. Beneath the pain in her eyes sparkled something more, but he could not identify exactly what. Whatever it was convinced him yet again of her unusual spirit. She was a woman like none he had met. Perhaps it was the passion of her religious beliefs, but he did not fully credit that explanation. He looked toward Catherine, who had been studying the silent interplay. Catherine offered a gesture—half nod, half shrug—as though to say that she, too, saw the dangerous quality in Jane. Jane held herself up for a few moments more, then without a word sank back onto her elbows. Catherine ushered Massaquoit out of the room and into the hallway. She half shut the door behind them.

"You see," she said, "what has befallen them. They must learn to govern their tongues."

"The boy might," Massaquoit replied. "He felt the whip. I do not think the girl did."

"Surely you saw her back, as bloody and torn as his."

"Yes. But I see in her eyes that she did not feel the pain in the same way."

Catherine sighed. "You only give voice to my own thought. She will not be instructed, but still I must protect her as I can."

"Why not send her back to her parents?"

"And do the colony's work for them? I think not."

Massaquoit smiled. "Ah, so, you agree with her protest?"

Catherine lowered her voice. "More than I can show."

"You want to protect her, then?"

"Yes. As best I can. And while they recover from their grievous hurts, I have a little time to find a weapon to fight back on her behalf, and"—she paused—"perhaps to right another wrong as well. I attended a birth . . ."

"And you would like me to bring back the father."

"Why, yes," Catherine said.

"Do not be surprised. Newbury might be English, but it holds secrets no better than my old village. There is no man about the house where the babe was born. All can see that."

"He is at Niantic."

"Helping us find the English god."

"Yes."

"What if he does not want to return?"

Catherine permitted herself a small smile. "I am

sure you can find grounds persuasive enough to convince him."

A soft moaning drifted out into the hallway where they stood.

"I must attend their hurts," she said.

"It is the boy."

Catherine opened the door and looked into the room. She saw Roger's pained stare in her direction.

"It is indeed," she said.

"I leave with the morning sun," Massaquoit said.

Catherine looked into the room and sighed. "I do not think they will find any more trouble before you return."

"Only if it finds them in this room," he replied.

He heard the soft tread outside his wigwam and he knew that the person making it could have been quieter had he intended to be. Massaquoit had been lying on his back, looking up through the smoke hole at the dark sky, waiting for it to lighten. He had already eaten a breakfast of cold corn bread, which would hold him until he reached Niantic, a five-mile walk up the river that emptied into Newbury harbor after cutting its way through the woods to the north and west of the town. He waited for his visitor to announce his presence. A moment later a soft whistle made its way through the thin summer matting of woven reeds that formed the shell of his wigwam. He pushed out the flap at his door and emerged. Wequashcook, wearing his beaver hat as always, was waiting for him.

"You sleep light," the older Indian said. "Or you are up early to begin a journey."

"And you are here to advise me not to go, are you not?"

"I am here only to confirm my suspicion."

"You have done so. As you have correctly guessed, I am about to leave." He glanced back at the entrance to his wigwam. "There is a little of my breakfast left."

Without replying, Wequashcook crawled into the wigwam. Massaquoit waited. It would be rude to leave before the other emerged. When he did, Wequashcook was wiping the crumbs from his lips with one hand and holding the remains of the slice of corn bread with the other.

"Thank you," he said. He took another bite, chewing the hard bread slowly. He picked at a crumb that had stuck between his front teeth. "I am to track you and prevent you from reaching Niantic," he said.

Massaquoit nodded. "You must do as you must."

"I am glad that I find you so agreeable."

"I do not think you will succeed in catching up with me. Your legs are older than mine."

"That may be."

Massaquoit took a few walking steps and then broke into a trot. He permitted himself a quick look back over his shoulder. Wequashcook was squatting in front of the wigwam, munching the last of the bread.

Catherine looked across the table, first at Roger and then at Jane. Both leaned on their elbows. Roger dipped his pewter spoon into the samp that filled his wooden trencher. He moved his arm with great care, and Catherine felt herself grimacing in sympathy with him as the pain registered on his face with the slow progress of his hand back toward his mouth. When he had raised the spoon almost level with his lips, he gasped and dropped the implement with a dull clatter onto the table. Phyllis, who was standing nearby, picked up the spoon and tried to hand it back to him. He shook his head.

"I cannot," he said.

"But I have added extra molasses. It will sweeten your tongue."

"I cannot bring it to my tongue," he said. "It is not possible."

"I will have a go," Jane said.

She forced her arm to move against the pain that the movement sent searing across the ruined flesh of her back. She brought a spoonful of the steaming samp to her mouth even as she had to close her eyes to shut out the agony. She swallowed and managed a weak smile.

"Thou art right, Phyllis," she said. "It is sweet enough, perhaps, even to sweeten his disposition."

"Aye, I warrant," Roger said, "but I will have none of it." He rose clumsily from the chair.

"You must eat," Catherine said, "that you may mend."

Roger began to say something but then had to set his jaw against another spasm of pain. When it passed, he nodded and walked out of the room.

Jane ate her samp in silence, her face set as she brought the spoon to her mouth at even intervals until she was done. She then rose, and with a nod at Catherine and Phyllis, went to join her brother in their room upstairs. Phyllis looked after her as she dragged herself, one step at a time, up the staircase.

"I must tell you, Mistress," Phyllis said in a voice just above a whisper, "that I heard them talking this morning when I passed by on my way down to the kitchen."

"Think you that odd?" Catherine asked.

"It is not that they were, but what they said."

"And what might that have been?"

"I could not hear their words," Phyllis replied.

"But did you not just now say . . . ?"

"I did. And I meant what I said. It was not what they said, but their manner of conversation I refer to."

Catherine frowned. "You know I must go to Abigail."

"It was not right," Phyllis insisted.

"But in what fashion?" Catherine asked as she stood up.

Phyllis brought Catherine her midwife's bag from the peg in the corner of the kitchen. "It just was not. If you had heard it, you would know."

"Then, perhaps tomorrow and the next day I will, although I fear what you heard was no more than their groans."

Phyllis considered for a moment. "I do not think so, for it was words I heard."

"Words that you did not make out."

"Words nonetheless, angry words, I think."

Catherine strode to the door. "You may tell me more when you know more. Until then, do not fill your head and my ears with such fanciful tales."

Phyllis muttered something under her breath that Catherine could not hear, and then busied herself clearing the table as Catherine closed the door behind her.

Catherine walked with a rapid, rolling stride up the path that led to the King house, her mind turning over Phyllis's remarks, giving them a bit more credence now as she had time to consider them, for she, too, felt something odd in the relationship between her young guests. Up to now she had attributed whatever it was to a combination of their awkwardness as strangers in Newbury and the intensity of their religious convictions, and she still believed she was right in that view. Yet, she left her mind open a crack to admit Phyllis's suspicions, so she could examine them at her leisure. Whatever else she was unsure of, she was most certain that their injuries would prevent Roger and Jane from getting into mischief for at least a little while.

Her thoughts thus engaged as she came within sight of the hut, she did not immediately take note of the figure coming toward her. She was slow to see that it was a man of substance, as indicated by the ruff collar and broad-brimmed hat adorned with a buckle, an extravagance permitted under the sumptuary laws only to a man of two hundred pounds a year. She brought herself to a sudden stop as she realized she was about to walk right into the governor.

Governor Peters was apparently absorbed in thought, for as he walked, he shook his head back and forth as though in sorrow or anger, his eyes staring at, but not seeing, the ground immediately beneath his feet. He looked up just in time to catch Catherine's eye as she came to a halt in front of him.

"Ah, Mistress Williams, is it? Come to check on mother and babe, I do not doubt."

"Indeed I have." She felt the tension in the governor's face and chose not to explore its source. He seemed to have come to the same tacit conclusion, for he straightened up, as though dismissing whatever had been troubling him, and nodded his head.

"A very good thing," he said, "that the whore and her bastard should have you to look after them."

She felt her anger rise, but she also recognized that Peters wanted to provoke her. She should not take the bait. "I trust you left them well," she replied, and without waiting for an answer, she turned herself sideways to pass him on the narrow path.

"Well, Mistress," he called after her, "for that you must inquire of them inside."

Miriam King stood hunched in the low doorway. The wrinkles on her face seemed deeper, and she twisted something tightly between her hands. As Catherine approached, she retreated into her house. Catherine followed. Inside, Abigail sat on a stool, her babe at her breast. She glanced at her mother, her eyes bright with anger. She started to say something, then stopped herself. Catherine looked from one to the other. Neither woman returned her glance. She approached Abigail. The babe, its eyes closed, sucked, unaware of the new presence in its tiny world. Abigail looked up at Catherine. "We have just had a very special visitor," she said.

"That I know," Catherine replied.

Abigail gestured with her shoulder toward her mother.

"You can ask her about it," she said. "I have nothing to say."

Miriam looked down, and Catherine saw that she was unwilling to meet her glance. She waited. The babe continued sucking. He pulled back his head and screwed up his face. Abigail was staring at her mother. The babe tried the breast again, then howled.

"You had better give him the other," Catherine said.

Abigail started, then nodded. She switched her babe to her other breast and he grabbed it between his tiny fingers. He fastened his lips to the nipple, sucked once hard, his cheeks extended like a squirrel carrying nuts, then drooped his head and was asleep.

Something clunked onto the floor. Catherine turned to see Miriam stooping, her hands groping beneath the door, which still stood open. She dropped to her knees and ran her hand along the floor until she found the little sack. She stood up and dropped the sack into the pouch she wore around her waist.

"How much did he give you?" Catherine asked.

"Enough," Miriam said, "and that is all I intend to tell you."

Ordinarily, Catherine's sympathies would be engaged by the obviously desperate plight Miriam King, her daughter, and now her grandson, faced. As a widow with no male relatives to provide assistance, Miriam scraped out her sustenance any way she could, mending garments of the rich although she was not gifted with a needle, or begging when all else failed. As a servant in the governor's house, Abigail was paid with room and board and an occasional coin, the main economic benefit of the arrangement for her mother being removal of the daughter from the mother's daily responsibility. But now daughter and new babe were back where there was little food or money, and little hope for improvement.

Catherine understood all of this, but she knew that Miriam had just sold not only her self-respect but also that of her daughter for the coins in that pouch. Moreover, it was likely that she had traded away any chance of the child having its father, or her daughter a husband. But if she were honest with herself, what probably rankled her most was the untenable thought that Jonathan Peters would escape any responsibility.

"You have made your bargain," she said, "and well I can understand why you have."

"Can you indeed?" Miriam replied, her tone edged with the weight of the eternal contempt of the poor when faced with someone of better circumstances who claims to understand their misery. "I think not."

"But yet I can," Catherine insisted. "I was not born rich."

"Well, then, remember when you were not, and you will have nothing further to chastise me with," Miriam said.

"The governor called your daughter a 'whore,' and her child a 'bastard.' In your pouch you have coins that perhaps have bought your silence on this matter. But not mine."

"What do you intend to do, Mistress Williams?" Abigail asked. There was hope in her eyes.

"What I can, child, what I can," Catherine replied, and then she left.

• • •

The thought took Massaquoit by surprise. For that matter, it was less a thought than an image, one that caused a stirring in him that had been an everyday occurrence when his wife was alive, but which he had now almost forgotten. He had seen the woman behind the image years before, in a clearing not far from where he now was as he approached Niantic. At that time, he saw her as the mother of two angry young sons who would not accept the English god as the others in the village had. However, his history with her went further back to a time neither wanted to remember, and so they had parted. He had thought of her from time to time when some news from the village reached Newbury, but he had resisted the urge to renew their acquaintance.

Now, though, he felt anticipation rise in him. He had begun to tire after his walk, but his feet regained their spring, and he quickened his pace along the path that led from the clearing to the outskirts of the village. He saw smoke curling up between the trees, and he heard dogs barking. The path circled a small rise, then straightened again. He paused at the point where it emerged from between two tall pines onto a flat field of brown weeds. A scrawny dog lifted its head and growled. The smoke was rising above the wigwam that sat on the far edge of the field. It was one of a dozen or so that ringed a central structure, built in the English fashion of frame and planks with a thatched roof. Massaquoit recognized that building as the meetinghouse, provided after years of acrimonious debate, by the English of Newbury to house Christian Indians.

Of a sudden, he felt a weariness that had nothing

to do with his journey to the village. Rather, he seemed to be breathing in the settled apathy of the village's residents. As he looked about, there were few signs of activity. Here a man sat in front of a wigwam, his eyes vacant; there a woman mashed corn in a pestle and mortar. Behind the wigwams were gardens, most overgrown with weeds and offering corn and beans no more than half their usual size. As he walked among the wigwams, children looked at him with bright and curious eyes, but the adults either glanced away or stared at him with suspicion. He had heard that Rawandag, an old warrior recently returned from a distant village, still had his heart hardened against the English and had gathered a few of the younger men to his cause, but Massaquoit saw no sign of either them or their energy in the lifeless atmosphere he now entered.

In front of the meetinghouse, he saw someone he thought he recognized. He walked closer and confirmed that the young man in his early twenties was the same individual he had seen years before in the clearing with his mother and his younger brother. The young man smiled.

"Matthew, have you come to join us? Meeting is tomorrow."

Massaquoit studied the confident face, searching his memory for a name to attach to it. He could not remember.

"I saw you last in the woods, when your younger brother wanted to put an arrow into my chest. But I do not recall your name," Massaquoit said.

"It is no matter, for that name no longer exists. I am Peter, as you are Matthew."

"Only in Newbury," Massaquoit replied.

"I do not want to quarrel," Peter said.

Massaquoit nodded. "I have not seen your brother in many years."

Peter hesitated, sadness in his eyes, but then with an internal shrug that manifested itself in an audible exhalation, he answered. "After he helped you, he lived with your mother for some time. He was confused. He did not know if he was an Indian or a white man, and so he was neither. He has come back, and I think he is still uncertain. He says he has something to sell to the English that will buy him an English woman."

Massaquoit remembered the figure that dashed onto the beach to retrieve whatever the gull had dropped.

"Do you know what he is selling?"

Peter shrugged. "As I said, he is confused. You did not come to seek him, did you?"

"No," Massaquoit replied. "I am looking for an English." He looked toward the closed door of the meetinghouse.

Peter's face darkened. "Then you will not find him inside there."

"Is he not a minister?"

"He wears the clothing of one. I was preaching here before he arrived."

"So you are angry that he has replaced you?"

Peter shook his head. "I would be happy to have one better informed open God's Holy Word with more skill than I can with my own poor abilities. If he did that, I would be more than content."

The idea struck Massaquoit, just a variation on a

story that was now very stale. "He has found other interests, then, away from his uncle's eyes."

"Yes," Peter said, "and we are powerless to control him."

"But I am not," Massaquoit declared. "Where might I now find him?"

Peter turned around as though looking through the closed door.

"There is a wigwam on the other side. Its owner went away, and is not coming back. A girl plays in there sometimes. The English minister. . . . ."

Massaquoit heard what Peter did not want to say.

"And you did nothing?"

Peter hung his head like a beaten dog. "What could I?" he asked, his voice plaintive. "He is the governor's nephew, and the governor raised the money for our meetinghouse."

"A child who plays in a deserted wigwam," Massaquoit snapped. He started to trot in the direction of the wigwam.

Peter put his hand on Massaquoit's arm as though to stop him. "Do not make trouble for us."

Massaquoit stared at him until Peter relaxed his grip. "I have a message to him from Mistress Williams. That is my business here. I intend no trouble for you more than you have already created for yourselves by abandoning our ways and pretending that you have become as the English."

"We do not pretend," Peter said. "The old ways failed us. Nobody should know that better than you."

The remark stung, because it was right.

"That may be," Massaquoit said, "but I must be about my business."

He walked around the meetinghouse, and at its rear he saw a wigwam with an untended garden some fifty feet straight ahead. He approached it. As he did, his eyes caught a movement beneath a tree to the right of the wigwam. He made out the shape of a woman. She put up her hand as though to stop his approach. He continued, although his pulse quickened at seeing Willeweenaw again. He considered for a moment, then veered toward her.

"I have just spoken with your son," he said.

"He told you about this," she said, pointing to the wigwam.

"He did."

"And you came anyway. You have a nose for trouble."

"I have a commission."

"From the English woman?"

"Yes, to bring back the English inside there."

She shrugged. "I cannot stop you."

"Do you want to?" he asked.

She did not hesitate. "No."

He nodded and turned to the wigwam. He heard a loud slap, and a muffled moan. He hastened his pace. He pulled open the flap and saw the white buttocks of Jonathan Peters, who was crouched above a girl no more than twelve or thirteen. His hand was over her mouth, and her eyes were wide and starting. Jonathan was about to descend onto her when Massaquoit reached him, and with one blow to the back of his neck rendered him unconscious. He rolled off the girl, who jumped to her feet and pulled down her dress. She stared wildly at Massaquoit for a moment. He expected her to flee, but she dropped to her knees and reached under the mat on which she had been lying. She pulled something out, and fled through the flap. As she did, she caromed off of Willeweenaw.

Willeweenaw watched the departing girl and then turned to Massaquoit. "You see how it is," she said.

Massaquoit began to nod, but Willeweenaw put her palms on his cheeks. "No, that is not all," she said. "She is Minnehaha, my sister's daughter. She runs now to her cousin, my son Ninigret."

Jonathan moaned from inside the wigwam, and Massaquoit looked in that direction.

"I must take this English back. I need to know what the girl carried with her."

Willeweenaw shrugged. "I am sure your old friend can tell you that."

"Wequashcook?"

"Of course."

Jonathan crawled out of the wigwam. Massaquoit took a step toward him, and he cowered. "I will offer you no resistance," he said.

"That is very wise," Massaquoit replied.

FIVE

❦

MINISTER DAVIS STOOD in Catherine's front room. He was accompanied by his niece Grace. Catherine saw the fearful expression in the young woman's eyes. She could not give voice to her assurance that she would not reveal Grace's secret, but she took her hand and gave it a warm squeeze. Grace returned the pressure, and her countenance almost audibly relaxed.

"I hope you will permit me to talk to the young people," Minister Davis said.

"To what purpose?" Catherine asked, although she well knew the answer.

"Why, to see if they have been lessoned by their punishment."

"You believe the whip opens the mind?"

"Surely, it is well known."

"How do they mend?" Grace asked, and then blushed as her uncle frowned at her. "I did witness their correction," she added. "The young man's back, as he was on the ground, all I could see was the blood, and I had to avert my eyes."

"Please excuse my niece's impudence," Minister Davis said. "She would accompany me here to see for herself that he and his sister do not suffer overmuch. She has too tender a heart."

Catherine knew that Grace's interest in Roger had nothing to do with her uncle's concern for the young man's soul. For a moment, she was back in Alford, a young girl captivated by the dark eyes and broad shoulders of a clerk who worked in her father's textile business. Her father had frowned upon a romance that promised no material gain—the young man was poor, with no prospects of becoming rich—and Catherine had dutifully turned her eyes elsewhere. That memory flickered before her mind's eye, and she felt, so many years later, a pang of regret.

"My servant is dressing their wounds now," Catherine said. "Perhaps Grace can assist."

Minister Davis looked at her for a moment, and she thought she saw there an expression not unlike that which she had seen in her father's eyes when she had announced that the young clerk might seek permission to court her.

"I have come to pray with them, Mistress Williams, not to play the surgeon. And if they are able, perhaps to dispute with them, so as to show them their errors."

The stairs creaked under a heavy tread, and they turned to see Phyllis coming downstairs. She was holding an empty jar in one hand and a rag in the other. She gave a quick, almost imperceptible bow to-

ward the minister and a suspicious glance toward
Grace.

"I need more poultice," she said to Catherine. "I
have dressed Jane's wounds, and she is resting comfortably. Roger waits."

"I see that this is not a good time for my visit,"
Minister Davis said to Catherine. "When might you
advise me to return?"

"In a day or two," Catherine replied. She did not
want to encourage the minister's attention, and she
also felt he should recognize the severity of the
wounds inflicted on her young charges. "I can send
for you when they are better able to profit from your
counsel."

"Then we must take our leave," Minister Davis
said. He stepped toward the door. He paused when
his niece, whose eyes were fixed on the stairs, did not
follow him.

"Come along, then, Grace," he said.

She turned to him and nodded. "Yes, uncle."

Catherine was sitting at her desk, going over accounts, later that afternoon when she was aware that
Phyllis was greeting somebody at the front door. A
moment later, Phyllis entered the room.

"It is that young woman," Phyllis said. "She is
here again."

Catherine knew immediately which woman it
must be.

"Send Grace in, if you please," she said.

Grace appeared in the doorway, eyes downcast,
her pale face warmed by a blush.

"Does your uncle know you are here?" Catherine

asked. "Or that you have been here without him more than once?"

The young woman lifted her head, and Catherine noted the spark of defiance in her eyes.

"I see," Catherine said. "What am I to do? Countenance your deceit and anger your uncle, or send you away to satisfy him and deny you what your heart seeks?"

Grace did not respond, but hope shone in her eyes, and Catherine was forced again to remember her father's clerk, and her lost opportunity. Her head and heart argued, fiercely and silently.

"I will call him down to you," she said. "I will not have you visit him in his bed."

But before she could, the stairs creaked, and there stood Roger, towering over Catherine, his eyes fastened on Grace. Catherine raised herself on her toes until Roger noticed the movement and looked at her. Catherine motioned to the front room where she had been sitting at her desk, but where guests also were entertained.

"You may talk in there," she said, "but after today I must seek, and obtain, Grace's uncle's permission."

She stood in the hall as the two young people walked into the front room. She heard the scraping of wood against wood, and she knew that Roger was moving the two heavy side chairs closer together. There was silence for a few moments, and then the low murmur of voices. Catherine sensed Phyllis now standing behind her. She turned to face her servant.

"Do not say it," she said. "It is foolishness."

"And worse," Phyllis replied.

"Perhaps, but to save me from further embarrassment, stand you near the door, where they cannot see you, and wait no more than ten minutes before coughing loudly."

"I am well," Phyllis said.

"But you will cough, nonetheless, as though your very life depended on it, and then you will enter the room and tell them that I require my desk to finish overlooking my accounts."

"Ten minutes?" Phyllis asked.

"Indeed, and no more."

Catherine sat at the table in the dining room. She busied herself trying to remember the particulars of the account page she had been examining when Grace arrived. It listed the various items unloaded from *The Good Hope*, amounts of trading goods, supplies, prices, and so forth. The numbers swam. She closed her eyes. She snapped them open with a start, not sure whether she had dozed or not. She heard the stairs creak again, this time under a rapid and much lighter tread. A moment later she heard Jane's sharp voice answered by Phyllis's gruffer tones. She could not make out the words. She rose and went out into the hall to find them jaw to jaw. Roger was approaching; Grace remained seated in the front room.

Phyllis's face was red with confusion and anger. She turned from brother to sister and back again. "Mistress Williams . . . ," she began.

"What of her?" Jane asked.

Phyllis stared past her and caught Catherine's eye. Relief spread over her face. "Why, ask her yourself," Phyllis said to Jane. "For she is right behind you."

Jane spun around, her jaw thrust with determination to make her point. "What meanst thou," she asked Catherine, "to leave these two alone?" She nodded in Roger and Jane's direction.

"Do you fear your brother's reputation?" Catherine asked. She expected a quick and sassy reply, but instead Jane seemed to consider her response.

"No," she said with deliberation. "As for that— why, as he is in thy house, under thy governance, I shall leave him to thee." She turned on her heel and headed for the door.

"My sister is impulsive," Roger said.

"That she is," Catherine agreed. "Her tongue and her actions know no rein."

Grace now stood up and joined Roger. She looked up at him, her eyes moist with affection.

"I fear I have overstayed," she said. "My uncle will miss me."

"Perhaps you should have thought so beforehand," Phyllis said.

"Walk with her to her uncle's house," Catherine said. "I have an errand to run."

"She need not," Grace replied.

"No, but I prefer it," Catherine said.

"My sister . . . ," Roger began.

"She is my errand," Catherine said, and walked toward the door, which Jane had left open.

The footpath in front of Catherine's house quickly took a sharp bend as it headed south toward the center of Newbury. However, in the other direction it lay straight for a mile or more as it worked its way through the open fields of the huge tract owned by the governor that was worked by several tenant farmers. Beyond those fields the woods had been cleared only occasionally by lesser landholders.

Catherine did not hesitate after walking down the hill from her house. She turned north towards the governor's land. Far ahead she saw a tiny figure who, she surmised, must be Jane. The figure was moving at a fast pace and would soon disappear. However, Catherine did not hurry after it, for she knew, almost to a certainty, where Jane must be heading.

The rumors had been bruited about even before Roger and Jane arrived. And now that they had been in Newbury for several weeks, the stories about the secret meetings had so increased in frequency and intensity that Catherine had concluded that, though exaggerated, the gossip must be rooted in fact. She set out, therefore, at a deliberate but unhurried pace while she worked out in her mind what she would say when she knocked at a door where she had no reason to expect a friendly welcome.

It had been a hot and dry summer. The fields through which she walked evidenced the drought. The rows of corn were only a couple of feet high, with browned stalks and stunted ears. The beans straggled up their poles and bore only scattered blossoms. Cows lay in pastures of parched grass. The air was hot and thick, and Catherine felt her feet getting heavier with each step. As the path narrowed at the end of the governor's fields, it entered a pine wood. Dried needles crackled beneath her feet, and it was cool in the shade of the trees. She knew she was getting close to her destination. The house she sought sat just past this section of the path, where it opened again into fields surrounding a low hill. Rumor in Newbury had it that squatters had occupied some of these fields, which they were now cultivating without permission from the town.

Catherine half expected to hear voices lifted in prayer as she approached, but the only sound was the chirping of birds and the scurrying feet of a chipmunk, fleeing at the sound of her feet crunching the dried needles on the ground. Her face glowed with perspiration, and she paused in the last shade at the edge of the woods before venturing onto the field between her and the house.

The last time she had approached this house, it was to treat a young girl ill with a fever. The child lived with her mother and father, new arrivals from England, who had agreed to farm this land in return for their shelter. The girl lay in the bed shivering, and Catherine had nursed her with a tea brewed from boneset, an herb she was introduced to by Massaquoit, who had learned of it from his wife's mother. The girl recovered, but the family fortunes declined. The man had been a weaver in England and did not take to farming. They lasted one season, and then Catherine arranged passage for them back to England. Since that time the house had been vacant.

It was a structure no more than thirty or so feet square, with one large front room that had served the family's daily needs and two small rooms in the back, one a bedroom, the other an oversized pantry. Now, as Catherine had heard, that front room was used for meetings of the Friends. There was one window, low to the ground, beside the door she now approached. She stooped and looked through the window. The sun was shining over her shoulder into the room, and she could clearly see the benches laid out to form a

square, leaving the center of the room bare. There
was no pulpit or lectern. The Quakers sat, men,
women, and children mixed together with no separa-
tion by gender or social status. She looked for a minister but saw none. She listened for preaching, but
heard none. Sitting by herself on the edge of the
bench directly across from the window was Jane.

Catherine studied the pretty face and the bright,
determined eyes. Those eyes were not half or entirely
closed, or cast upward, as were those of the others in
the room. Instead, they were restless, moving from
side to side, as though looking for someone who had
not yet arrived. Then they settled off to her left.
Catherine moved her head so she could, too, could
look in that direction, but her view was blocked by a
bookcase or cabinet on the inside wall next to the
window on that side. She looked back toward Jane
and saw a small smile form on her lips, followed by
an almost imperceptible nod. Catherine heard a step
behind her, then felt a hand on her shoulder. She
straightened up and formed her face into her most determined and dignified expression as she gazed up at
a large man wearing the same kind of broad-brimmed
hat favored by Roger. She did not recognize him.

"Can I help thee?" he asked.

"I think not."

"Dost thou look for someone inside, or dost thou
want to join our meeting?" His voice was kindly—
too kindly, Catherine thought—for she sensed men-
ace behind the soft words. It revealed itself in his next
sentence.

"Then thou wouldst better be off, Mistress, for

though we would welcome thee to join us, we also know how to entertain those that would spy on us."

"You are not from Newbury," Catherine said, "else you would not presume so to speak to me."

"Nay, I am not from here. I am Nathan Whitehead, and I travel God's kingdom. But I have heard of thee, Mistress Williams."

A woman's voice floated through the window. It spoke of the spirit moving within her. Whitehead nodded his head with the rhythms of the woman's speech, his eyes partly shut, but he kept his hand on Catherine's shoulder. She removed it, and he did not resist.

"I do not want to join your meeting," she said. "Nor do I wish to disturb it. A young woman among you is my responsibility."

Whitehead shook his head.

"Thou shouldst seek her elsewhere. In our meeting, only God is invited."

Catherine caught the heated reply that was half out of her mouth. It would do no good to argue theology with this itinerant Quaker preacher. She knelt down again and looked through the window. The place on the bench where Jane had sat was now empty. Everyone else's eyes were directed toward the woman who was offering her testimony. Next to the woman sat a young girl, no doubt the woman's daughter, looking with rapt eyes toward her mother. An older boy and a man, probably the girl's brother and father, sat with heads bowed as they listened to the woman's spontaneous preaching.

She felt Whitehead's presence behind her. He was looking over her shoulder. He pointed to the family in the meetinghouse. "That family, the Martins, have felt God's love touch them. It would do thee well to hear Rachel Martin preach, or mayhap her daughter Susan, who, if anything, speaks with more authority than even her mother, for the Lord does work powerfully within her."

Before Catherine could reply, she heard a door open at the rear of the building. She strained to see, but could not. A moment later, the door slammed shut. She turned to Whitehead. He shrugged.

"The woman thou seekest is no more one of us than thou art," he said.

"She left with someone," Catherine said.

"That I cannot tell thee. Thou wast at the window, not I. Couldst thou not see?"

"No. I will take my leave."

Whitehead tilted his head. "Thou art welcome to join us at meeting. But if thou comest back, I must insist thou use the door, and not the window."

"Perhaps," she said, and began to walk away. She did find the Friends interesting. She recalled Minister Davis affirming with satisfaction the Apostle Paul's injunction against women speaking in church, and therefore the notion of a woman preaching was startling, but not unattractive. She well knew that she would never be permitted to speak in Minister Davis's meetinghouse. "So much the worse for him," she muttered, as she quickened her step.

She had no serious intention of overtaking Jane, but she thought perhaps she would be able to see the direction the young woman had taken. She rounded the corner at the back of the house and saw a path leading into the woods. Standing in front of it was

Wequashcook. He looked back over his shoulder to the path, and then turned his steady gaze toward her. She noted the deep wrinkles on his face, the bright sparkle of intelligence in his eyes, and the inevitable beaver hat, worn at all times and seasons to cover the hideous scar left by Massaquoit's sharp blade so many years ago. Wisps of white hair showed beneath the hat, and a thin line of perspiration beaded his forehead. He remained still as she approached. When she was before him, he spoke.

"They were here some minutes ago."

"Who accompanies the young lady?"

For the first time, Wequashcook's face revealed a thought, as surprise lifted his eyebrows. "I was sure such a wise woman as you must know that the young English lady has found a young Indian man."

Catherine did not react. She knew Jane loved to shock, and therefore the news of her liaison with an Indian seemed almost fitting. Catherine now felt more weariness than dismay. Jane was simply too wild a creature to be tethered. But one question remained, and Wequashcook guessed it.

"He met her here because he knew she came here to these secret meetings. He has no god. Certainly not the Quaker god, which he sees as just another English god to persecute him. No, it was not religion but business."

This time Catherine could not suppress her surprise. "They are not lovers?"

"I do not think so. He wishes to sell her something that she wants very much."

"What could that be?"

Wequashcook glanced up to the sky for a moment, then shrugged.

"He did not tell me, although I offered to be his agent. He is young, and unpracticed in the ways of the English. He bade me get in touch with the young woman."

"And you did his bidding?"

"I try to be helpful," Wequashcook answered. "They attended the service for a while. Then they came out the back door while you were in the front."

"And did you help them with their business?"

Wequashcook shook his head. "No. I said I could not at this time, although perhaps in the future. Then they said farewell to each other. The young Indian went toward his village. The young English woman walked toward Newbury, no doubt to your house. I do not think you can overtake her."

"I did not so intend. As for the young man, he will no doubt encounter Massaquoit, who is even now in the village."

Wequashcook smiled, a quick movement of his lips.

"Ah, so you know," Catherine replied. "Perhaps you mean to find him there?"

Wequashcook shook his head. "I was offered that commission, but I did not find the pay sufficient for the risk. Still, there is no doubt our paths will cross."

"I see," Catherine replied. She did not pretend to understand the tangled relationship between Wequashcook and Massaquoit. She had asked Massaquoit once, and when he indicated that it must remain a private matter, she had left it at that. Nonetheless, she knew that the two men were bonded in some powerful fashion. Wequashcook seemed to be waiting to see if Catherine had further questions.

"I think I have told you as much as I know," he said.

Catherine gazed steadily at the old Indian's face, which offered an impenetrable mask of specious geniality.

"Yes," she replied, "but I do believe you are not now telling me all."

Wequashcook did not change his expression, although his eyes seemed to sparkle a little more brightly. "For that, perhaps you should talk to the young woman's brother."

And then the Indian bowed in a manner that suggested ironic respect, and walked up the path. Catherine watched him disappear around a bend, and then she looked back toward the little house. The congregants were leaving, but not as the citizens of Newbury left their meetinghouse, pausing to congratulate Minister Davis at the front door and then walking in family groups, exchanging greetings and gossip. These Friends came out of the doors of the house, front and back, one at a time, stopping to look in every direction and then scattering into the fields and the surrounding woods, ignoring the road that led to the house.

A moment or two later, and Catherine fully understood the reason for their behavior. Two men in armor came hurrying across the field. As they neared, she positioned herself behind a tree, then watched as one approached the front door and the other the rear door. Each paused a moment or two, and then they rushed into the house. Catherine waited to hear sounds of resistance or dismay, but there was only silence. The two emerged red-faced and panting. They met on the side of the house with a shrug of their shoulders. Catherine permitted herself a smile at the escape of the congregation, but her expression darkened as she thought that with a little worse timing the soldiers might have gathered all of the Friends in their net, including, and most especially, Jane.

When Catherine arrived at her house, Phyllis was waiting at the door, her face flushed with anger and shame.

"Much has transpired in your absence, Mistress," she said. "They deceived me. I should not have believed them."

"Did you not attend them on their way?"

Phyllis nodded.

"Right to her uncle's very door, I did," she declared.

"Well?"

"And then as I was walking back here, taking my time, as you were off and Edward don't never care for my company, so I strolled, thinking maybe I would see some of those flowers you had me pick a while back. . . ."

"The point?" Catherine demanded. "I sent you not to gather herbs."

"I am coming to it," Phyllis declared. It was clear to Catherine that her servant was not just babbling on mindlessly, as often she did, but purposefully, for she did not want to say what she knew she must. She stopped, and took a deep breath. "And then I met him," she declared, her face relaxing in relief at having disclosed the source of her shame.

"Who?"

"Why, Minister Davis," Phyllis said emphatically, as though it were obvious whom she must be talking about. "The very one they told me was behind the door waiting for them."

"Oh, I see," Catherine replied. "So you left Roger and Grace alone in her uncle's house."

"Not by intent," Phyllis declared.

"But indeed in fact," Catherine replied, her voice soft with understanding. "You could not have known." And unsaid, although each knew the other was aware, was the recognition that as a servant Phyllis had no choice but to assume that her betters were being truthful. Catherine gave that idea voice. "And even had you known, little there is you could have done."

Phyllis's face relaxed a little. "That is the truth," she said. "And. . . ."

"No. Tell me what else you can about our young lovers, for that, apparently, is what we must now call them."

"I know nothing of such matters," Phyllis sputtered.

"Well, then, a simple question or two. Did Roger indicate when he was to return here?"

"No."

"Did you say aught to Minister Davis?"

"Surely not."

"We can do no more, then," Catherine said, "but wait for Roger, or Minister Davis, for surely he will insist on satisfaction from me for having let this affair progress to such a dangerous place."

Catherine and Phyllis sat across from each other, but neither touched the potted beef and boiled peas that Phyllis had prepared. Edward, though, at the far end of the table lowered his head toward his wooden trencher and shoveled the food into his mouth with a loud, slurping sound. Catherine and Phyllis turned toward him, then resumed their silent meditations. Every once in a while, one or the other would cast a hopeful glance at the two unoccupied place settings, as if doing so would cause Roger and Jane to appear. A knock on the door dispelled that hope. Phyllis rose to her feet as though propelled by the energy that had been bottled up in her all the long afternoon of waiting for the brother and sister to come home from their separate and equally dangerous adventures.

"Go ahead, then," Catherine said. Unlike her servant, she felt drained by the waiting and did not know if she could rise to her feet. She closed her eyes and listened to the sounds made by Edward, who continued eating as though unaware of the interruption. In a few moments, her worst fears were confirmed as she heard male voices jangling against Phyllis's. Among the men, she clearly could make out Roger's tenor and the deeper tones of Minister Davis. The third, she concluded, must belong to Constable Larkins.

She hurried from the kitchen to the entryway and the voices. Phyllis was now almost shouting.

"I must remind the gentlemen that this is Mistress

Williams's house, and this young gentleman himself is a guest under her roof."

"That is the point," Minister Davis said, as Catherine arrived. His face was purple with anger. Roger, towering above the others and wearing his broad-brimmed hat, looked bemused. Constable Larkins wore an expression that indicated he wished he were somewhere else.

"And what is that point?" Catherine asked.

Minister Davis looked up at Roger.

"Your guest, Mistress, welcome as he may be in your house, is not in mine, where he abuses my niece."

Catherine watched for Roger's response—a sign of embarrassment, a confession in the twitch of an eyelid or the quiver of a lip, the rise of color to his cheeks. Instead, he smiled.

"If I abuse Grace by loving her, then I abuse her indeed," he said, his voice gentle and lilting. Catherine could only admire his composure before the minister's wrath.

"You cannot love her without my permission, which I do not grant."

"Have you asked your niece if she returns his affection?" Catherine asked.

"No."

"And why not?" Catherine insisted.

"Look at the man," Minister Davis said. "Does his back not bear the scars of our displeasure?" He shook his head. "Grace cannot love him. I forbid it."

Catherine glanced at the constable. "What is your business in my house?" she asked.

"Nothing, Mistress. Only to accompany him here." He looked at Roger.

"I would have come of my own volition," Roger said.

"I summoned the constable," Minister Davis said. "I did think to have him take this young man to the jail to await the pleasure of the magistrates, but decided instead to return him here."

"That was kind of you," Catherine said.

"No, not kind at all, for I have given you a burden. In your hearing I tell this young man that he is not to come near my house or my niece, at peril to more than the flesh of his back." Minister Davis spun on his heel. "Come," he called to the constable, and together they walked to the door. However, instead of continuing out of the house, they paused, and Minister Davis turned back to Catherine.

"Your other stray sheep returns," he said. "And if I am not very much mistaken, she has been studying heresy whilst her brother practiced fornication." He and the constable stepped aside as Jane walked in. She passed by them without a glance and then, without looking back, pushed the door shut with her foot. Roger took a step toward her, but she stopped him with a stone-faced shake of her head and went upstairs. Roger shrugged, waited a moment or two, then followed.

After a little while, as Catherine sat at the kitchen table, muffled words came from upstairs, and then the volume of the voices rose to angry tones. The anger behind the words was clear, but the words themselves had become indistinct. Then there was silence.

SIX

MASSAQUOIT SAW THE movement behind the tree and grabbed Jonathan's arm.

"Wait here," he said.

Jonathan's face was wet with perspiration from the rapid pace of their walk. He began to smile at the prospect of a rest when Massaquoit directed him to a fallen log at the side of the narrow trail they had been traveling.

"Sit, as though you are resting," Massaquoit said. "Then begin walking again. If there is more than one, you can then run."

Jonathan nodded and hunched himself on the log. Massaquoit took a quick step over the log and into the cover of the pines that lined the trail. The ground was covered with dried pine needles, so he walked as though over hot coals. He sensed the motion from the trail and knew that Jonathan, doing as he had been instructed, had now gotten up and was walking. Massaquoit worked his way a little deeper into the woods, to a line of oaks where he felt hard dirt beneath his feet. He trotted parallel to the trail until he saw the figure crouched with his back toward him. For a second he contemplated letting the assailant have a free opportunity at Jonathan, but he dismissed that idea. In a couple of quick steps he was within reach of the figure, who turned to face him. Massaquoit relaxed as he looked into the familiar countenance of Ninigret, whom he had not seen in years, but whose mature features had not changed so much from the boyish ones Massaquoit had known. Ninigret shrugged.

"So you are the keeper of this English?" Ninigret asked.

"I take him back to Newbury," Massaquoit replied.

"To be hanged, I hope."

"I do not think so. What is your interest in him?"

Jonathan's steps now indicated he was about to draw abreast of them. Ninigret tensed, then looked back over his shoulder. Massaquoit followed his glance and saw the girl.

"He has taken something from her," Ninigret said.

The girl came forward, her head bowed. She was holding a pouch. She handed it to Ninigret, who untied the leather string that held it closed. He pulled the pouch open so Massaquoit could peer into it.

"It is empty," Massaquoit said.

Ninigret did not answer. Instead, he tossed the pouch to Massaquoit and jumped out onto the trail. Jonathan grunted as he was hit. Massaquoit took two quick steps onto the trail. Jonathan was on his knees, holding his head.

"I did not hit him so very hard," Ninigret said. "I

do not want him dead yet. Not until he can tell us what he did with what was in the pouch."

Jonathan stood up. Blood trickled from his lower lip. He spat a stream of mixed spittle and blood. He stared at Ninigret with undisguised contempt.

"I came to bring you God's word," he declared.

Ninigret beckoned the girl forward. "Were you preaching to her when you were lying between her legs?" he demanded.

Jonathan shrugged. "My flesh is weak. She invited me to lie with her."

The girl, who had been keeping her eyes steadfastly on the ground, now raised them and they flashed anger. She shook her head violently from side to side.

Jonathan seemed unperturbed. "What I say is true nonetheless."

"We want what was in the pouch," Ninigret declared. "Then, perhaps, I will not kill you."

Massaquoit was standing a few feet away, listening and ready to intervene at the first hint of violence.

"He is under my care," Massaquoit said to Ninigret. "I will bring him back to Newbury. You can accompany us and make your report to the magistrates."

Ninigret sneered. "And do you think the English might punish him?"

Massaquoit remembered the bloody backs of Roger and Jane, along with other victims of the English's justice: blasphemers whose tongues had been bored through, thieves whose hands or foreheads had been branded. He nodded. "It is possible."

"And if not?" Ninigret demanded.

"Then there will come a time when he will not be

in Newbury, when you can do with him what you want."

Ninigret seemed to consider for a moment or two, although Massaquoit knew the young man would not challenge his authority or his strength.

"The letter," he said simply.

"I know nothing of a letter," Jonathan said.

"It was in the pouch," Ninigret replied. He held out his hand and the girl placed the pouch in it. "This pouch."

Jonathan shrugged. "I tell you I know nothing of that pouch or its contents."

"I will question him further as we walk to Newbury," Massaquoit said.

Ninigret stepped back. "As you say, there will come a time." He took Minnehaha by the shoulder and led her into the woods beside the trail.

Massaquoit watched them disappear. When they were out of sight, Jonathan nudged Massaquoit. "I believe this is what they wanted," he said, holding a folded piece of paper in his hand. Massaquoit noted the smooth flesh and the trimmed fingernails, denoting a man who did not labor with his hands, if he labored at all. "I heard them talking in their tongue. They did not think I understood. I followed the girl. I entered the wigwam. She was lying on the mat so I would not see where she hid the pouch. I meant only to take its contents. I told her to close her eyes, and she obeyed. I took the letter and replaced the pouch, but still she was lying there. I did not think she would mind."

Massaquoit brought the back of his hand hard against Jonathan's cheek. "She did," he said.

Jonathan staggered back, rubbing his cheek where the skin reddened. "That is twice today I have suffered the indignity of being hit by a savage."

"The letter," Massaquoit said. Jonathan unfolded the letter. "I can read your English words," Massaquoit said, holding out his hand.

"A wise savage, how marvelous," Jonathan said raising the letter to shoulder height. Massaquoit puzzled over that gesture for a moment, and then he sensed somebody behind him. Even as he began to lift his arm to protect himself, he knew he was a half second too slow. Then he felt something crash against his head.

"He must have left during the night," Phyllis said as she placed the bowl of steaming samp on the table. "And she still sleeps. I looked in on her and she did not rouse. If you ask me. . . ."

"I did not," Catherine replied as she spooned some samp into her trencher.

Phyllis continued as though Catherine had encouraged her. "She is worn out from traveling into the woods last night, and as for him, he went with her and did not come back. That is what I think— witches, the both of them."

Catherine studied the earnest conviction on her servant's face, and chose not to argue the point. Phyllis waited for a reply for a few moments, and then she, too, began to eat. Just as Catherine was almost finished, there was a knock at the door. Phyllis rose to answer it. Catherine heard a male voice she did not recognize. She sighed in relief, for she was in no mood to deal again with Minister Davis, the constable, or anybody else who might trouble her about her young guests. She waited for Phyllis to bring the stranger in. He turned out to be a young man with the remains of what had been a deep bruise under his right eye. Catherine noted the slight discoloration, just a little yellow where the skin should have been pink. It was a bruise that had been healing for some time.

"Good morning, Mistress," he said. "I am sorry to trouble you. I am Henry Jenkins, and I sail on *The Good Hope* under your good Master Gregory."

"I do not think you will find him here," Catherine replied.

The young man smiled, showing a gap where his front teeth should have been. "Aye, that I know," he said. "It is your lady guest I seek, as I have a message for her."

"From Master Gregory?"

Henry shook his head.

"Then who?" Catherine asked.

"I am sorry, Mistress, for I am sworn to secrecy."

"Why, then, take your secret home with you. I will have none of that kind of business in my house. And at my breakfast, no less."

Although Catherine had intended her sharp rebuke to shake the sailor's confidence, he gave her a quick smile, made a little bow of his head, and took a step back.

"As you like, Mistress. Just tell the young lady that a friend of Billy Lockhart was here to see her, to take up their arrangement, seeing as Billy himself can no longer do his part."

After the visitor left, Catherine sat at her desk, poring over her account book. She stared at a column of figures, but they made no more sense to her. Her mind was busy seeking the connections among the sailor who had just been at her door; the dead sailor Billy Lockhart, whose burial she had authorized in Newbury cemetery; and Jane. So absorbed was she in these contemplations that she did not hear the light footstep until it was almost upon her. She looked up to see Jane's face fixed into an expression of almost childish sweetness.

"I thought I heard a visitor come," she said.

Catherine looked up from her figures. "Indeed? Were you expecting anybody? Perhaps your Indian friend?"

Jane smiled more fully, and Catherine chastised herself for thinking she could disturb this young woman's self-control. She wondered if this calm might derive from Jane's religious convictions, which focused on the nurturing of the spirit within. But a glance at the sparkle in Jane's eyes discredited that notion; her expression spoke more of the passionate nature, barely controlled, beneath the calm surface. Catherine, remembering what Nathan Whitehead had said, along with her own observations, was coming to the conviction that Jane's profession of spiritual intensity was specious.

"Hast thou been spying on me, Mistress Williams? I do not think my parents thought thou wouldst be so extreme in thy watchfulness that thou wouldst follow me about."

"I have, and an arduous business it has been," Catherine replied, not attempting to mask the sharpness of her tone. "I do not think your mother and father expected that their son and daughter would be imprisoned and whipped almost as soon as their feet found Newbury's shore. I am only trying to do a better job of my governance, which I will continue, whether that please you or no."

"I, we, mean no harm," Jane said in her most conciliatory tone. "We are strangers here, beholden to thy hospitality, and not familiar with thy ways."

"I am sure that is true insofar as you have no Indians in Alford, as I recall."

"Indeed not."

"And perhaps that is why you find ours so interesting."

The slightest blush reddened Jane's cheek, and Catherine was glad to see that the young woman's armor was not impenetrable.

"But it was not an Indian at our door just now, was it?" Jane asked.

"A sailor, he said he was, a friend of Billy Lockhart. Do you know such a person?"

"Poor Billy," Jane murmured. "He did much to make me comfortable on the voyage when the waves so sickened me that I could not leave my cabin."

"This sailor said that you and he had business, which he now wants to complete."

Jane shrugged. "As for that, I cannot guess what he has in mind."

"Perhaps something to do with your Indian friend."

"I do not think so," Jane replied. "But if I see him, I will surely inquire. And inform thee fully," she added in a tone that suggested irony more than sincerity.

"You would be well advised to let your business with that dead boy die with him," Catherine said.

Jane's face brightened into a manic smile. "Ah," she said, "I find such good advice so difficult to accept."

"The scars on your back should instruct you otherwise."

"Indeed, they are forceful teachers."

"I do not think they have taught your brother very well."

The smile disappeared from Jane's face. "He does go his own way. I do believe he is secretly visiting his harlot."

The word struck Catherine like a slap to her face. "You have no right. . . ."

"Oh, but I do," Jane answered, "more than thou knowest. But I will go seek him. If I find him, I shall bring him back and thou canst ask him thyself where he has been." Before Catherine could remonstrate, Jane had closed the door behind her.

The sun was setting, and there was no sign of Jane or Roger. Edward sat at the table, sopping up gravy with a crust of bread.

Phyllis looked up from her plate. "I think it is a good idea," she said.

"I do not think so. What do you expect to find out in the tavern? Did I not know you better, I should think you had another reason for suggesting you go to the Lion's Paw."

Phyllis reddened. "You have no cause. You know me that well."

"Of course," Catherine replied.

"It is only that the other servants can be found there. And they are the ones who can help us."

Catherine stood up and walked toward the front door. "Well, then, what do we wait for?"

"I did not intend. . . ."

"Well I know it. But I cannot rest here while you are there. I want to know the moment you find out something."

"I do not know if the others will speak freely if they see you."

Catherine reached into the midwife bag she wore around her waist, pulled out several coins, and handed them to Phyllis. "These should loose their tongues and blind their eyes to my presence," she said.

It was dark by the time they reached the tavern. Beneath a huge maple on one side of the tavern two shadow figures came together so that their bodies blended beneath the outlines of their heads. Phyllis tripped over a large stone in the path, and it went bouncing toward the figures. The taller shadow's head turned toward them, and then the shadows separated into two distinct bodies. Their heads bobbed back and forth toward each other for a few moments, and then a male voice uttered a few angry words. The larger shadow pushed the other figure away and trotted off into the darkness.

"Take it home to your good wife," a woman said, punctuating her words with a cackle. The smaller figure leaned against the tree, staring at Catherine and Phyllis. She walked toward them on unsteady legs and stopped a few feet in front of them. Her breath smelled of beer.

"You are interfering with my trade, you are," she said. She leaned a little closer toward Catherine. "Mistress Williams, is it now?" she asked.

"Yes," Catherine replied.

"That is my good luck, isn't it?" the woman said. "I was to come looking for you, because my man is sorely hurt, and he said in particular that I should bring you to him. But as you can see, I stopped here, being thirsty as I was, and then I met that fellow there who you frightened away, so now I figure that you are in my debt."

Phyllis took a firm step toward the woman, using her broad body to shield Catherine from the woman. "Here, now, you do not speak to Mistress Williams that way. Be off with you. Maybe you can run after that fellow and finish your business."

The woman glanced in the direction the man had gone, then laughed in Phyllis's face. "In truth, I do think he was looking for you when he found me by mistake."

Phyllis raised her arm as though to strike, but Catherine seized her elbow. "Do not be provoked," she said, and pulled gently on Phyllis's arm until she stepped back. "I think I would like a word with this woman."

"Now, that is right sensible of you," the woman said. "Because I think you will want to hear what my Timothy has to say."

"Is he hurt?"

"That he is. But his mouth works fine, and he says to me, 'Tell Mistress Williams that I cannot pay her in coin for her help, but maybe she will want to pay me for what I have to say to her.'"

"That may be," Catherine replied. "How badly is he hurt?"

"For that, I am no judge, other than to say a knife has cut his side, and he still bleeds. You must see for yourself, if you care to follow me."

"Go. We will follow."

The woman led the way through Newbury toward the harbor. When they were close enough to the water to smell it, she turned onto a narrow path that led to a wigwam. The woman pulled back the flap and motioned for them to enter. Inside was a man lying on a mat, a stump of a candle flickering next to him. He raised himself slowly, with a grunt, onto one elbow when they came in.

"Mistress Williams, I take it. I have no doubt Bess here stopped for a swallow of somethin' afore she found you."

"Just a nip and a bit of business, Timothy. You know we can use the coin," Bess replied.

"Aye, while I wait here with my lifeblood running out."

"Why, then, I would need the money to bury you, wouldn't I?" Bess said with a snorting laugh, which Timothy soon joined.

"That you would, my love."

"Can I see your hurt?" Catherine asked.

For answer, Timothy lay back down and pulled up his shirt. A dirty cloth, stained a dark reddish brown from dried blood, lay across his wound. He lifted the cloth. Catherine held the candle over the wound, which was mostly covered by congealed blood through which a few bright red drops of fresh blood oozed. The blood trailed down to the leg of his breeches, where it left a dark brown stain in the fabric.

"You will live," she said.

"And so you can use her money for drink," added Phyllis, who had been standing near the entrance.

"Is there water about?" Catherine asked.

"There's a stream on the other side of the hill," Bess said.

Catherine handed her the dirty rag. "Clean it in the water, and bring it and a bowl of water back."

Timothy watched her leave, his eyes warm with affection. "A good woman, she is," he said. "She does take care of me after her fashion." He looked around the bare interior of the wigwam. "How do you like my house? It is a present to me from a friend of yours, the one they call William, who always wears that beaver hat."

"A present?" Catherine asked. "I know William to be a man of business who exchanges goods for services."

Timothy began a laugh that dissolved into a coughing fit that had him clutching his side. The blood oozed a little more strongly. He looked down, shook his head, then smiled. "Service, yes, that is what he seeks."

"And in this case?" Catherine persisted.

Before Timothy could gather himself to answer, Bess returned with a bowl of water in which floated the rag, only a little cleaner than it had been before. Catherine dipped the cloth into the water and wrung it out. She lifted Timothy's hand from the wound and daubed around the edges, removing the congealed blood and working to where the knife had entered the flesh. The wound was a deep puncture, but fortunately the knife had gone in and back out without tearing the flesh beyond the entry point. Once she had the area free of dried blood, she pressed her palm over the wound. The skin was at ordinary body temperature, and there was no sign of inflammation.

"You will keep bleeding unless I stitch this," she said. She looked at the bloodstain on his breeches. "And you have already bled quite a bit."

"That I have, Mistress," Timothy said, his voice still filled with good humor.

Catherine handed her bag to Phyllis. "Thread the needle, if you please."

Then she looked to Bess, who was squatting in the corner of the wigwam, seemingly uninterested. "Do you have any rum?"

Bess looked up and smiled. She pointed to her belly.

"I see," Catherine said. Phyllis handed her the bone needle with the catgut thread. "Take a deep breath," Catherine suggested to Timothy, "and close your eyes if you like."

Instead, Timothy focused his glance on the needle and watched as with a few quick stitches, Catherine gathered the flesh over the wound. She motioned to Phyllis, who handed her a rag dipped in the poultice of coneflower. She smeared the poultice over the wound while Timothy watched her every motion. When she was finished, he lay down and closed his eyes.

"If you want to find the man what done this to me, who now has my very own knife, which he put into me, you can follow the blood it dripped to your own house, and if you find him not there, seek him at the Minister's house." His last words were swallowed in a snore, and he was in a deep sleep.

Massaquoit trotted down the path toward Newbury. He winced each time his foot landed on the ground and sent the pain radiating from the base of his skull down his spine and up the back of his head, extending its reach to the spot between his eyes. He slowed his pace to a walk, and the pain eased after a few steps. He stopped for a few minutes, and the pain ceased. He took a deep breath and launched himself again into a jarring trot. He bit down on his lower lip and grunted against the knife that seemed to be probing from the back of his head to the front. He had no intention of giving in to this discomfort. Instead, he held his fingers against the lump at the back of his head, as though to press the swollen flesh and remove the pain. He knew that was a foolish thought, but it somehow took his mind off the shocks that tore his head each time his foot hit the ground.

The pain, of course, only fed his anger and humiliation at having been surprised by an assailant. Age must have made him careless. He must have considered how little resistance he could expect from Jonathan and ignored the possibility of an accomplice, or if not an accomplice, perhaps somebody who was just as interested in gaining custody of the English minister as he was. In any case, he was certain that Jonathan would not travel very fast, whether he was with someone who had freed him or someone who had taken him from Massaquoit for his own purposes. Either way, Jonathan would not be made to hurry.

It took even less time than Massaquoit expected to overtake his quarry. He had not traveled half a mile when he heard a moan coming from the side of the path. He waited. A red squirrel scurried in front of him, an acorn in its mouth. Birds twittered in the trees above where the moaning came from. Whoever was making that sound had been there long enough for the local wildlife to become comfortable with the intruder into their environment. A few steps through the underbrush brought Massaquoit to Jonathan, lying on his side with his hands tied behind his back and bound to his feet. He was facedown in a pile of moldy leaves, and he seemed unable to lift himself for more than a few seconds, during which time he gasped for air and moaned. Then his head dropped back into the leaves and he flailed like a beetle on its back, trying to right himself.

Massaquoit watched this struggle for a few moments, wondering if this helpless man could have been responsible for the knot at the back of his own head. Jonathan became aware of Massaquoit's presence and struggled to hold his head up long enough to plead.

"Help," he said, and then dropped into the pungent leaves.

Massaquoit bent down and rolled him onto his back. "I have a lump on my head," Massaquoit said. He placed his foot on Jonathan's stomach and leaned his weight on it until Jonathan gasped. "Do you know anything about that?"

Jonathan shook his head and then looked down at

Massaquoit's foot, which was still on his stomach.
"Please," he gasped.

Massaquoit lifted his foot, and Jonathan sucked in
a deep breath. Massaquoit took his knife from the
sheath on his belt. He passed the bright blade in front
of Jonathan's eyes and watched the man's eyes open
in terror. Then he rolled the minister back onto his
side and sliced through the knot in the rope binding
his feet. The rope had been wrapped through several
turns about Jonathan's legs so that a length of several
feet fell to the ground. Massaquoit picked it up and
watched as Jonathan staggered to his feet. Jonathan
turned his back toward Massaquoit and held out his
bound hands.

"No, I do not think so," Massaquoit said. "I have
an even better idea." He picked up the length of rope
and knotted it to the piece binding the minister's
hands. He wrapped the free end firmly about his own
wrist.

Jonathan shrugged. "I do not suppose it will do
any good to tell you I know nothing of who hit you."

"It will not. But I remain most interested in the letter you were showing me the moment before."

Jonathan gave a half laugh. "It is gone. Taken by
the one who tied me up. Find him, and maybe you
will find the one who attacked you. I think you know
the man. He wears. . . ."

The image of a beaver hat flashed into Massaquoit's mind, and he pressed his palm across
Jonathan's lips. He did not want his suspicion confirmed by the lying mouth of this English.

"Never mind him," Massaquoit said. "As we walk

together to Newbury, you will tell me all about that letter, will you not?"

Jonathan did not answer. When it was clear that he would not, Massaquoit yanked the rope up with a sharp, brutal gesture that brought Jonathan's bound hands toward his shoulder blades. Massaquoit held the rope taut with one hand, and placed the other beneath Jonathan's hands and pushed even harder until he heard a crack in the minister's joints. Jonathan grunted in pain.

"I will tell you," he said, "for all the good it may do you."

"I do not know if it will do me any good," Massaquoit responded, "but that piece of paper has already caused me some pain and trouble, and has raised my curiosity about why so many people seem so interested in it."

"That I do not know. I have read it, and I confess I do not know why that Indian boy or anybody should want it."

Massaquoit looked up at through the trees at the darkening sky. "We will stay the night here."

"I do not fancy that," Jonathan said.

"And I do not fancy walking with you through the woods in the dark," Massaquoit said, "for you have not convinced me that it was not a friend of yours who attacked me."

"It was not."

"So you say. But now, before we sleep, tell me what you know about that letter."

"It is from the parents of the Quaker brother and sister to Mistress Williams, placing them in her care."

"That does not seem to be all," Massaquoit replied.

"There is one more thing. It is probably nothing at all, and now that I do not have the letter, I cannot check my memory."

"What is it?"

"Something about the woman."

Massaquoit leaned toward Jonathan, holding his gaze. He saw there more strength than he had anticipated. The English minister was not a man of physical courage, but when he saw a way to gain an advantage without exposing his flesh, he could be very stubborn. Massaquoit concluded that although he could probably coerce more information from him, he would rather wait and observe to see if Jonathan revealed more.

"Let us sleep, then," Massaquoit said. "In the morning, your memory might be fresher."

SEVEN

ᗧ•ᗣᗧ•ᗣ

CATHERINE SAW THE movement out of the corner of her eye as she approached her house, and then the man staggered onto the path in front of her. His face was bruised, and he had a bloody rag tied around one hand. In his other hand was a blood-encrusted knife. He pressed the palm of his wounded hand against his ribs, and he seemed to be having difficulty catching his breath.

"Roger!"

He dropped to his knees in front of her. "Somebody attacked me."

"I think I know who," she replied. "Phyllis, help me with him."

Phyllis and Catherine each took an elbow and helped the young man to his feet. They placed his arms around their shoulders and started to walk the remaining distance to Catherine's house.

Roger stopped walking so abruptly that both

women lost their balance. Catherine freed herself
from his arm and stepped back. His face was frozen
in shock.

"What is it?" she asked.

"I just remembered. I must find the man."

"The one who attacked you?"

Roger looked down at the knife still in his hand.
He threw it into the darkness.

"You need not worry about him," Catherine said.
"He will live."

Roger started, then bowed his head and permitted
himself to be led into the house. He took one look at
the stairs leading to his room, and he shook his head.
"I do not think I can."

Catherine pointed to her front room, and Roger
followed her into it. There he maneuvered his long
frame onto a settee covered in an ornate scarlet velvet fabric decorated with gold thread embroidery. He
placed his bloody hand against the fabric and sighed.
He had a wallet on his hip, and he kept his good hand
firmly over it.

"At least I cannot stain it," he said, looking at the
red fabric.

"Hush," Catherine said. "It is only cloth. Let me
see your wound."

Roger glanced down at his hand. "It is nothing."
He coughed and doubled over, spitting blood.

"Phyllis," Catherine said, "fix some chamomile
tea. He will need his rest." She took his hand and un-
wrapped its bandage. A deep, clean gash cut into the
palm. He winced as she examined it. She daubed it
with goldenrod poultice and wrapped it in a clean
piece of cloth. She studied his face. His cheek under

his right eye was swollen. She touched it, and he winced. She traced down his cheek to his neck, where she found a shallow scratch.

"His knife did that," Roger said, "before I could grab it." He held up his wounded hand. "Better this than my throat cut. After I wrestled the knife from him, he hit me hard, here." He pointed to his sternum. "Then, then I used the knife on him."

Phyllis returned with the tea in a saucer, and Roger drank it down. Catherine took a rug from a chest and spread it on the floor next to the settee. He looked at the rug and nodded.

"Yes, I am weary." His head dropped to his chin. "He put the knife to my throat, he did," he mumbled. "He said I must leave Newbury, for such as I am are not welcome here."

"Is that all?" Catherine asked.

Roger nodded. He knelt on the rug and stretched out. In a few minutes he was asleep, his good hand still on top of his wallet. Catherine waited a few moments, then attempted to lift his hand from the wallet. He stirred, and she desisted. She would have to wait to discover its secret, for she assumed that was why he kept such close guard on it. As if to confirm her judgment, Roger rolled onto his side so that his body now covered the wallet.

Later that night, Catherine tossed in her bed. She had drunk some of the same tea she had given to Roger, because she knew that she needed a good rest. But she had not remembered how powerfully the tea could act on her, and so as she lay in bed, her head flashed images, merging past and present. She heard her front door open. She heard hushed voices, and saw Frederick coming through the door, clutching his side, from which a steady stream of bright red blood flowed. He was her older son, whom she had not seen in twenty years, since he moved west seeking land for his growing family. Rumors had recently reached Newbury that Frederick's village was threatened by Iroquois in the service of the French. Now he stood before her, dripping blood from the stump where his hand used to be. Then her son's handsome features hardened into the coarse mien of Timothy, and then the aristocratic face of Roger, bloodied and bruised. She stirred herself awake, and separated the thoughts of her son and the young Quaker. She pushed away her fears for Frederick and concentrated on what had happened to Roger. She knew that somebody had paid Timothy to attack him. And Timothy's cryptic comment suggested that Minister Davis might have been that sponsor. She was surprised at that thought, but not shocked. She fell back into a fitful sleep.

Toward dawn, Catherine heard the floorboards in her front hall creaking under somebody's weight. She turned her head away from the noise for a moment until her mind cleared, and then she got up. She heard the door shut. She looked out of her window, which was directly above the door, and saw a figure loping into the darkness.

She went downstairs to look in on Roger. He was gone, leaving behind a fresh red stain on the settee. Whoever she had heard in what she thought was a dream had brought a summons to which Roger had responded.

* * *

For some reason, Massaquoit was not surprised to see the young Englishwoman whose back had been whipped sitting on a boulder at the edge of the path as it left the riverbank and veered toward the harbor. She was in an intense conversation with a young man who kept shrugging his shoulders and shaking his head as though to indicate his inability to tell her what she wanted to know. A small wooden shipping crate lay at his feet. Jane pointed at it, and the young man shook his head vehemently.

"I needs must talk to her," Jonathan said. "About the letter. It would be a courtesy, one more than I deserve, perhaps, but I will be in your debt."

"You are now."

Jonathan snorted a half laugh. "You are an arrogant savage," he said. "But you are also right."

Massaquoit chose to ignore the term. He was well used to the English habit of designating what they did not understand as beneath them. "For a moment, only, with me in attendance," he said.

"That is all I ask."

"Good, for that is all that you get."

Massaquoit had been keeping his eye on Jane and her companion as he fenced with Jonathan. He saw the young man now strap the crate to his back and walk in the direction of the town center. Jonathan, too, watched this bit of business. He shrugged and turned back to Massaquoit.

"I can make nothing of that," he said. He presented his bound hands. "Can you untie me now?"

Massaquoit took out his knife and sliced through the rope in one swift motion. Jonathan stretched his hands out in front of him and rubbed his wrists. He started walking toward Jane, and Massaquoit followed a few steps behind. Jane looked at them as they approached, her glance switching from one to the other and then remaining fixed on Jonathan. He arrived at her side and bowed his head toward her. Massaquoit stood a few feet away, a look of bored indifference on his face as they spoke in hushed tones. He knew what they were talking about as well as if he were part of their conversation. He waited for the exclamation to come from the young Englishwoman when her disappointment would move her to speak loud enough for him to hear. When it came, it was short and very much to the point.

"Thou art a damnable fool," she said. "Thy folly will be my ruin."

"Peace," Jonathan said in his best ministerial tone, which Massaquoit had come to recognize as English preachers' way of soothing with style more than substance. "All is not lost, only misplaced."

"Indeed," Jane said. "But I have run out of time."

Massaquoit stepped forward and seized Jonathan's shoulder. "Your time, too, has run out," he said.

Jonathan looked almost relieved. "You see how it is," he said to Jane. "This savage is now my master."

Jane contemplated Massaquoit as though seeing him for the first time. "I would not have thought so a little while ago, but it is not so terrible to have a savage for a master."

Jonathan's face expressed dismay, but Massaquoit understood.

"In the first place," Massaquoit said, "I very much doubt that any man, white or red, can claim to be your master. And in the second, Ninigret has enough difficulty mastering himself."

"Then you know my friend?" she asked.

"Is that what he is? A friend?" Jonathan interrupted. Jane kept her eyes on Massaquoit.

"Yes," Massaquoit replied.

"Well?" she insisted.

"Well enough," Massaquoit said.

"Then next thou see him, tell him I am fond of him still."

"In spite of his failure?" Massaquoit asked.

She only offered a bright smile and turned to leave. She walked away from the town, toward the river and Ninigret.

"She is disappointed in you," Massaquoit said to Jonathan.

"So you understand. . . ."

"Of course," Massaquoit said, his hand rubbing the bump on the back of his head. "She wants from you what everybody seems to be looking for. Who do you think now has it?"

"I do not know," Jonathan replied. He did not blink or look away, yet Massaquoit was quite sure he was not telling the truth. Lying was so natural to this English, Massaquoit thought, that he probably no longer knew the difference between truth and falsehood. He seized Jonathan by the arm.

"I am to take you to Magistrate Woolsey," he said.

Jonathan tried to pull away, but Massaquoit squeezed his arm harder.

"Why the magistrate?" Jonathan asked.

"I do not know," Massaquoit answered, in a voice as flat and opaque as Jonathan's denials. He could

have told the English minister that he was going to be
questioned about fathering a bastard child, but then
he might try harder to free himself, and he had already been quite enough trouble.

Catherine stiffened when she heard the knock at the
door. She heard Phyllis greet a woman. She relaxed a
little. She did not think a woman would be sent to tell
her that Roger had been arrested again. The woman
struggled to articulate her words, and Catherine knew
that Charity, the servant in Minister Davis's house,
was at her door. She was given her name by the minister when he had taken her into his household as a
slave at the conclusion of the war with the Pequots.
She was then a child of ten whose legs had been
badly burned when the English attacked her village.
She had bitten through half her tongue in her agony.
For a long time thereafter she would not speak. Minister Davis's persistence paid off, finally, when she
relented and learned to speak the words of those who
had so badly hurt her, even evincing sufficient ability
to form the stump of her tongue into the words of her
catechism and so be baptized with her new name, one
that Catherine had always thought to be more than
passingly ironic. She hurried to the door to find what
Charity, now a young woman of twenty, wanted.
Charity stood there, her head bowed. She took a shuffling step forward on legs that had healed imperfectly
from their burns. She looked up and spoke slowly.
Her mouth searched for the right alignment of lips
and stump of tongue.

"Minister Davis asks that you attend his niece on a
matter of great urgency and delicacy."

The words, clearly a speech carefully memorized at the minister's direction, with a vocabulary no servant would have ever used, came haltingly. Charity's eyes again sought the ground in front of her feet. Catherine understood the meaning behind the words, and in that moment of comprehension her gravest fears seemed to have been realized.

"Go, then," she said, "and I follow." She looked out of the window toward the field of corn behind her house, where Phyllis was hoeing the weeds with Edward. She decided not to wait for Phyllis. Charity still stood in the doorway, her glance following Catherine's out to the field. "Go on," Catherine said, and Charity, without a word, turned and walked away at a pace almost fast enough to smooth her limp.

Minister Davis's wife had died in birthing their first child. He had married late, and he chose to remain a widower. The child, a son, went to England to study at Oxford and, much to the father's displeasure, turned Anglican and lived in London. Thus, the minister lived alone except for Charity and occasional young relatives who were sent to him by their parents to profit from his guidance. Grace was the most recent of these.

His house stood across the town common from the meetinghouse. It was a modest structure at a time when many New England clergy were beginning to shake off more austere years of colonization and were building formidable houses to match their status as members of the ruling elite. Minister Davis took his calling very seriously—too seriously, in fact—to live in a grand house. He chose instead a decent but restrained comfort in his dwelling, which Catherine and Charity now approached. Catherine saw him peering out of the front window, but when Charity opened the door and ushered her into the hallway, he was nowhere to be seen. Charity led the way to the small bedroom to the left of the entrance hall. She stepped aside to permit Catherine to pass and then stationed herself against the wall next to the door. In the corner of the room was a cradle. And lying on the bed in the middle of the room was a very pale Grace.

Next to her, her ample size filling a deep blue gown trimmed in lace, was Francine Peters, third wife of the governor, balanced uncomfortably on a three-legged joint stool. Both she and the governor had lost their second spouses after their children were grown, and so they married more out of economic ambition than romantic interest. Their union joined two of the richest Newbury families into an even wealthier combine. The governor was fond of Francine for the money she added to his fortune, and she was grateful for the protection he offered in securing her widow's inheritance. They were civil toward each other, but did not spend overmuch time together. As a result, Francine often sought company elsewhere, and she had become a kind of surrogate mother to Grace, not trusting the minister to provide adequate counsel to a young woman. She pressed her fingers to her lips, with a nod toward Grace, who was sleeping fitfully, and with some difficulty she lifted her bulk from the stool. Her expression mingled concern for Grace with a recognition that she had been right in fearing for the young woman living in a house presided over only by a man, albeit the minister, and a sad acknowledgment that her attempts to provide the necessary feminine guidance had been too little and too late.

"She bleeds," Francine said to Catherine, "where she should not."

Catherine nodded. "I feared as much," she said.

She lifted the rumpled bedclothes from Grace and raised her shift. A napkin that had been pressed between the young woman's legs was stained a dark brownish red with dried blood. In one place it showed bright red drops. Catherine removed the napkin and daubed the fresh blood where it gathered on Grace's inner thighs. She replaced the napkin and covered Grace again. She beckoned to Charity, who limped to her.

"Go back to my house," she said, "and tell Phyllis to come immediately. Tell her that Grace is losing her babe and to bring what is necessary. She will know what to do."

She and Francine watched Charity hobble out. Grace groaned as a cramp convulsed her. She pressed her hands to her belly.

"Can I not keep it?" she asked.

Catherine hesitated, forced to choose between a truth the young woman would not want to accept and a lie that would offer her temporary comfort. "The Lord must decide," she said.

"Then I am ruined, for I have sinned," Grace said, "and now He is taking my babe from me."

"The Lord's will be done," Francine intoned.

Catherine rebuked Francine with a sharp glance, and then stroked Grace's hands, which were still pressed against her belly.

"Hush," Catherine said. "I am here now, and all will be well."

Grace nodded and closed her eyes. A few minutes passed, and then another cramp, not quite so violent, seized her. Catherine continued stroking her hands while Francine cradled her head. When the cramp subsided, Francine leaned toward Catherine.

"I should not say so, but some say her uncle has put her in this bed."

"Do you think it?" Catherine asked.

Francine leaned a little closer, and Catherine could smell the beer on her breath. "Indeed," she said, "with no proper woman here for guidance."

"Surely the minister can watch over one lamb," Catherine replied, surprising herself by defending Minister Davis.

Francine bent even further toward Catherine, so that their noses almost touched. "Some say," she whispered, "that he was a little too close to this lamb." Then she threw herself back, as though dismayed at the very thought. "I, of course, do not believe such idle and vicious talk."

No, Catherine thought, *but you do not hesitate to repeat it.*

Grace stirred. Her face reddened, and her mouth quivered in anger. "Do not say such things about Uncle."

Francine smiled as though she had seen the mouse take the cheese in the baited trap. "I meant nothing," she said. "Fault me for my idle tongue."

Grace was not mollified. She looked at Catherine. "Mistress Williams, I think you know right well enough that my uncle is blameless. He only did what he thought right in keeping Roger from me. He failed in that, as all the world can see, but as for the other suggestion, that he, himself . . . why, that is unspeakable."

"Yes, child, I do," Catherine said, as her eyes noted the new red stain on the napkin. "Now, lie still. I am sure Mistress Peters does not intend to upset you further. Is that not so, Francine?"

Francine moved away from the bed as though to signal her compliance. Grace again closed her eyes. After a few moments, Francine leaned toward Catherine.

"What I do mean to tell you, and not in the way of gossip, is what I have seen with my own eyes, and that involves *your* young woman guest."

"Jane?"

Francine nodded. "She has been often a visitor in my house, seeking the company of my nephew."

"Your Jonathan does seem to find his way among the women of this town," Catherine said.

She expected a defensive response from Francine, but the governor's wife only chortled. "He is an energetic young man, he is."

"And he will have much to answer for," Catherine replied. "I have taken the liberty of informing Magistrate Woolsey about his desertion of Abigail King. I have sent for your nephew so he might answer."

"He is the governor's nephew. I do not claim him. I only say what anybody can see: these young men, Jonathan in my house and Roger in yours, this poor young woman here and Abigail bearing a bastard child. "

Catherine felt the sting, although she would not for

a moment place Roger and Jonathan in the same category. She stared hard at Francine, seeking malice in her expression, but found only the weary wisdom of a woman who had managed to prosper in a world dominated by rich and powerful men who routinely took advantage of poor and powerless women. On that level, Catherine could not disagree. She chose, instead, to seek information.

"You were talking about Jane. Did you mean to suggest that Jonathan and she. . . ."

"Oh, no, not at all. I am quite certain their relationship was a matter of business."

"Indeed? Of what sort?"

"That I cannot tell you. But I have seen them together often enough. They talked like two merchants negotiating the price of goods, not lovers deciding where next they might meet." She again leaned close enough for Catherine to smell her breath. "I do not know what they were trading, but I can tell you this. It involved a young savage."

"Who might that be?" Catherine asked.

"For that, you can ask your own Matthew. I warrant he knows." Francine settled back on the stool with a contented smile, but with a motion too sudden for her weight that caused her to nearly lose her balance. Catherine reached a hand to steady her.

"Thank you," Francine said. "I am sometimes too exuberant."

"You are not the only one."

The voice came from the doorway, where Minister Davis now stood. His face was dark beneath its skullcap, and his tone carried an anger that Catherine could not remember hearing.

"Mistress Williams," he said, "it is the exuberance of your young ward that not only has ruined my niece's reputation, but now threatens her life. Surely, it is the Lord's hand upon her for her sin. And his."

At least, Catherine thought, the good minister was not placing the full blame on the woman, on the model of Eve and all those other temptresses sprinkled about the Bible that ministers so liked to point to as examples of woman's perfidy. On the other hand, Minister Davis's placing responsibility on Roger showed the depths of his anger and feelings of betrayal. He seemed to understand what she was thinking.

"You should have looked to him, as he was in your house. But now I have taken measures. He will not again bother my niece."

"I have seen the results of your measures," Catherine replied.

Minister Davis smiled. "Good," he said. "Then it has been done. I trust he has been lessoned well."

"The whip did not seem to do that office," Catherine replied.

"We will chastize him until he permits himself to be corrected," Minister Davis said, and left as silently as he had come.

Francine had shifted her glance from one to the other during this exchange. Now she rose to her feet. "Perhaps it is well for me to leave now, as you can tend to Grace far better than I."

"Indeed," Catherine said, as Francine peered out of the window. "I need only wait for Phyllis."

"As for that," Francine said, "I do believe I see her

coming up the walk now. I leave Grace in your excellent care."

Phyllis stood on one side of Grace's bed, stroking her
arm, and Catherine sat on the stool on the other,
pressing Grace's fingers between her own. Grace
looked from one to the other, her eyes expectant. She
removed her fingers from Catherine's grasp and ran
them over her belly.

"It is quiet," she said. "Is it not possible?"

Catherine shook her head. "I do not think so." She
pointed to the glass that contained the chamomile tea.
"That it is that has brought you relief. But it was too
late. It was not to be."

"Because I so bled?"

Again Catherine shook her head. "The blood was
the consequence, not the cause."

Grace's eyes flashed. "As for that, the cause was
mine and Roger's."

"I would not judge so harshly," Catherine replied.

"Aye," Grace responded, "but I do believe the
Lord has." She looked about her distractedly. "Where
is my uncle?"

"Asleep," Phyllis answered. "Charity told me this
past hour."

"I fear for Roger, though mine uncle is in his bed.
Those he pays are up and about."

"Hush," Catherine said, although she, too, feared
for the young man's safety. "Try to sleep. I am quite
sure Roger is even now in his bed at my house, and I
will send for him in the morning."

"Will you indeed?" Grace asked. "But my
uncle. . . ."

"I will send for him, nonetheless," Catherine said, "for he should be here with you."

Grace smiled, and Catherine grimaced behind her own fixed expression. She did not know where Roger was, but she was quite sure he was not at that moment safe in his bed. When she did arrive home, she found neither Roger nor Jane, only a shipping crate in her front hall.

"I forgot, in all the excitement," Phyllis said. "A sailor brought it over. He said it was for Jane."

"Indeed?" Catherine said.

"From the ship what just arrived from England," Edward added. He had opened the door for them, and now stood next to the crate. "He gave me this letter with it," he added.

Catherine looked at the letter and recognized the hand of Jane and Roger's mother. The letter was addressed to Jane. Catherine placed it on top of the crate.

"If you please," she said, "take it up to their room."

Phyllis lifted one end, and Edward the other, and together they carried the crate, the letter perched atop it, up the stairs.

Magistrate Joseph Woolsey, now approaching seventy, often found his thoughts alternating between contemplation of his death, which he did not fear, and his youth back in Alford. This morning, he sat by the window in the front room of his house, sipping a glass of tea, which calmed his stomach. As the warm liquid slid down his throat, his memory slipped back forty years, when he was a lawyer trying to keep

Catherine's father out of prison, and Catherine was a young girl who did not blame him for his failure to save her father, who had abandoned his textile business to become the lay preacher of a dissenting congregation of Puritans. Woolsey would take Catherine to visit her father as he wasted away in Newgate Prison, one of the many swept up in Archbishop Laud's net and left with the choice of conforming to the official church or languishing for indefinite periods of imprisonment. His cell was comfortable enough, and Woolsey saw that he had enough to eat, but as was fairly common, he caught a chill from the pestilent prison air and died one day, his head in Catherine's lap. Before he died, he secured a vow from Woolsey that he would look after his daughter, now orphaned as his wife had died shortly after giving birth to Catherine's brother.

Woolsey had taken both children into his household, only to see the brother fall sick and die within six months of his father. Woolsey, a childless widower, raised Catherine. He tried, gently but persistently, to steer her away from the adamant and aggressive nonconformity of her father, but she had inherited his spirit as well as she had imbibed his instruction, and so it was she who led Woolsey to become a Puritan. He was a sensible man whose religious convictions did not run as deep as his affection for the wild young woman he had sworn to protect. When, some years later, she and her young husband announced their intentions to come to the New World, he agreed to accompany them, for they were his only family. He prospered in the new colony, and never regretted his decision.

But this morning he reminded himself that the woman the young girl had grown into still presented him with problems he otherwise would never have confronted. And he was never more sure of that thought than now as he watched Matthew walk toward his house, leading a bound Jonathan Peters. He felt himself recoil. Unlike Catherine, he had never become comfortable with the Indians, and he remembered well this one's fierce demeanor on that unhappy day when his companions were drowned by order of Governor Peters.

For his part, Massaquoit was aware that he was approaching the house of a man who did not trust him, even though Catherine stood as a nexus between them, with strong relationships extending to the Pequot sachem on one side and the English magistrate on the other. Her strength, however, was inadequate to bring them together. Rather, they orbited, like two contrary planets, about her fixed center, each always wary of the other.

Jonathan tried to hang back. "A moment, please," he pleaded, "to gather my thoughts."

"You have had more than enough time to do that," Massaquoit replied. "And I find my present responsibility as unpleasant as you find it difficult. I am tired of your company." He gave a hard yank on the rope, and Jonathan stumbled behind him to Woolsey's door. The magistrate's servant, Dorothy, opened it, and without a word pointed to the front room where Woolsey awaited them, seated behind his desk with a look of pained exasperation on his face.

"Matthew," Woolsey said, "what do you here, towing the good reverend like a recalcitrant mule?"

"Delivering him to your governance," Massaquoit replied, "as I am sure you know Mistress Williams has asked me to do."

"But he is a man of God, to be treated with proper respect. Unbind him."

Massaquoit did not respond at once. As Woolsey spoke, Massaquoit remembered how he had come upon this minister on top of the Indian girl. He could tell this English magistrate about that, but he did not think he would be believed. A time would come, he figured, when he could teach this minister some respect, but that time was not now. Jonathan held out his bound hands, and with one quick motion, Massaquoit's knife sliced through the rope. He nodded slightly at Woolsey. "I have delivered him into your hands," he said.

"On what authority, might I now inquire?" demanded Jonathan.

Woolsey frowned hard at him. "Mine," he said.

"To what purpose, then?" asked Jonathan.

"You know a young woman named Abigail King, do you not? She. . . ." Woolsey stopped himself, for Dorothy now stood at the door.

"The governor," she said simply, and turned aside as Peters' tall figure strode into the room. He crossed the room in two steps and stood between Woolsey's desk and Jonathan.

"Nephew," he said, "come with me."

Woolsey looked hard at the governor. He placed his palms flat on the desktop and pushed himself up. He waited a moment to catch his breath.

"Your nephew is before me at my request, and I am not finished with him."

"Ah, but you are," Peters said. "You had no authority to summon him." He glanced at Massaquoit. "I suppose you hired this savage to fetch him."

Massaquoit shook his head. "I am not for hire."

"He treated me most offensively," Jonathan said, his voice tinged with a whining quality that caused Massaquoit to look away in disgust.

"Never you mind, Matthew," Woolsey said. "You have done what you should have done, right and proper, and I will so report to Mistress Williams."

"I should have known," the governor sneered, "that I would hear that name in connection with this affront to my family."

"Indeed," Woolsey replied, "and you can add my name to hers, if it please you."

"It does not," Peters said. He yanked Jonathan's arm to turn the young man toward the door. Massaquoit looked at Woolsey. The magistrate shook his head.

"In time, and in a proper fashion," he said, "we will have opportunity to hear what Jonathan has to say about Abigail King's bastard child."

Peters, who was now at the door with his nephew still firmly in his grasp, looked back at Woolsey, opened his mouth, sputtered an inarticulate syllable, and left, pulling Jonathan behind him.

EIGHT

L ATER, MASSAQUOIT WOULD conclude that he must have been unusually distracted. How else could he explain that he almost tripped over the young Englishwoman as she was trying to drag the body off the road? He had left Magistrate Woolsey's house feeling more rage welling in him than he had experienced in years, and he did not understand why. His mind was on the insolence of the English magistrates as his feet found the river road north out of Newbury. The road followed the riverbank and paralleled the main artery that took a more direct route toward Catherine's house. Today, though, he was not interested in making haste to his wigwam beneath the ancient maple. His anger had almost boiled over as he found himself caught between the dueling English magistrates, the arrogant governor and the well-intentioned but still subtly condescending Woolsey. And all of this effort was expended to protect the English man of god whom he had pulled off an Indian girl, and who seemed to be in possession of something that all the English wanted.

None of it had anything to do with him, he had decided as he walked along, his eyes on the lengthening shadows of trees riding the slow-moving current of the river. The black of the shadows and the deep blue of the water mingled in places to form one ebon blotch, and somehow that merger soothed him, as though he, too, could merge his troubled spirit with the waters of the river.

It was the Englishwoman's grunt that brought his eyes back to the side of the road away from the river. She looked up, perspiration beading her forehead, her hands around the ankles of the man.

"Matthew, canst thou help me?" she asked. She looked down at the body and then over her shoulder to the thick undergrowth between two pines at the edge of the road.

He did not respond immediately as he stared at the body, which was lying on its back. Its face was covered by a piece of dark blue fabric. The man was tall, and although Massaquoit could not see the face, the thick black hair was not covered by the cloth, and he recognized it. He had seen it close up in the meeting-house some weeks before. If he could turn the body over, he knew he would find its back scarred from the whips of the English. He closed his eyes for a moment and felt another presence. When he opened them, he sensed only the woman.

"Do I have to call thee Massaquoit, then?" Jane asked. She rose to her feet and looked at Roger. A piece of her blue gown had been crudely torn off below the knee, and he could see the flesh of her lower leg. Her gaze followed his eyes as they moved from the fabric over the dead man's face to her torn gown. "I want to put him there in the shade."

"I do not think he can feel the sun on his face," Massaquoit said.

"I covered it because it was a beautiful face, once, and although he was untrue, I do not want to be unkind."

Something in her eyes revealed a passion as confused as the thoughts she expressed. Massaquoit knelt behind the body, and lifted the fabric from the face. The eye sockets, nostrils, and mouth had been attacked by maggots, leaving ragged flesh in those orifices. The flesh on his cheeks was bruised, as though he had been struck repeatedly. An artery in his throat had been cut, and his blood had spilled over his white shirt so that its entire front was one rust-colored stain. Massaquoit paused, waiting to feel the dead man's spirit. He sensed nothing, but out of the corner of his eye he detected a slight movement behind a tree, and he knew that they were being watched by someone who was very much alive. He was fairly certain who that was, and so he turned back to Jane.

"His spirit is nowhere about. Perhaps it seeks his killer."

"I saw him only a little while ago," she said.

"Who?"

"Why, the man who slit his throat. He ran away when I came upon them, but I have seen him before."

Massaquoit looked again at Roger's face. He wondered how so much damage could have been done to the man's flesh in so short a time, but he said nothing. Jane, too, now leaned forward to examine the ruined face. He noted that she did not seem moved by what she saw.

"Dost understand, now, dost thou not? About his poor face?" She leaned over and ran her fingers over each of the ruined eyes, and then down over the nose to the mouth. She let her fingers linger on the ragged lips. She placed the cloth again over his face, and smoothed it over the ruined flesh. She stared up at the sun. "They say, do they not, that the sun breeds these worms that have so feasted on him?"

"I do not know," Massaquoit replied, keeping his voice gentle. He thought she must be mad with grief, although something in her manner did not strike him as absolutely sincere. She returned to her position at Roger's feet and again grasped his ankles. Her face was set in granite determination.

"We must move him," she said. "It is not only the worms, I fear. He must be hidden for the sake of thy friend, the savage with the beaver hat."

"I would not think so."

She threw up her hands and then shook her head as though to clear it of confusion. "Mayhap thou art right. He is such a strange old man, wearing that heavy hat in the sun, is he not?" Massaquoit did not answer, and the smile disappeared. "I meant to say it is the sailor. The one that was on the ship I came on."

Massaquoit wrapped his mind around her disjointed words, and finding them incoherent, he nodded and seized the body underneath the armpits while she lifted its feet. They walked unsteadily over the few feet to the undergrowth. Massaquoit, moving backward squeezed his shoulders between the pines. He let his end of the body drop to the ground. Jane remained holding the feet.

"Turn him over, if thou pleasest," she said. She looked up through the pines as a ray of sun found its way to Roger's face. Massaquoit shrugged and then grabbed Roger by the waist, above the purse he wore around his middle. He pushed the purse aside to grasp the shirt and saw that the purse had been cut open. He felt Jane's eyes on him all this time, but she said nothing. He pulled hard on the shirt, and the body flopped onto its face. By the time he stood up, Jane was back on the road.

When they reached the path that ran from the river road to the main way, Massaquoit turned onto it. Jane stayed on the river road. She looked in the direction of Catherine's house.

"When thou getst there, tell Mistress Williams I could not return. It is because of him that lies back where we left him, and if that does not satisfy her curiosity, why then she can open that crate and see if she finds an answer there." She smiled brightly, curtsied like a little girl, and half skipped up the road. Massaquoit watched until she had almost disappeared. When she was not much more than a dark spot in the lengthening shadows, it seemed as though another figure emerged from the side of the road and accompanied her into the distance.

Massaquoit shifted his gaze to the river, now almost black as the sun set behind the trees. It was full dark by the time his slow pace brought him to the path leading up the slope to Catherine's house. Candles were lit in the front windows, and the door opened as he reached it. Phyllis stood in the doorway and beckoned him in.

"Mistress has been waiting for you."

"I bring unhappy news."

Catherine, sitting on the ornately embroidered settee in her front room, still stained with Roger's blood, could not hear the words of this conversation, but she could detect the hushed tones in which it was conducted, and she knew that her fears had been realized. She took a breath and squared her shoulders. When Massaquoit appeared before her, she did not wait for him to speak. "Where did you find him?" she asked.

Massaquoit was not taken aback at the question, for he had long ago stopped being surprised by the intuitive sagacity of this Englishwoman. "On the river road, just a little way above the harbor."

Catherine recalled the shipping crate that had just arrived, and the body that had been floating in the shallow water shortly after Roger and Jane arrived, and she imagined the breeze lifting from the waters of the harbor now carrying miasmic fumes. The place, she realized, was the center from which radiated the troubles of the brother and sister. She gave this notion voice.

"Was she there as well?"

"Yes."

She took the idea a step farther. "Is she hurt?"

"No."

Catherine relaxed a little.

"But she is not right," Massaquoit said. "Her words did not make sense, and her actions were peculiar."

"I am not surprised," Phyllis interjected.

"Please explain," Catherine said to Massaquoit after a quick, stern glance at her servant.

"She said she must hide her brother's face from the sun, which was breeding the worms that fed on his flesh. She insisted I help her pull it into the shade. And then she told me to tell you that if you wanted to understand why she could not come back to your house, you should look into that shipping crate."

"Such babble," Catherine said. "I cannot fathom her meaning."

She looked at Phyllis. "You have not opened that crate yet, have you?"

Phyllis reddened. "Why, it does not have my name on it," she sputtered.

"Then do it now, and see what you can discover. I am too weary at this moment to try that puzzle."

Massaquoit watched the broad back of Phyllis as she slowly walked out of the room. It seemed as though the servant was torn between her curiosity to see what was in that crate and her desire to hear what conversation would ensue between Catherine and Massaquoit. He waited until her heavy tread on the stairs indicated she was out of earshot.

"Jane had other things to say," he said.

"Touching upon who killed her brother?"

"Yes. She first said her killer was Wequashcook."

"Pshaw," Catherine exclaimed. "She could have been more original than to cast blame on an Indian. . . ."

Massaquoit felt the smile begin to stretch his lips. Over the years of his acquaintance with this strange and marvelous woman, he had come to believe that she did not share the racial hatred of the other English toward the Indians.

"Do you credit that idea?" Catherine asked, her voice now quite serious, as though she had decided that Jane's words, however bizarre their author, must be given due consideration.

"It is possible," he replied with a shrug. "But she changed her story immediately, and said she did not mean Wequashcook, but a sailor from your ship."

"I think I know who that might be," she replied. "A lad with a bruised face who came here looking for her one day."

"I know that lad. He was there when I found that dead sailor."

"Yet, it is remarkable how that lad keeps turning up near dead bodies," Catherine said. "Where think you he might be found?"

"He is a sailor," Massaquoit said.

"Of course," Catherine agreed. "There is another one to suspect," she added. "I patched Roger up, as you know, once before, and his assailant that time was an Englishman in the employ of Minister Davis, I suspect."

"To discourage his interest in the niece. But not to rob the young man."

"Certainly not. But why do you mention robbery?"

"Because Roger's wallet was cut open and there was nothing in it."

"Aye, there was nothing, for he had nothing. He has been borrowing coin from me this past fortnight."

"And yet somebody wanted what was in that wallet. I do not think it was money."

"What, then?"

"A letter. One that the English man of god you had me fetch had."

"Had?"

"It was taken from him. Perhaps by Wequashcook, with the help of that same sailor. I will seek them both in your ship."

"Both?"

Massaquoit nodded. "If Wequashcook has been using this sailor in his business, he will keep him close so as to have his eyes on him. I will tell you what I find out."

"And I, you," Catherine said. "For as you seek this letter from one side, I will look for it on another."

"Jonathan Peters?" Massaquoit asked.

"Indeed. I have business with him on behalf of the woman he has ruined."

"There have been more than one," Massaquoit said.

"I know. All the more reason to hold him to account."

At first, nobody answered Catherine's knock at the King house. She stood outside the crude plank door, which permitted the sun's rays to pass through cracks into the interior. She put her eye to one of these cracks, but could not see anything. Yet, she sensed a presence inside. A moment later a baby's cry, followed by an adult's hushing sound, confirmed her feeling. She knocked again, and this time she heard feet shuffling toward the door. It opened, and Abigail peered out, her face set in a hard look of despair.

"My mother says I am not to speak to you."

"Where is she?"

"She works now, she does. And we have enough to eat for us and the babe."

"I see. I suppose the governor can be generous when he chooses."

Abigail's face widened in surprise. "I told you nothing."

"In words, you did not. But your expression spoke what you would not say. I am not young, Abigail, and it is a long way back to my house. And it would do my heart good if I could see your babe."

Abigail exhaled, her breath smelling of something spicy. She shrugged and opened the door. "I don't suppose it can do any harm to have you come in and sit for a few minutes. Mother does not come home until after dark."

A cradle beside the table seemed to be moving of its own volition. Catherine walked over to it and saw the infant looking up at her, waving his arms and legs strongly enough to upset the equilibrium of the cradle. The babe's face glowed with health.

"He is a fit one, he is," Catherine said.

For the first time, Abigail permitted herself a quick smile. "He is that, my Jonathan."

Saying the name, however, erased the smile. She picked up the infant and held him to her chest. "What good is there in my calling him that name?"

"Are you going to baptize him?" Catherine asked.

Abigail scowled. "I hoped to baptize him Jonathan, with his father in attendance, as he should be."

"That won't happen," Catherine said gently. She recognized that the turn this conversation was taking might work toward her purpose, but she did not want to distress the young woman more than was necessary. Still, Abigail's anger could motivate her to risk the small comforts brought to her household by Governor Peters's money, which was no more than a bribe to shield his own family from disgrace. It was that shield which Catherine intended to penetrate. And, if in so doing, she also came closer to understanding who had killed Roger, so much the better.

"I did see your mother the other day wearing a new gown," Catherine said.

Abigail recoiled, and then cast her eyes down at her own gown, a shabby affair mended in several places, stained in others with all the various shades of dirt to be found inside and out of her house.

"Aye, she has become the lady, hasn't she?"

Catherine decided on one more bold stroke. "Unacknowledged bastards do not wear any finery," she said.

Abigail rose from her chair, her eyes ablaze. "He is no more a bastard than your own."

Catherine took the young woman's hand. "Then come with me," she said in her gentlest voice. "Let us visit the governor."

Abigail withdrew her hand, her face again sullen. "I can see no profit in that," she declared. "He has made himself very clear that he will have nothing to do with me, or my babe."

"But the babe's father is now in his house."

Catherine expected Abigail to rise to this bait, but instead the young woman seemed to withdraw more fully into her sullen depression. "I do not know that I want to see him."

"But you have said. . . ."

"I know what I did say, and what I am saying now is"—Abigail paused—"that I do not think he wants to see me, and that will pain me too sore."

"I see," Catherine said. "I am just now on my way there. I thought you might wish to accompany me."

"I will consider."

"I do not walk fast," Catherine replied, "and I believe you know the way."

It did not take long. Within ten minutes, Catherine heard footsteps behind her, and then labored breathing. She turned to see Abigail, babe in arms, hurrying after her. She waited for her to catch up, and then, with a nod and quick smile, she resumed walking. Together, they made their way to the governor's house.

Massaquoit approached the ship tied up at the dock in the harbor. It was so unlikely a place for the old Indian to be that it made sense that he would be there. For Wequashcook had not lived so long and so successfully by being predictable.

A rope hung down the flank of *The Good Hope*'s wooden hull. Massaquoit eyed it and waited. There was no sign of activity on board the ship, which had been emptied of its cargo some time ago. A young man wearing the rough leather doublet and breeches of an apprentice walked off the dock toward him. Massaquoit offered him his stone-faced stare; and the young man averted his eyes and continued walking. The dock was now deserted. Massaquoit seized the rope and, hand over hand, lifted himself to the ship's rail. He then heaved himself onto its deck.

As his feet hit the planks, a sailor approached him, as though he had been waiting. Massaquoit noted the stubborn discoloration beneath the right eye, and he knew he was looking into the face he had last seen peering down at the corpse of Billy Lockhart.

"Aye, so you have a good eye, and a better memory," Henry said, with a mocking smile that permitted saliva to drip between his missing teeth and onto his chin. He swiped the drool off with the back of his hand.

"I did not come to find you," Massaquoit replied.

"Of course you did not. The last time we met, you did not see me neither."

The bump on Massaquoit's head seemed to throb with his understanding. He felt a strong urge to pay back this audacious pup, but that would take him away from his present business.

"I think I prefer seeing you face to face," he contented himself with saying.

Henry smirked. "I was this time sent to greet you proper. Him you do seek set me to watch for you, for he says it won't be long afore you figure that you must talk to him."

"Is it not strange for an English to be in the service of an Indian?" Massaquoit asked.

The smile that had been playing on Henry's face disappeared as the young man thrust out his jaw and narrowed his eyes to form a fierce scowl. "I take orders only from myself, I do."

"Like your mate that was found floating dead in the water?"

"He was a fool."

"I see, and you are wise."

"Smart enough to know my own interest," Henry

replied. "But here, now, we are passing the time, and your mate waits below."

Massaquoit followed Henry down a ladder that led to the cargo area. As they pushed through a door that led to the hold, a strong stench of urine and excrement assaulted Massaquoit's nose. The floor of the hold was lined several feet thick with ballast stones, some smooth river cobbles and other roughly hewn pieces of granite. The smell seemed to rise from these stones. Massaquoit paused in the doorway and waved his hand in front of his nose. Henry gave a smirking grin.

"The lads come down here in foul weather," he said. "You gets used to it, after a while."

"A long while."

The voice belonged to Wequashcook, who was sitting cross-legged on a blanket some fifteen feet into the hold, almost against the timbers of the hull. The blanket lay on a wooden platform, and it seemed that the stones immediately about it had been kept clean of excrement or urine. Wequashcook lifted a wooden spoon from the iron pot on his lap and extended it toward Massaquoit.

"I see you still have your appetite," Massaquoit observed.

"I've been keeping him fed," Henry said.

"It is not bad," Wequashcook said.

Massaquoit looked past the spoon to the pot, in which he saw and smelled soup. A fish head floated on the surface of the liquid. He squatted and took the spoon from Wequashcook. As he was about to bring the spoon to his mouth, he felt something brush against his lower leg, left bare by the English-style breeches that ended just above his knee. He recognized the hard bristles of a rat's face against his flesh. He saw the animal, poised on its hind legs, nose twitching and red eyes glaring, a short distance away. With a quick motion he swatted it with the back of his hand. The rat flew toward Henry, who was standing at the foot of the ladder leading down into the hold. The animal landed on its back, and before it could right itself, Henry skewered it with the knife he wore in a sheath at his waist. The rat spasmed for five or ten seconds on the end of the knife and then was still. Henry made a downward throwing motion but held onto the knife, hurling the dead rat toward his feet, where it landed with an audible splat against the stones. Henry offered himself a self-congratulatory grin. Wequashcook motioned him away, and Massaquoit now brought the spoon to his lips and swallowed. The soup was hot and not a little salty, but it felt good going down into his stomach. He handed the spoon back to Wequashcook. Wequashcook scooped the spoon into the soup and brought it to his mouth with a smack of his lips. He shook his head.

"A very complicated business," he said.

"And here you are at the center of it, eating soup made for you by an English."

Wequashcook glanced toward Henry, who had not moved. Henry looked away, and with a shrug climbed up the ladder toward the deck. He paused after climbing a little way and turned back.

"I cannot vouch for your safety down here any longer," he said. "I hear that the cargo is to be loaded on the morrow."

Wequashcook sighed. "That is unfortunate," he

said. "But I tire of the food, and the company. And the rats."

"You need not come back, then," Henry said. He pointed to the dead rat at his feet. "But if you do, this fellow and his mates will be what you will have to eat." He sheathed his knife and disappeared up the stairs.

"An irritating boy," Massaquoit said. He rubbed the back of his head.

Wequashcook smiled. "I did not intend that. He is a clumsy boy, like most of the English, but he has his uses, if you know what to do with him." Wequashcook took a swallow of the soup. "But now he is no longer useful, and I will be rid of him."

"He seems to be free to go where he likes," Massaquoit said.

"For a short while, but I have set the dogs on him." Wequashcook waved his hand in a dismissive gesture. "Forget him. He is not important."

Massaquoit shrugged. "I did not come here to talk to you about this boy. I have been to a great deal of trouble with no more to show for it than this bump on my head. And somehow, I think you have the answers I seek, if it was not your hand that hit me."

"Your head will heal like mine did, only better. But I will pay you for your pain with the information you seek. Your young friend Ninigret comes to me. He is involved with this Englishwoman. They want to retrieve a letter. I find out that the English priest has it, the one you were taking back to Newbury. I catch up with him after Henry has"—he paused—"distracted you." He dipped his spoon again into the soup and slurped a large mouthful. The soup dribbled down his chin, and he licked it with his tongue. "That boy is a good cook. That is what he does on this ship. He works in the galley."

"The letter," Massaquoit prodded.

"Ah, yes, the letter."

"Did you not read it?"

"No. It did not concern me, and could burden me with unnecessary information. I tried to trade with the priest, but he was insulting to me. I did what I had to and took it from him, and then I watched as you caught up to him."

"Who has it now?"

Wequashcook shrugged. "I know who did have it a little time ago. The dead English. I sent the boy to meet him where he went to pray in his strange fashion, in that abandoned house where the Quakers meet. When he did not find him there, he was very bold, more than I would like. He went to your woman's house. In the night. He brought him to me." His face brightened. "Do you think the Quaker god is the same as the one they pray to in the meetinghouse in Newbury?"

"I do not know."

"I find this English god very puzzling," Wequashcook said, "but he seems to keep the English content, and that is good for us Indians."

"You gave the letter to Roger?"

"I sold it to him, for future considerations. He had no money. Bad business."

"Yes, he's dead, and you have nothing in your pocket."

Wequashcook shrugged. "I should know better. As

for the letter, whoever killed him must have it. Perhaps his sister knows."

"She says you killed her brother."

Wequashcook's expression did not change except for a slight twitching of his lips, which could have been the beginning of a smile or a scowl.

"Then she changed her mind," Massaquoit said.

"I am not surprised. Her mind is not steady."

"She said your sailor friend did it."

"I do not think so." Wequashcook shrugged, a gesture that said he had dismissed the matter from his mind. He scraped his spoon across the bottom of the pot, and scooped up the last of the soup. He offered it to Massaquoit. Massaquoit shook his head.

"Thank you for the soup, and the information." He stood up and ran his hand over the sore spot on his head.

"Unfortunate," Wequashcook said, "but only in the way of business. Only business."

Massaquoit walked up the stairs and took a deep breath of the fresh air that greeted him as he emerged onto the deck. He blinked against the sunlight that struck his eyes. Henry was leaning against the railing where the rope was suspended. Massaquoit looked past the dock to where it met the harbor road. He saw the unmistakable glint of sun against steel.

"I think I have had more than my belly full of your friend," Henry said, "and of this ship, for that matter. And there's this woman I knows at this tavern." He took hold of the rope and began to swing himself over the railing. Massaquoit considered warning him, but for once decided to operate on Wequashcook's well-established principle of not interfering where he had no genuine interest. Let the English have one of their own, he thought, and chuckled to himself at We-quashcook's duplicity.

"Well, I am sure she is better company than an old Indian living among the rats in the hold of a ship."

"He has the special accommodation, he does," Henry replied, "for all the good it can do him." He swung himself over the railing. Massaquoit heard his feet striking against the hull as the sunlight flashed off the pikes of the approaching soldiers.

Catherine and Abigail had walked in silence from the King hovel to Newbury, where they now approached the governor's mansion. Catherine recalled the grim poverty that rose from the dirt floor beneath Abigail's feet, its smell so strong that it seemed to permeate her spirit and burden her with an implacable despair. She saw in Abigail a spirit like a candle flame flickering in a black wind, threatened at any moment with extinction and yet flaring from time to time in defiance. The young woman's expression had remained fixed during their walk, but now she hung back as she faced the grandeur of the governor's house—as though, Catherine thought, wondering what business she might have with such majesty. Catherine took her arm and gently urged her forward.

"It is because he has so much that we are here," she said. Abigail nodded, although her eyes betrayed her fear. Still, she permitted Catherine to lead her to the grand double doors of carved oak at the front of Peters' mansion. At her knock, the doors swung open as though they had been expected. Francine stood in the doorway, her face set in a civil but cool expression.

"I expect you are here to see the governor," she said.

Catherine put her arm about Abigail. "Yes."

Francine stared hard at the young woman. "She has no business in my house, and the governor is sick in his bed."

"Perhaps I can minister to him, then," Catherine replied.

"I fear not," Francine said.

"You seem not yourself," Catherine suggested.

Francine looked back over her shoulder as though she thought she would be overheard. "My tongue feels wondrously heavy," she replied.

"So I see."

"Is he not here, then?" Abigail asked. She stepped forward, and her eyes were now bright with determination.

"Did you not hear me, girl?" Francine demanded.

"Not your husband, Mistress," Abigail said, "but his nephew, the father of my baby."

Francine leaned forward, her hand cupped to her ear. "I am afraid my ear is as clogged as my tongue is heavy."

"Try a little, for me," Catherine said.

"For you, then," Francine replied. "Jonathan is not here, and the governor forbids me to tell his whereabouts, though truth be known, I could not tell you if I wanted. He left early this morning, his fowling piece on his shoulder."

"And yet I will have him own his babe," Abigail said.

"As for that," Francine began, then paused. Behind her a figure appeared. Francine turned. "What is it, Miriam?"

"The governor," Miriam said, "calls for you."

Francine shrugged and began to close the door. Abigail seized the handle and held the door ajar.

"Mother," she said.

Miriam looked at her and shook her head. "He was most insistent," she said to Francine.

Francine nodded and let go of the door. "I will go to him directly."

She left, and Miriam advanced. She started to push the door shut while Abigail still held the handle on her side. For a moment, mother pushed against daughter, then both dropped their hands.

"You should not have brought her here," Miriam said to Catherine, then put her shoulder to the door and closed it.

"Do not despair," Catherine said as they turned their backs on the governor's mansion. "Francine will report our visit, and Governor Peters knows I am not easily discouraged."

"But my mother, how could she be so cold?"

"Do not blame her. She only does what she thinks she must, even if she is mistaken."

A woman with a hobbling gait hurried toward them. "Mistress Williams," she said, "I needs must talk to you."

Abigail looked at Charity with the contempt one downtrodden person can feel toward another even half a step lower.

"I cannot imagine what she might want with you," Abigail said.

"No doubt she does not speak for herself," Catherine replied. She saw that Abigail was still very agitated.

"Go ahead to my house, if you please, and ask Phyllis to give you some chamomile tea. It will soothe you."

"Do you think I need soothing, then?" Abigail snapped.

"You have had a difficult day," Catherine replied.

Charity was now standing a few feet away, and Abigail leaned her head to whisper to Catherine. "Do you not want to know where Jonathan might be?"

"Indeed, I do."

"He told me once that he likes to hunt near where the savages live—for the adventure, he said. I did not know whether to believe him at the time, he is so fond of a good jape." Her eyes brightened as though with a pleasant recollection, then narrowed into a frown that creased the otherwise smooth skin at the corners of her eyes. "That was then, and this is now. I will think about your tea." She looked once more at Charity, who returned her glance without expression, then hurried up the road toward Catherine's house.

Charity waited until Abigail was out of hearing, then she took the one step that still separated her from Catherine. She opened her mouth to begin talking, but first she ran the stump of her tongue over her lips as though to orient it so as to form the words she wanted to speak. "There are two things I must tell you." She glanced over her shoulder toward Minister Davis's house. "And I can tell you only beyond his hearing."

"And what are they?"

"The first is what the minister say when he find that young man under the covers with his niece. He say that this Roger Whitcomb be a devil come to test his faith and that of his niece, and the Bible tell him to fight that devil as hard as he can. And once, why, I see them together with mine own eyes, and I tell you what I think. The minister is a wise man, but he does not see this affair the right way, for if he did, he would know that these Quakers are witches, and that is why that girl lose her baby and a just God has struck down that young man for casting a spell on her and her babe."

"I see," Catherine said. "Is that what you wanted to tell me?"

Charity shook her head in a slow determined motion. "That is only the first thing. The second is this. Just this morning that man Timothy. . . ."

"The one hurt attacking Roger?"

"He is that one, the very devil, only this devil have the minister's coin in his pocket, and he come to the house. I overheard them talk while I was cooking the morning meal. They pay me no mind like I was not there, so I listen to what they say. They have their heads together, and I do not hear everything, but then Timothy stands up and says in a clear voice that he will tell the governor that he saw who killed that Quaker, and it was the sailor from your ship. And then the minister say that very good, and he hands him a little leather pouch, and I hear the coins jangle in it." Charity stopped, as though suddenly aware that she had said too much. "I must get back to my work."

"But why do you tell me all these things?"

"Don't you see? That man, he take me in, and he is a man of God, but he forget what he teaches."

"And what is that?"

"That vengeance is the Lord's," Charity said, then turned and hobbled across the town common to the minister's house.

NINE

ABIGAIL WAS ALREADY gone by the time Catherine
reached her house. Phyllis stood in the kitchen,
examining a piece of clothing that she had draped
over her arm.

"Did you give her the tea?" Catherine asked.

Phyllis looked up with a confused expression on
her face. "Tea?"

"Yes, for Abigail, to soothe her nerves."

Recognition lit Phyllis's eyes. "Surely I did, just as
you bade me do."

"Seemed she grateful?"

"I do not think so. She was in a temper."

Catherine waited and watched while her servant
turned her attention back to the garment on her arm.
Phyllis looked up to see if she had Catherine's attention.

"Well?" Catherine asked. "What is it?"

Phyllis's face brightened. "Something that will

make us forget Abigail and her foul mood." She held the garment out in front of her. It was in two pieces, a bodice and a gown of rich blue velvet. The bodice was edged with fine linen lace. Phyllis ran her fingers over the lace.

"It is the gown of a rich woman," she said.

"So it is," Catherine replied.

"I would never be able to wear such a thing."

"But that is surely not your revelation."

"Indeed not, it was just holding it this way put me in mind of that thought." She clasped the bodice to her chest with one hand, and pressed the gown to her waist with the other. Both pieces were far too small for Phyllis's ample frame.

"Do you not see?" she asked Catherine. "It is not only the lace that would make this an improper garment for such as myself."

"I see that indeed. Came these garments from that crate I bade you open?"

Phyllis nodded. "As usual, you do see right through me, like the sun through a window. So you know that these were indeed in that very crate you asked me to examine."

"I do see, now," Catherine said, as the realization began to settle in her mind. "Those clothes were sent by Jane's mother, intended for her so she would have some variety in her dress. And Jane, of course. . . ."

"Could no more fit in these than I could. Why, these are of a size more like for a child. I do not think a mother could be so mistaken about her own daughter."

"Nor do I," Catherine replied.

"There can be only one answer to this misfitting,"

Phyllis said. "The person what this gown and bodice was supposed to be for, is not the person who has been living in this house." Her face was alive with the excitement of her discovery.

"And if she is not. . . ."

The excitement drained from Phyllis's countenance, replaced by a blank stare of confusion. "I can go no further," she admitted.

"Well, then, you need not," Catherine said, taking the garments from her and holding them against her own much shorter frame. She noted that they would be a little small even for her if she were as thin as she had been as a girl, and Jane was a good four or five inches taller than she was. "You have gone quite far enough, indeed."

"Do you see, then?" Phyllis asked.

"I begin to. And what I do see is not very pretty. For our Jane must be an impostor."

"Then what of the Jane who these clothes were for? Perhaps we could inquire of her brother, if he was not dead." Phyllis sat down with a sigh at the bench next to the table.

"Dead or not, he was not her brother," Catherine said with a frown.

Massaquoit found Catherine sitting at the table in the kitchen while Phyllis rinsed the wooden trenchers in a large wooden tub. Phyllis looked up. "If you are hungry, you are too late," she said.

Massaquoit smiled. "I dined earlier with a friend."

"Did you indeed?" Catherine said. "Would that have been Wequashcook?"

"He is a generous host," Massaquoit replied.

"Did he offer you more than food?"

"He did, but I do not know how helpful he has been."

Phyllis had been leaning over the tub, and now she stood up with such energy that her leg pushed against the tub, almost causing it to tip. Water sloshed onto the plank floor. Phyllis bent over the wet spot, dabbed at it with her rag, and then strode toward Massaquoit.

"Did he tell you how it is that Jane is not Jane?" she asked.

"He did not."

"Well, that is the mystery," Phyllis declared. "If you can tell us that, we can figure the rest."

"I cannot tell you that, but I believe I know where I can find this Jane who is not Jane."

"And so think I," Catherine said.

Phyllis looked from Catherine to Massaquoit. "She does not credit my idea," Phyllis said.

"And what is that?" Massaquoit asked.

"Why, that it all has something to do with Roger climbing in the low window into Grace's bed. Her uncle found him there, you know. And he set that villain to attack Roger."

"I thought we were talking about Jane," Massaquoit said.

"Men!" Phyllis said to Catherine. "They do not see what is in front of their nose. Because, don't you see, it is at that time when Roger is sneaking to see Grace that Jane, who is not Jane, starts behaving most strange, and then this crate arrives just when he is killed."

Catherine stood up and put her arm about Phyllis.

"Now that you have explained your theory better, I begin to see its merit."

Phyllis looked stunned. "But I do not understand it quite."

"Nor do I," Catherine said, "but I believe you are right, in any case."

Massaquoit studied the two women, who now seemed to understand each other thoroughly.

"I believe," he said, "that I need more instruction."

"Phyllis is pointing out," Catherine said, "that several circumstances converge, and at the root is Roger's relationship with Grace."

"Jane was jealous?" Massaquoit asked.

"Yes, but only . . . if they were not brother and sister," said Catherine.

"As they were not, surely." Phyllis continued.

"Because Jane is not Jane," Massaquoit finished the thought. "From one root grows a tangle of weeds."

"Weeds, indeed," Catherine added, "for no flower grows in this garden."

"Only corpses," Phyllis concluded. She looked at Massaquoit as though he had just arrived. "But can you not tell us anything?"

"Only this," Massaquoit replied. "Whether part of the root, or another weed, I do not know. But I believe Roger was killed because of a letter he had in his possession."

"Jealousy, I say," Phyllis insisted. "He did die for love."

"If so, the letter must be the key. Wequashcook told me he sold it to Roger after he took it from the

English priest. Although why the priest should want it, I do not know."

"Perhaps for Jane," Catherine said.

"My head begins to whirl," Phyllis murmured, and as though to emphasize the point, she sat down at the table, cradling her chin in her hands.

"In time, " Catherine said, "all will come clear."

"I do not think so," Phyllis replied.

Edward came in, his hands covered in dirt from hoeing. Narrow bands of perspiration gathered in his wrinkles. He ran his hand across his eyes to clear the sweat from them, and left a streak of moist dirt across his forehead and cheek. He looked toward the front door.

"There is a soldier or two coming up the path," he announced.

"I know their errand. They come to seek your help for the sailor," Massaquoit said.

Phyllis, her face red, rose from the table. "How would you know that?" she demanded.

"Never you mind," Catherine replied as a loud knock sounded on the front door.

"I can explain," Massaquoit offered.

"In time," Catherine said. "Phyllis, get me my bag, if you please, and see that there is clean cloth in it for bandages."

Edward had gone to the door, and now he returned. "The soldiers," he said. "There is a boy at the jail who is about to die. The governor himself desires that you keep him alive long enough to get a confession."

Jailer Drake sat on a joint stool in front of his prison house, picking his teeth with a twig. He got up as

Catherine and Phyllis followed the two soldiers. As was his custom, he offered Catherine a halfhearted bow, which demonstrated that he recognized her superior social status but did not in his heart believe she warranted it, perhaps because he did not believe a man should ever feel subordinate to a woman. Still, he was a man who always looked out for his own interests, and in this case that meant showing a degree of respect toward Catherine.

"Ah, Mistress Williams, your arrival is timely." He turned to the door, which was half open. "I have but the one guest at the moment, and he is in no condition to leave. In fact, I would not swear that he still breathes."

"The soldiers here have explained the circumstance, how the young man attempted to flee as he was being arrested and did struggle so mightily," Catherine replied.

One of the soldiers, a boy of no more than sixteen, stepped next to Drake and then turned to face Catherine. His lips were puffy and one eye half closed. He held out the blade of his pike, which was encrusted with dried blood.

"He did that, as I have told in truth to Mistress Williams. My face bears the imprint of his fists, as you can surely see, but he did not profit from his encounter with me, I warrant." And with that, he thrust out the pike blade. "It caught him between the ribs, and that is a fact."

The other soldier, a grizzled man in his early forties, a head shorter than the tall, lean boy, shook his head. "I do believe he will be telling the story of how he captured that lad inside to his grandchildren."

"That I will, Nathaniel, and you can tell yours how you watched from the ground, where he did shove you."

"Enough of this chatter," Catherine said in exasperation. "You say the boy is near death, so let me pass to see what I can do." She stared hard at the young soldier. "Step aside, if you please."

"Let be, Oliver, that's a good lad," the grizzled soldier said. The boy shouldered his pike and moved away from the door.

"This way, then, Mistress Williams," Drake said as he motioned Catherine inside. Phyllis followed, and after a moment so did Oliver.

There, lying on a thin blanket on the floor next to the table on which Drake took his meals, was Henry. His face was pale, his eyes were closed, and his hands were pressed against his left side. Catherine knelt next to him and gently lifted his hands. He opened his eyes and moaned. Oliver peered over Catherine's shoulder until she looked up at him.

"My pardon, Mistress," he said.

"No doubt you hope to see the reward of your efforts," Catherine snapped.

"I thought only that he might die."

"That is what I meant. Now stand back."

Oliver retreated to a position by the door. A hacking cough preceded the entrance of a wizened little man who pushed past Oliver and walked toward Henry, stopping a few feet away. Henry looked past Catherine, then shook his head with enough force to cause him to grimace in pain. Catherine stood up and faced the visitor, who was a little taller than a dwarf and had wispy white hair and beard. The little man held a foolscap sheet of paper in one hand, and a quill pen and small jar of ink in the other. His beard was smudged here and there with ink stains.

"I trow the governor has sent you, Will Best," Catherine said.

"Aye, that he did," Will said, and pointed to Henry. "His excellency wants a record of anything he might say."

"You are wasting your time, then," Henry said, "if you believe I will say anything worth your writing down."

Catherine pointed to a corner of the room. "If you hear anything, it will be from over there, Will, for I will not have you in my way, or causing this lad any discomfort."

Will scurried to the corner and sat cross-legged with the paper on his knees. He uncapped his ink jar and dipped his pen.

"As you like, Mistress Williams. I serve my masters and mistresses each as well as the other. Unless," he cackled, "they be of different minds, and then it is the master I heed, as any wise man would."

"Your master is not here to contradict me," Catherine replied. She turned toward Oliver. "This is a small enough room, with little air to breathe."

Oliver's face expressed his disappointment, but he shuffled through the doorway. Catherine turned her attention back to Henry. "Never mind Will Best," she said.

"I fear," Henry replied.

Catherine lifted Henry's bloody shirt and probed the wound in his side with her forefinger, pressing it in until she encountered resistance. Then she ran her finger the length of the gash and found it to be about six inches. The wound had bled copiously, and that was the danger; it did not appear that the blade of the pike had struck any vital organ. If Henry were given a decent chance to recover, given his youth and strong constitution, the wound would not prove mortal. However, she concluded that he was far from out of danger because he had lost so much blood.

"Drake," she called. The jailer, who had remained outside, came in, scratching his chin. "Have you any water about?" she demanded.

Drake ambled past the table to the far end of the room, where a pitcher sat on the floor. He brought it back to Catherine and handed it to her. Then he walked back through the door and out into the sunshine. Catherine looked into the pitcher and saw a dead beetle floating in it on its back. She grabbed the insect between her fingers and tossed it aside.

"Phyllis," Catherine said, and her servant handed her a clean rag from her midwife's bag. Catherine dunked the rag into the pitcher and then ran it over the wound, washing off the congealed blood. Henry bit down on his lips.

"That's a good lad," Catherine said. Phyllis, in the meantime, took out another rag, which she dipped into a small jar containing the coneflower poultice. She handed the rag to Catherine, who applied it to the wound.

"There, now," Catherine said in her most reassuring tones. "A couple of stitches is all I need to close this. You should mend before long." She looked toward the door through which Oliver had departed.

"I am sure that one would be disappointed so to hear."

"You are not fooling me, are you?" Henry demanded. "I do not want to die."

"No," Catherine said. "You may die, surely, but not from this wound." She eyed the little man across from them. "That one poses you a far graver threat."

"But I am innocent," Henry said.

"Innocent, he says," Will cackled. "Why, who did say you did anything? Why, then, you must therefore be guilty, else why would you protest your innocence?"

"I know well you think I killed that Quaker," Henry said. "Else why would you be here?"

"Only to record," Will said. "That is what I do."

Henry, now clearly agitated, started to sit up, but then the color drained from his face and he clutched at his wound. He collapsed, and the back of his head thudded against the floor.

"Phyllis," Catherine called.

Phyllis lowered herself onto the floor next to Henry and cradled his head in her ample lap. Catherine lifted his hands from the wound. The rag was red with fresh blood. She removed the rag and threaded the catgut thread through the fishbone needle. With quick and deft movements, she held the flesh together and pulled the needle through. Henry jerked each time the needle entered his flesh, and Phyllis cooed in his ear while leaning her weight on his upper body to keep him still. After the last stitch, Catherine rummaged in her bag and removed a long strip of cloth. "Just lift yourself a little," she said, and when he did, she passed the strip under his back and then over the cloth on top of the wound, forming a bandage.

"Now lie down and stay still," she said.

He nodded, but his eyes darted back and forth toward the little man. "He is going to see me hang," he said.

"Hang," Will repeated. "I do not hang men. I only write down their words." He held his pen poised over his paper. "Now, lad, what words can you give me, for you must speak, now or later."

"You need say nothing while you regain your strength," Catherine said. "I am witness to your condition."

Just then the door, which Oliver had shut behind him, swung open and Timothy barged in. He looked down at the wounded sailor, and then he clutched his own side.

"Ah, Mistress Williams is a good one with her needle and poultice," he said. "I can vouch for that. But she is wasting her talents on a murderer."

Charity's words flashed in Catherine's mind. "Be careful," she said to Timothy, "for the Lord hates a false witness and will not abide your lies."

"Begging your pardon, Mistress Williams, but I knows what I have seen with mine own eyes, and there is no lying that way. And I saw him kill that Quaker."

Will Best dipped his pen in his ink and wrote rapidly. "Words," he murmured as he wrote. His pen made a quite audible noise. Henry started up, and Catherine pressed her hand on his chest. When he settled back down, she moved her fingers to his lips. He nodded. She stood up and stepped toward Timothy.

"There are fresh coins in your purse, I warrant," she declared.

"Only honest wages."

"Jailer!" Catherine called out, and Drake entered. "Remove this man, or instead of a prisoner you will soon have a corpse."

"That is what I know full well," Drake said. "But then corpses don't eat very much, do they?" He took Timothy by the elbow and whispered something in his ear. Timothy hesitated, then followed the jailer out of the room. Henry watched him depart, then looked first at Will and then Catherine.

"With respect, Mistress," Henry said, "he has written those lying words that will put my neck in a noose. I do not know how I may mend, or what may befall me, so words he wants, words I will give him while I have a little strength." He rolled toward Will. "Hear me now, you troll."

"Troll, he calls me, and he the one facing the hemp," Will sneered. "Speak, my pen awaits."

"Then write first that I killed nobody. It may be that someone might say I was nearby, and that is no lie, but I did no harm to him what is dead. You would do well to look for his sister, for she was there, along with her Indian lover. I saw them there. I never went near him that got killed. I wanted only to retrieve a piece of property I knew he had."

He paused, and the air was filled with the scratching of Will's pen, which he moved with marvelous efficiency over the paper, pausing only long enough after several words to dip his pen into the ink. Henry glared at him until he again held his pen suspended over the paper.

"Do you not have questions for me?" he demanded.

"Questions? I only record, have I not said to you that is my only function?" Will replied.

Catherine put her fingers to Henry's lips.

"I can no more," he said.

After a few moments, when he did not continue, Will closed his ink jar and folded his paper with elaborate care, creasing it once in half with his blunt fingernail, and then once again before tucking it into the top of his breeches.

"Pity," he said. "I do think he has more words for me."

"I think not," Catherine replied. She ran her hand over Henry's eyes and saw that he was asleep. "Leave him now," she said, and stood up. Will nodded, and scurried out as suddenly as he had entered. A moment later Drake came in.

"Are you through with that one?" he asked, pointing at Henry. "I do want my living quarters back. There is a room where I can lock him up proper."

Catherine reached into the bottom of her bag and pulled out a couple of coins. She held them out to Drake. "Put him where he will be comfortable, and feed him what he will eat when he awakes."

"Are you sure you want to feed a dead man?"

"Do what I say," Catherine snapped. "It is not for you to be saying who will die."

Drake offered an insincere smile. "Why, Mistress, of course such be in the hands of God."

"Remember that," Catherine replied, "and tend to that lad."

"Speaking of God," Drake said, "Minister Davis waits outside."

"I do not doubt it."

Catherine saw the minister and Timothy leaning over Will as the little man glanced down at his paper. Minister Davis nodded and stroked his chin. Timothy looked confused, and it was clear to Catherine that he could not read. He turned toward her and said something to the minster, who motioned him away. Timothy left. Then Will folded his paper again and he scurried after Timothy. Minister Davis held his heavy Bible clutched under his arm. He took off his skullcap and wiped the sweat from his forehead.

Catherine strode toward him. "Are you here to offer that boy comfort?"

"You tend to his wounds. I will provide balm for his spirit," Minister Davis replied.

"I have done what I can for him."

"He has told an interesting tale," Minister Davis said. "About that whore you entertained in your house. I believe she conspired with that lad inside, and now she appears to have run off with an Indian. Will is even now on his way to the governor. Timothy goes with him to complete the part of the story the boy did not tell."

Catherine felt the heat rise in her cheeks, and took a deep breath to calm herself. It would do no good to confront him at this time and place. Perhaps later, with Magistrate's Woolsey's support, she could pierce the minister's aura of self-righteousness. For now, she saw a net being dropped over both Henry and Jane, and she could not help but feel that the minister was holding one end of it and the governor the other. Both men, for different reasons, were more concerned with preserving their family's honor than with discovering the truth. The minister's niece had been deflowered in his very own house by a man who had now himself been murdered after having tried to pass off another woman as his sister. The governor's nephew had given Abigail King a bastard child, had raped an Indian girl, and had somehow become involved in the deceit of Roger and Jane. She looked hard at the sweating man of God and wondered if the perspiration came more from the heat of the sun or the anger in his blood.

And then, restraining as best she could any tone of irony, she said, "I leave him to your tender care."

Massaquoit sat with his back against the tree next to his wigwam. He had chosen not to follow Catherine on her mission of mercy to nurse the wounded sailor. He would be of no use there, and his mind was heavy with confused thoughts that he hoped an hour or two of solitude might help clarify.

Two English were dead, and they were linked by a piece of paper. And that piece of paper had passed through Wequashcook's hands. Massaquoit did not think that Wequashcook would kill for that paper, for the old Indian preferred commercial transactions that did not involve spilling blood, on the very sound theory that violence often turns back on its source. But Ninigret was another matter. He remained, to some extent, the angry boy Massaquoit had first met some years before. That anger had alienated him from his own people and had also made it impossible for him to adapt to the ways of the English. He lived on the line between the two cultures, much as Massaquoit and, in his own way, Wequashcook did, but Ninigret absorbed only the hostility between the two peoples and none of the occasional reconciliations or accommodations.

Thinking of Ninigret filled his mind with the scenes of slaughter he had witnessed since the English arrived. When he looked at the setting sun, it was ringed with a reddish aura, as though his imagination were casting its bloody thoughts onto it. A cloud with a ragged edge drifted in front of the sun, and it looked like flesh torn asunder and bleeding. The cloud moved on, and Massaquoit stared hard at the ground beneath his feet until he felt he had cleared his mind. When he again looked at the sun, it glowed pale yellow.

Yes, he concluded, Ninigret was capable of such violence. And then Massaquoit recalled the sailor's deft handling of the knife as he killed the rat, and he figured that the young English could use that skill just as well on a human target. He sat until he felt the rough bark of the maple tree through his shirt. He closed his eyes and sat forward so that he could clasp his knees with his hands. He remained that way until he heard the steps of Catherine and Phyllis as they made their way up the hill toward the house. He stood up and walked to meet them. Phyllis continued on to the house, carrying Catherine's midwife bag, while Catherine remained with Massaquoit.

"Will the boy live?" he asked.

"He will recover from his wounds," Catherine

replied. "But it is likely that he may live only to die at the end of a rope."

Massaquoit was surprised at the feeling of relief that surged through him. He had not realized how strongly he wanted to believe that the sailor would be found guilty and so, at least this one time, spare an Indian from being held responsible. Still, he felt he must ask. "Do you think that just?"

Catherine did not answer right away, and then she shrugged. "I cannot say. But he thought he was near death, and he was being hounded by the governor's scribe and the minister's witness, who I think is lying for pay, and so he maintained his innocence."

"What else would a man say who is looking in the eyes of death?" Massaquoit asked.

"Truly," Catherine replied. "But I have seen the fear of death straighten a tongue that otherwise would lie for a farthing or a drink of beer."

"Ah, I understand, I think. Your English god's punishment in the life after death."

"Yes." Catherine studied his face. "I see that you hope he is guilty, whatever his reasons for denying it." She hesitated, for she knew what she must say next, but she could not shield him. "Not only did he insist on his innocence, he pointed his finger at Jane. And Ninigret."

"To save his skin," Massaquoit replied. He, too, paused as he considered what next he would say. He realized, as she no doubt had done, that the relationship they had established over the years was like planks suspended over the embers of a fire. Most of the planks were solid and had shown their ability to withstand the weight of misunderstanding or suspi-

cion. But there were some, perhaps weakened by
contact with the ancient flames, that would snap if
asked to bear too much. Yet, he felt he must try their
strength. And his own. "I have known Ninigret for
some years," he began.

"I do recall," she replied in a tone she hoped indicated that continuing would be strictly his choice. He
nodded his understanding.

"He was an angry boy, and now, as a young man,
he seems to have fallen in love with a dangerous
woman. That is an explosive combination."

"You credit the possibility that Ninigret might be
implicated, then?"

"I cannot deny it."

"But you would not want to see an innocent man
hang, would you?"

"No."

"I thought not. Even to clear one of your people."

"Even so," he replied. "So it appears that we must
find the truth. And I think I know where to pursue it."

"Jane?"

"She is the link that holds all together," Massaquoit said.

"It will not be long before the governor seeks her,"
Catherine said.

"Then I must be first," Massaquoit replied.

Massaquoit paused as he approached his wigwam.
Although it looked just as he had left it some hours
before, he sensed a difference. Instead of proceeding
directly to the flap that covered the entrance, he
walked around its outside, his foot touching the
ground so gently that his step was soundless. His

wigwam had its summer sheathing of reed matting, through which he would be able to discern the outline of an intruder if there were any light from inside, but it was dark. As he reached the back of the wigwam, opposite the entrance, he thought he could detect a slight bulge in the line of the reed sheathing. He studied it, but he could not be certain whether it moved or not, or whether his eyes were being deceived by the shadow of a branch from the maple that overhung the wigwam.

He kicked at the bulge, and his foot thudded against something solid. He trotted back to the opening of his wigwam and waited. He heard movement inside, and then a hand emerged in a tentative movement. Massaquoit seized the hand and pulled. He met a moment's resistance, and then a body tumbled out at his feet. He let go of the hand as he recognized the face.

"I did not mean to startle you," Ninigret said, "but I did not think it wise to wait for you outside."

"In that you are correct. Now that I have pulled you out of my house, let us both go back into it."

They crawled back through the flap and squatted across from one another, the stones of Massaquoit's fire circle between them.

"I have no food to offer you," Massaquoit said.

"Do not concern yourself."

"You are under a cloud of suspicion for murdering the English. They will come for you."

Ninigret pulled his lips back into an ugly sneer. "That is not all they will find if they come to Niantic. We have the English priest. Rawandag and some young braves took him as he hunted. As you said, a time would come."

"And the woman?"

"She is with me. She says she wants the English priest to marry us. But Rawandag says the English priest must be tortured for what he did to Minnehaha."

"And what do you think?"

Ninigret's expression softened, and Massaquoit realized the young man loved Jane at least as much as he hated Jonathan.

"I think I will live with this woman."

"And the priest?"

"I want to see terror in his eyes."

"If you kill him, the English will want payment ten times over in your blood."

Ninigret considered, and his expression turned grave. "I am sure you know about their revenge," he said in a low voice.

"Yes," Massaquoit replied.

They sat in silence for a while.

"I must return. My mother sits with Jane. They do not understand each other."

"Your mother," Massaquoit repeated.

"What?" Ninigret asked, and Massaquoit realized that he was thinking about Willeweenaw in a way that had nothing to do with her son sitting in front of him.

"I was just remembering," Massaquoit said, "a long time ago."

"Yes, when I was a boy."

Massaquoit was thankful that Ninigret's self-absorption prevented him from reading Massaquoit's mind.

"I will follow after you later tonight. Maybe I can talk to Rawandag."

"Yes," Ninigret replied. "That would be good. I see you standing in the middle between my brother, who has given himself to the English and their god, and Rawandag, who wants only to return to a time that is gone."

Ninigret reached across and seized Massaquoit's arms in a firm grasp. "I have no father," he said, then dropped his hand and made his way to the entrance.

After Ninigret left, Massaquoit was struck by the force of a thought that he now realized he had been attempting to repress. There was another reason to be anxious about what he might find in Niantic. Ninigret's passing reference to his mother now brought back the memory of Willeweenaw, not as he had last seen her, but as she had been when they were both young in the house of Uncas, the Mohegan sachem, and then again in the forest not far from Niantic when she told him about her husband, who had come back only in body, not in mind, from the slaughter at Mystic. He remembered her determination to retain her hold on Ninigret, her angry son, and how he had seen in her eyes the realization that her efforts would be futile.

And in those eyes, passionate and deep, he had also felt the pang of memory of his own wife, killed at Mystic along with their son. Willeweenaw and he, he understood, shared the pain and disappointments of their people, both of them having lost spouses and children, either in fact or in effect. Perhaps that is why he felt such a strong emotion as he contemplated seeing her again.

Or perhaps he was remembering how he felt when he was young and his blood stirred in the presence of a beautiful woman, as Ninigret so clearly evidenced now.

TEN

❧❧❧

MASSAQUOIT HEARD THE drums and the singing from a half a mile away, and he shook his head at Ninigret's brazen nerve. If the English were coming to take Jane, the music of the feast would draw their clumsy steps right to the village. He followed the path around the rise before the village, and paused at the beginning of the field. A scrawny dog came out of the shadows, baring its teeth and growling. Massaquoit took one quick step toward it and waved his arms, and the dog disappeared back into the shadows. He saw the square shape of the meetinghouse rising above the cones of the wigwams. He passed the nearest wigwam and where smoke rose from two fires in a cleared space before the meetinghouse. The drummers were squatting by the fires, and dancers whirled in a circle about them. On a spit over each fire was the headless and legless carcass of a roasting deer. A woman stood in the shadows behind the dancers and near a wigwam, her arms clasped in front of her chest. He knew it must be Willeweenaw.

Massaquoit walked to the edge of the first circle of dancers, all men, and watched as they passed before him, sometimes whirling, sometimes hopping first on one foot and then the other. Now that he was close enough to see them in the light, he could make out the paint on their bodies, bright shades of red and blue and green in fanciful shapes on bare chests and faces. He looked past them to the next circle of dancers, all women; they, too, wore paint on their faces, and their tunics were elaborately decorated with brightly colored beads. Each of the two circles danced as though the other were not there. Massaquoit studied all the faces in both circles as they presented themselves to him; he saw neither Ninigret nor Jane.

As Massaquoit approached Willeweenaw, he took note of the wigwam next to which she stood as still as a tree on a calm night. It looked newly constructed of freshly cut saplings. It was covered by reeds still green and only loosely woven together. He saw that Willeweenaw's face was not painted, nor was her tunic decorated with ceremonial beads. She looked at him as he approached and then, with the slightest motion of her head, turned his attention to the wigwam.

"They are inside. They wait for you," she said.

"You do not approve," Massaquoit said.

She shrugged. "Ninigret, as you know, has not heeded my advice since that day when his father came back from the war with eyes that no longer focused, and a heart turned to stone. Why should he listen to me now?"

"He said to me that he has no father."

"Yes, but he could also have said he has no mother."

"And his brother, who now speaks the words of the English god?"

Willeweenaw's face softened in sorrow. "Peter tries only to convert him. And me. When he saw that Ninigret was set on living with this English woman, all he could suggest is that he baptize both of them, and then marry them the English way. Ninigret listened with a blank face and then he sent Peter away. He said he would marry this woman in our traditional way."

The drumming had stopped, and Massaquoit turned back toward the dancers. They stood still, their chests heaving. A moment later, two men detached themselves from the circle and walked toward Massaquoit and Willeweenaw. As they came abreast, they stared hard at Massaquoit, then continued past the wigwam and into the shadows behind it. Massaquoit watched their backs until he could no longer see them.

"Wait, and you will understand," Willeweenaw said.

Two different men emerged from the shadows and walked toward the circles of dancers. They were not sweating or breathing hard. They took their places among the other men, and the drumming resumed.

"The English priest?" Massaquoit asked.

"There must come a time when we push back."

"Now you sound like Ninigret."

Her eyes flashed. "Is that so strange?"

"Not at all," he replied, and took a step toward the wigwam.

"Rawandag is inside. He plays the role of father to my son. What will you say to him?"

"That the English priest must not be killed."

"And to my son?"

"What he surely knows: that the English will be coming after them, perhaps as early as tomorrow."

"We heard about the dead English, this woman's brother."

"Ninigret and she are suspected."

"Of course," she said, and then her face darkened. "It may be that my son has killed an English. If he did, I will not blame him." She took a step toward Massaquoit, and he could feel her breath on his cheek. "Help him if you can. I do not want to lose him."

He put his arm around her, expecting her to pull back, but she did not. Instead, for a few moments she pressed her head against his chest, and then looked up.

"Please," she said. She put her hands on his chest and pushed him away. "There is not much time, and maybe he will trust you."

Massaquoit walked the few steps to the new wigwam. It had an uncovered opening for an entrance, and its reed sheathing was so loose that it admitted the light of the moon with little interruption. He stooped and entered. The moonlight took the edge from the darkness inside, and in its pale glow he could see two figures sitting together on one side, and a third a few feet away on the other. He waited for his eyes to adjust to the semidarkness. When they did, he could make out the white line of Ninigret's smile. Jane's face, however, remained obscured by the darkness. The white hair of the other figure also was visible, and Massaquoit concluded that the man below the hair must be Rawandag, an elder of the family that included Ninigret and the girl Jonathan Peters had attempted to rape. The old man held a pipe in his left hand. His right arm hung limp at his side. He sucked in the smoke, held it in his mouth for a few seconds, and then expelled it. He held out the pipe to Massaquoit. Massaquoit took it from him and inhaled. It had been a long time since last he had been offered a ceremonial smoke, and he savored the pungent taste. He let the smoke out of his mouth slowly and waited for its acrid scent to reach his nostrils. He handed the pipe back to Rawandag, who gave it to Ninigret. Ninigret took a puff and passed the pipe toward the old man. Jane intercepted it and held it in front of her mouth. Ninigret started to reach for the pipe, but Jane stopped him with a quick shake of her head and a look that seemed to convey some secret understanding between them.

"I have wanted to try this tobacco," she said, "to see if I can taste your god, as I think mine has abandoned me."

"I do not think you will find him in the smoke," Massaquoit said.

"But still I will try." She took a deep puff, and coughed until the tears came to her eyes. She tried again, and this time held the smoke in her mouth. She then let it out between lips that were only slightly open. She gave the pipe to the old man.

"I am Rawandag," he said. He put the pipe down, then used his good left hand to lift his useless right arm. "And this is a present I received from the English in the war that you, Massaquoit, know well." He picked up the pipe and puffed on it again before handing it back to Massaquoit. "Smoke, and remember what happened to you and your family."

As if on cue, a man's scream drifted into the wigwam from somewhere behind it. Massaquoit began to get up, but Rawandag reached across to grab hold of his arm.

"You do not intend to interfere, do you?" Rawandag asked.

Massaquoit did not answer immediately. Instead, he focused on the hard anger in the old man's eyes, and it stirred a sympathetic emotion in his own heart. He saw again, with startling clarity, the white skin of Jonathan's buttocks above the dark and flailing legs of the young girl, the terror, mixed with contempt, in her expression as she struggled to free herself. The incident epitomized the fifty-year history of his people's dealings with the English. And yet, across from him sat Ninigret, a young man at least as angry as the old man, about to join his own dark skin to the fair-complexioned woman at his side. From some perspectives, perhaps, their union might appear to be a reconciliation between the two cultures. Massaquoit, however, did not think so, for there was something unremittingly selfish in this woman's demeanor, and he could only conclude that she was using Ninigret, perhaps to escape the wrath of the English. All of this flashed through his mind before he responded, but he chose to answer with an understatement bordering on duplicity. Later, he would chasten himself, when recalling his answer, that he unwittingly permitted himself to sound more like Wequashcook than the proud and forthright sachem he, himself, used to be. It was small solace, at that time of bitter reflection, that he could charge the English with creating a situation in which his character yielded to the pressure of steering between two peoples who seemed intent on crashing violently into one another.

"I am a guest here," he replied. He looked across at Ninigret. "I have come to wish this young man a long and happy life with the woman he has chosen."

"That is good," Ninigret said. "Soon we will join the dancers, and then we will eat."

"We did not plan to have the wedding feast this evening," Rawandag said. "When Ninigret arrived here with his woman, we had already begun to prepare the English priest for his ordeal." He took another puff of the pipe and then handed it to Massaquoit. "The English priest thought he could hunt without fear, as though we were no longer men. When we captured him, he tried to preach to us out of his book that has the words of his god written in it. He did not believe we would hold him accountable for his actions. But our honor demands that we exact vengeance on him for his attack on Minnehaha. You saw that with your own eyes, and we are grateful for what you did in stopping him. But the English priest is here, and these young people are like cheese to the English rats who will seek them, and when they arrive in Niantic, they will also find their priest. It is a complicated situation."

Massaquoit envisioned his people's bodies strewn about, women and children along with the men trying to prove they were still men. As he inhaled on the pipe, he found a way to avert the slaughter he feared.

"You will need something to trade with, when the English come," he said.

"We have muskets, now," Ninigret said, "as well as our bows."

"They have more, and they are more," Massaquoit replied.

"We will give them their priest, then," Rawandag said, "in pieces."

"Yes," Massaquoit replied with a harsh smile, "pieces of the English priest's flesh that can be fed to the dogs. And then?"

"We will be gone," Jane said. "Leaving only the dogs and the priest's bones."

Massaquoit stared hard at this woman, then turned to Rawandag. "Do you imagine that the English will go home after arriving here to find the remains of one of their own—not just anyone, but their holy man?"

"Then we can stay to greet them," Ninigret offered. This time in voice and expression he seemed more like the surly boy Massaquoit had met years before.

Rawandag lifted his limp arm. "I have lost one arm to the English. I think that is enough. But perhaps the English priest, too, should lose part of himself."

Massaquoit felt a moment of relief. Perhaps the old man would abandon his anger long enough to accept a reasonable compromise. He set the pipe down between them, as a gesture of understanding. "Not too big a piece," he said.

"But a remembrance," Rawandag said.

"Maybe that part of him that he wanted to use on my cousin," Ninigret said. "That would be right."

"But not wise," Massaquoit said.

Rawandag picked up the pipe. He took a deep puff. "No," he said. "Not wise at all."

In the background all this time had been the drums, the singing, and the shuffling of feet in the dirt. Now there was silence.

Rawandag stood up. "We had better see to the priest," he said, "while there is still some of him left."

From outside the wigwam came a yipping sound like the howl of dogs. Rising above it, in clear English accents, was a voice that alternated between threats and pleas, and then finally settled on whimpers. Massaquoit led the way out of the wigwam. Willeweenaw stood where Massaquoit had last seen her, with her arms clasped. Emerging from the darkness behind the wigwam were several men carrying torches. Between them, naked and with his hands tied in front of him, staggered Jonathan. One man marched in front, holding Jonathan's huge Bible up over his head. Jonathan stopped every step or two until one or the other of the men encouraged him forward with a touch of a torch to the back of his legs, buttocks, or back. He then lurched forward, his eyes wide and staring and saliva dripping from his mouth, which was hidden behind lips puffed to twice their normal size. His eyes were almost closed, and his nose was crusted with dried blood. He walked gingerly on his toes, and Massaquoit knew, even without seeing them, that the soles of his feet must have been beaten until they swelled into massive bruises. The little procession paused in front of Massaquoit and Rawandag. Massaquoit could see the line of dried urine running down Jonathan's right leg from inside of his thigh to the top of his foot. Jonathan looked at

Massaquoit the way a drowning man might stare at somebody holding a rope just out of his reach. His eyes beseeched, and Massaquoit made an almost invisible nod. One of the warriors brought his torch down onto Jonathan's back and held it there until the minister shuffled forward. He left behind the pungent smell of singed flesh.

Massaquoit and Rawandag followed while Jonathan was led to a place between the two dancing circles. Nobody was dancing now. The drummers sat next to their instruments, and the men and women gathered in two lines. Between them was a thick tree stump. Jonathan was led there, and made to stand on the stump. The man carrying the Bible placed it, open, on the ground in front of the stump. Jonathan stared at the men, who began yipping at him as though they were wolves about to attack a crippled deer. Jonathan turned to the women, expecting mercy from them, but they put their hands to their mouths as though to muffle their laughter. They were staring at his exposed genitals and pointing to the line of dried urine on his flesh. He tried to cover himself, but two men sliced through the rope that bound his hands, and retied them behind his back. The women now approached, one by one, and each slapped or punched him between his legs. He staggered with each blow, but he was not permitted to fall; the men held him up by his elbows. When he tried to draw his legs together, two other men pulled them apart to give the women more ready access. Tears filled his eyes, but he no longer moaned. The last woman took a torch from one of those who had led Jonathan in. He now had closed his eyes against the pain and the humiliation. She waved the torch in front of his face, and its smoke settled over his head until he coughed. She moved the torch back to reveal his face, eyes now wide open, staring at the flame. His eyes followed the fire as the woman lowered it in front of him, from his face to his groin, where she held it as he struggled against those who were holding him. Finally, she pulled back the torch and spat in his face.

Jonathan was pulled down from the stump and a man holding a knife approached him. He began to whimper, but then stopped in relief as the man walked behind him and cut his hands free. His relief, though, was short-lived. The man with the knife signaled, and two others forced Jonathan to sit on the ground with his legs around the stump. His feet were tied together, and one arm was held down on the surface of the stump. The man with the knife leaned hard on his wrist, causing his fingers to splay out. He drew the knife across Jonathan's thumb, just hard enough to draw blood. Jonathan stared at his hand, his eyes full of terror.

Massaquoit stood not ten feet away. Every once in a while, Jonathan looked at him with an expression that shifted between despair and anger. But Massaquoit did not respond with word or gesture. Part of him celebrated the humiliation being heaped upon this English priest who had attacked Minnehaha without a thought, as though the girl's body was nothing more than servant to his lust. It was not so much the act itself as the indifference that had appeared in Jonathan's eyes, even after Massaquoit had pulled him off the girl. But on another level, Massaquoit was deeply troubled by what he was observing. He knew that he could not let it proceed too far. The more blood Jonathan was made to spill, the more his tormentors' appetites for even more blood would be whetted, and it would not be long before the humiliated English priest would be a very dead and mutilated one. And as pleasing as that image was, even to Massaquoit, the consequences of that act, inciting the English hunger for vengeance, would be too terrible to countenance. Massaquoit knew the English sense of justice would weigh twenty Indians as the equivalent of one English priest, corrupt as he might be.

For these reasons, he was about to step forward to see if he could say something to preserve this hulking, cowering priest, when from the fringe of onlookers near Willeweenaw came a man's voice yelling something that was swallowed by a chorus of dissenting exclamations. Massaquoit looked in that direction and saw Ninigret's brother, Peter, being restrained by Willeweenaw and another woman. With one strong shove, he managed to free himself from their grasp and hurtled himself forward until he stood in front of Jonathan. The man wielding the knife watched as Peter placed his own hand on top of Jonathan's. Jonathan looked up at Peter, his eyes filled with gratitude.

"Cut mine," Peter said.

"Is this what your English god teaches you?" Rawandag said with a sneer as he stepped forward.

Peter picked up the Bible. "It is."

Rawandag straightened himself to his full height, as though through that gesture he could erase the years that distanced him from the proud warrior he had once been. He swept the assemblage with his gaze, slowly, as though insuring that each would hear his words.

"Listen to the words of your brother who would lead you to worship the English god, and turn you into women who do not fight," he said in a loud and clear voice.

He was greeted with murmurs of approval.

"Then let us send him back to the English, where he belongs," Rawandag said. Several men moved forward and seized Peter. He struggled, but he was no match for their combined strength. They pulled him from Jonathan and sent him sprawling on the ground, where he was greeted with hoots from the men and scornful titters from the women. He reached for the Bible, which was in the dirt a few feet from him. A woman came forward, picked it up, and gestured as though she would hand it to him. When he tried to reach for it, she tossed it away from him. He stood up and looked once more at the Bible, and then at Jonathan. He walked through the crowd, and nobody tried to stop him. Massaquoit now took his place next to Jonathan. He put his foot on the Bible.

"Those who know my reputation know that I do not share Peter's enthusiasm for the English god."

"Yes, but you serve an English woman," a voice cried out.

Massaquoit stared in the direction of the voice, which had been supported by several others, and after a moment or two all were quiet again.

"You do not know him, if you say that," Ninigret declared. "He is a man, one of us. Listen to him."

"I say this," Massaquoit began, with a nod toward Ninigret. "I do not put my hand beneath the blade for this English priest. He must suffer for what he did. But we must also check our anger so it does not come back and lash us out of the barrels of the English muskets." He paused, his eyes on the ground. "We are no longer strong enough to fight the English on their own ground. We are alone, surrounded by them. Perhaps our young warriors will learn from the mistakes of their elders, and not fight until they have a chance of success. Until then, we must endure." He turned to the man holding the knife. "Continue. Take off his finger."

Jonathan tried furiously to free himself from his forced embrace of the stump. The man with the knife approached and again drew it across Jonathan's thumb, deeper this time, and the blood spurted. Jonathan cried out.

Massaquoit leaned over him and whispered into his ear. "I am trying to save your life, you fool. Not because I value it, but because I value the lives of those of my people that will be lost if they are foolish enough to kill you. Be still. You are going to lose one finger, maybe two. The more you show your cowardice, the slower he will cut you. Do you understand?"

Jonathan nodded, and Massaquoit stood up. "He is ready now," he said.

The man again approached. He held the knife over Jonathan's thumb, taunting him with feigned cutting gestures. When Jonathan managed to remain still and quiet, the man smiled and sliced again. The thumb was now half off, and covered with blood. Again the man held the knife over the thumb, and when Jonathan did not offer any plea or resistance, the blade came down again and sliced the thumb off. Blood spurted, and Jonathan's face turned white. He collapsed against the stump, and the onlookers began to chant as the drummers played.

Rawandag looked toward the women and nodded. An old woman, gray-haired and bent with age, came forward, carrying a rag that exuded a pungent odor. She passed it under Jonathan's nose, and he snapped his head back. She cackled and then pressed the rag over the bleeding stump of his thumb. Then another woman, young enough to be the first one's grand-daughter, joined her and wrapped another cloth around his hand to form a bandage. The two women stood up.

"He will bleed a little more," the old woman said. "But then my medicine will work, and the blood will stop."

"Pity," the younger one said.

Massaquoit recognized her as Minnehaha. She held his gaze. "I never thanked you," she said.

"It is not necessary."

"No," she replied, "especially now that you appear to have saved his life." She pointed at Jonathan.

"Only to protect you from more harm."

She looked as though she were about to protest, but then glanced at the old woman who was waiting for her.

"My mother calls me. I did not want to help her stop this pig's blood, but she said I must."

"She is wise, then," Massaquoit said.

The old woman nodded, and Minnehaha walked off with her. Jonathan stared at his bandaged hand, and then laid his head on his arms. His chest heaved with quiet sobs. Ninigret approached him and pressed his hand on top of Jonathan's head. With his other hand, he beckoned Jane forward.

"Let this English priest drink his own blood and wonder when we might take off his hand, or his head." He waited while the onlookers nodded and murmured their approval. He took Jane's hand and raised it high above their heads. "Let the feast in honor of my wife begin!" he cried. He dropped Jane's hand and took a long knife from a sheath at his waist. He knelt beside one of the roasting deer and sliced off a slab of meat. He cut the meat in two and handed one piece to Rawandag, the other to Massaquoit. He nodded at the drummers, who began playing their instruments. Rawandag and Massaquoit each tasted the meat and bowed their thanks to Ninigret. He cut another piece, which he handed to Jane, and then one more for himself. He jabbed his knife into the carcass of the deer and took his place in the dancing circle. The drummers increased the intensity of the beat. Ninigret began to dance by himself, and then he was joined by the others. One by one, the men approached the deer and sliced meat for themselves. The women led Jane to the center of their circle and she imitated their dance steps, at first with a shy hesitancy, then with exuberance. Her hair, flung about as she danced, matched the red of the fire. The women took their turn cutting meat from the other deer.

After a few minutes, her face glistening with sweat and shreds of deer flesh hanging from between her teeth, Jane exited the circle and walked to Jonathan. The drummers stopped, and all eyes followed her. She picked up his Bible and tore out a page. She held it aloft and spun in a slow circle. Her actions elicited loud hoots. She waved the page furiously around and around over head, and all eyes followed its whirling motion—all except Massaquoit's, who saw her reach into the waistband of her gown and pull out another paper. She brought her hands together and crumpled what she was holding. Then she grabbed Jonathan's hair and lifted his head.

"Open," she commanded. "It is time for you to eat."

Jonathan shook his head.

Jane beckoned to Ninigret. "Help me feed this priest," she said, her eyes bright with excitement. Ninigret clamped his fingers over Jonathan's nose with one hand and pressed hard on his jaw hinge with the other. Jonathan's mouth opened as he gasped for air, and Jane shoved the paper into his mouth. She spun away and took her place in the dancing circle as the drummers resumed, to a chorus of laughter. Ninigret released his hold, and Jonathan's head flopped back down on the stump. He raised it for a moment and tried to spit out the paper, but it was too far in his mouth.

Massaquoit watched and waited. When everyone seemed occupied either with eating or with dancing, or walking off in pairs into the shadows, he approached Jonathan and pulled the paper from his mouth. It was dripping with saliva. He folded it again until it fit into his hand, and then he walked to Willeweenaw and handed it to her.

"I may have need of this later," he said. "It may save your son."

She nodded, and tucked the paper into her mocassin.

Jane again left the circle and approached Jonathan. "So you have eaten, have you?"

Jonathan nodded.

"That is good," Jane laughed. "You must have been hungry."

Rawandag, who had been quietly munching on his slab of deer meat, now came forward. The drummers, as if on his command, ceased, and all eyes turned to the old man, who stood next to Jonathan.

"Take him to the house where he can pray to his god," Rawandag said. "We will meet again to decide what to do with him." Rawandag walked toward the meetinghouse, and Massaquoit followed as Jonathan was led, stumbling and falling. Peter sat huddled before the front door. He moved aside as Jonathan was taken inside. Massaquoit heard the thump of fists and feet against flesh, followed by exhausted moans. Rawandag took Peter by the arm and looked at the door.

"Do you want to join your English brother inside?"

"Yes."

"Are you sure?"

"Yes."

Peter walked into the meetinghouse, and the door was shut behind him. Two heavy logs were dragged to the door and jammed against it. Piles of dried reeds and twigs were placed around the perimeter of the building.

"If we must, when the English come," Rawandag

said, "we will see if their god can protect those two inside."

Willeweenaw strode to Rawandag and engaged the old man's eyes with her own fierce expression. "My son is in that building."

"No," Rawandag said, "that man inhabits the skin of your son, but your son is no more."

She stepped closer, so that he could feel the warmth of her breath, and she spoke in a low voice. "Save those words for others."

Massaquoit, who was a few feet away, stepped between them so that the width of his body drove them apart. He turned to face Willeweenaw, giving Rawandag only his broad back to look at. "It would be better if Peter came out, but if he will not, I will protect him."

Her expression softened for a moment, but then hardened as cold stone. "I no longer trust anyone. Even you, Massaquoit, who could not protect his own wife and child." She walked to the front door and sat down between the logs. "If you want to help me, you can help me open this door."

Massaquoit wanted very much to do just that, not for Peter's sake but because there was a warmth in Willeweenaw's eyes that touched that sliver of his heart that the years had not turned into adamantine. He felt the contemptuous gaze of Rawandag, and he looked out at the crowd of men and women, his people whose patience had been exhausted, and he knew that he must wait. He walked to Willeweenaw, and sat down beside her. "I cannot do that just now, but I will stay with you to show you that my word is good."

Rawandag followed Massaquoit's movements with a face set in hard disapproval. Then, using his good arm, he lifted his limp one in a gesture to his people that pointed them back to the dancing circle. The drummers began, and the people again gathered in their circles, with Ninigret in the center of one and Jane in the middle of the other.

Massaquoit gazed at the young people who would be in each other's arms in an hour or so, and he felt the warmth emanating from Willeweenaw. She, however, sat with her eyes straight ahead, as though she were sitting alone.

ELEVEN

❧❦❧

T HE YOUNG GIRL at Catherine's door looked at her
with an expression that showed she had over-
come her fear to complete an errand of the utmost im-
portance. The girl's face looked familiar, and then she
remembered.

"Susan Martin, what can I do for you? I trust your
family is well?"

The girl stepped back, startled. Catherine held out
her hand toward her. "Child, I did not mean to startle
you. I saw you one day at your meeting when your
mother was preaching."

"I did not see thee that day." The girl seemed to
have recovered her equanimity and now spoke with
quiet assurance

"Surely not, for I was not in the house, but looking
in through a window."

"How strange," the girl replied. "Thou wilt not
find the Lord in that manner."

Catherine was startled at the girl's audacity, but then she realized it was common among these Quakers, even the young, to speak their minds in a way that could be taken either as arrogant or as merely confident. She had reserved judgment as to which term she thought better fit, and she was not going to test her judgment on this little girl standing in front of her. Still, she did not feel comfortable letting the remark pass without comment. "Perhaps I have already found Him."

"Perhaps thou hast," the girl replied, but her tone conveyed her doubt.

"You did not come to my house to discuss my state of grace," Catherine said.

"Surely not. It is to ask thee to mend my father's arm, for he has had a grievous hurt and is in much pain."

"I will do what I can," Catherine said.

"Thou knowest the way to our meetinghouse. Walk a little way past it, up a little hill and down the other side. There thou wilt find our house. I can take thee there."

Just as Catherine and Phyllis were about to set off to follow the girl, the sound of drum rolls, carried by a gentle breeze flowing off the harbor, traveled from the town to Catherine's door. The girl looked toward the village.

"They say that the militia is being gathered to go to Niantic to bring back that apostate."

"Who says?" Catherine asked.

"Folks. And my mother and father."

"Do they mean Jane Whitcomb?"

"Of course."

"We must hurry, then," Catherine said. "For I, too, must away to Niantic."

"My father awaits thee."

"Then let us not tarry."

With Phyllis trudging beside her, and the girl dancing ahead, Catherine approached the Quaker meetinghouse. Standing in front of it was a knot of men. In the center was Nathan Whitehead, who appeared to be holding forth.

"Go on ahead," Catherine said to Susan. "Tell your father I am right behind you." The girl nodded and dashed ahead. "Follow after," Catherine said to Phyllis. "And make him comfortable. See if there is anything about the house for a splint."

Catherine walked toward Nathan, and he stopped talking. He looked in the direction taken by Susan and Phyllis, and then he beckoned Catherine forward.

"Mistress Williams. I see thou hast come to help Brother Martin. But his house is that way." He pointed toward the hill behind the meetinghouse.

"I did not think you would be meeting now." Catherine said.

The men, half a dozen ranging from late teens to sixties, seemed tense. They shifted from one foot to another. One young man had a knife on his belt. An older man was leaning on a thick staff, and Nathan held his clublike stick. He looked at his men.

"We have not come for that purpose."

"I can see that."

Nathan held his hands, palms up, toward the men, and then walked to Catherine. He took her elbow and steered her away a few feet, out of earshot of the others.

"We expect trouble. Thy townspeople will be happy to find a reason to come after us, and now that woman has given them one. We need to be prepared."

"I trust your fears are exaggerated," Catherine said, but she remembered Roger and Jane's backs opened beneath the whip and could not discount Nathan's concerns.

"Thy face tells me thou dost understand," Nathan said. He leaned down to her level. "Go tend to Brother Martin." It appeared he might say more, but he turned and strode back to the men. They huddled about him and seemed to resume their discussion. Catherine waited a moment, but she could not hear anything. It was clear that her presence was only being tolerated, and not for much longer.

She found Israel Martin lying on a straw mattress in the back room of a two-room house. The house, simply furnished with handmade stools and tables, was clean and in order. Susan Martin stood on one side of her father, and on the other, holding her husband's good hand, was Rachel Martin. Israel's face was white and beaded with perspiration, although a late afternoon breeze had cooled the air. His injured arm hung off the bed. His wrist was swollen and discolored, and his hand was turned at an unnatural angle away from his arm. Catherine reached to touch it, and he shuddered.

"He cannot bear to move it," Rachel said. "I told him about that horse, but he would not listen."

"He was kicked, then?" Catherine asked.

"I told him," Rachel repeated. "But he would have that big stump out where he took down that dead tree, so he goes to borrow the use of this animal from our neighbor, whose own leg is just healed after being broken by this same beast."

Israel looked as though he wanted to object to this characterization of his accident. He started to rise up from his mattress, but then the pain from his injured arm grabbed him and he settled back as slowly as he could, staring at his hand as though wondering how his own body could be attacking him so grievously.

Phyllis entered the room, red-faced and out of breath. She held a thin length of wood a foot long. She handed it to Catherine. "I found it out back."

"He was building a chicken coop," Rachel said. "He is always working, he is."

Catherine noted the affection in her tone, which had been lacking when she expressed her unhappiness with her husband's stubbornness that, in her mind, had led to his accident.

"I will need to set it," Catherine said. "But to do that, he will need to be calm." She looked at Phyllis. "In my bag, the dried hops blossoms."

"I can boil some water," Susan said, "if thou art thinking of a tea."

"I am," Catherine replied. She took Israel's good hand and pressed his palm.

"Patience," she said.

"As Job," he replied.

"And Job's wife, let us not forget," Rachel added.

The tea put Israel into a doze within a quarter of an hour. He lay back, his head lolling about. Catherine touched his injured hand and he stirred a bit, but did not shudder as he had before.

"Now," she said to Phyllis, who knelt next to her at the side of the mattress. Phyllis nodded and picked up the piece of wood. Catherine grabbed Israel's forearm with one hand and his wrist with the other. She knew that the effects of the tea would not be strong enough to block the pain for more than a second or two, so she must act quickly. In her mind's eye she saw how the hand should rest in a proper position. She slid her fingers to the top of his hand, and with one quick but gentle motion turned it to conform to the mental image. Israel convulsed in pain and groaned, but did not pull his arm away. Phyllis placed the length of wood along his forearm, and Catherine adjusted it so that it supported the wrist in a straight line. She wrapped the wood from his elbow down to his fingers with a long piece of sturdy cotton cloth.

"Try to see that he does not move it overmuch," she said to Rachel, and stood up.

They sat at the plank table before the fireplace in the front room.

"Dost thou think he will mend?" Rachel asked.

"My father is a sturdy man," Susan said.

Catherine looked at the child and then the mother. "I have every hope," she said. "I will look in on him when I return from Niantic."

Rachel's face darkened.

"What is it?" Catherine asked.

"Nothing."

"Tell, mother," Susan said. "Thou said thou wouldst."

"It is my son, Jethro," Rachel said after a few moments. "He saw something."

"Where is he now?"

"He is like his father. Stubborn. He has that horse harnessed, and he is pulling out that very same stump."

"What can he tell me? Something touching the killing of Roger Whitcomb? Or about his sister Jane?"

"Yes. And both," Rachel replied. "But thou knowest he cannot swear to anything he has seen."

"I have so heard," Catherine said. "But still, before I travel to Niantic, I must know whatever he can tell me."

"Thou wilt find him in the back of the field."

As they walked back toward town, Catherine was lost in thought.

"Do you think the boy told us the truth?" Phyllis asked.

"I am afraid so," Catherine replied.

They neared the town center, where a unit of a dozen or so militia had gathered. Minister Davis stood to one side of the assemblage and motioned for the women to come to him. "We go to seek that harlot and her savage," he said.

"We will go with you," Catherine replied.

Minister Davis looked back over her head in the direction from which she and Phyllis had just come.

"One of the Quakers, Israel Martin, was kicked by a horse. I set his wrist," Catherine said before he could ask.

"Touched by God for his blasphemy, no doubt. But come if you must, for you are the harlot's guardian."

"And so I will," Catherine answered, choosing not to respond to the minister's explanation of God's providence guiding the horse's hoof. From her point of view, Israel Martin was a thickheaded man who got kicked by an ill-tempered animal. She did not think that her God would so chasten a man who, whether rightly or wrongly, had devoted himself to a particular form of serving Him. As for Jane and Ninigret, her thoughts remained a tumble as she tried to factor in the story she had just heard from Jethro Martin.

The company of militia formed behind the drummer, a boy no more than fifteen or sixteen. Lieutenant Arthur Waters stood to the side of the column. Catherine recalled how the lieutenant had presided over the execution of the sachems years before, when she was permitted to save one of them and chose Massaquoit. Waters had done his duty, but it had been evident to her that he had taken no pleasure in it. In fact, he had returned to England shortly after that incident and had only recently arrived in Newbury, grayer and thicker of body. She wondered if he approached this new assignment with more enthusiasm. He lifted his arm and brought it down hard in the direction of the boy, who rolled his sticks over the drum. Just then, Catherine heard a shuffling of feet coming up behind her, accompanied by heavy breathing.

"Catherine," Joseph Woolsey panted, "I thought I might find you here, as you are ever where you should not be."

"Why, what do you mean?" Catherine said, although she was perfectly aware of his objection.

The magistrate swept his arm toward the soldiers, some with muskets, others with pikes on their shoulders.

"I know well I am not a soldier," Catherine said.

"Then you should bide with me until they return."

"I have not the patience."

"Then stay a moment while I tell you what has happened. That boy is to be indicted."

"The sailor?"

"Henry Jenkins."

"For killing Roger?"

Magistrate Woolsey was about to nod, but then he caught himself and shook his head.

"Not at all. For killing Billy Lockhart. He has confessed it all. Minister Davis came to ease his spirit, and he was so marvelously moved to accept our Lord in his extremity that he bade Will Best be summoned with his pen and paper so he could clear his conscience."

"Minister Davis is a marvelously persuasive man," Catherine said, but withheld the further thought that at times, while he served his God, he was also not unlike a vulture gnawing on the carrion flesh of a sinner.

"That he is," Magistrate Woolsey replied with an emphatic nod, and Catherine noted that, as usual, her friend failed to hear the irony in her voice. She did not know whether to attribute this habitual obtuseness to Woolsey's gradual loss of hearing or to his insistent belief, despite a lifetime of contrary experiences, that a person's morality accorded with that individual's title. Thus, by definition a minister would serve God, and a magistrate such as himself, or the governor, would promote the health of the community. She placed that question in the back of her mind as she looked past Woolsey to the militia company that was now beginning to move slowly out of the village common and toward the path that followed the river to Niantic. As it left the grassy common, a figure wearing a beaver hat slid from a small stand of pines and took its place at the head of the company. Phyllis, who had stepped a respectful distance away as her mistress spoke first with the minister, and then the magistrate, now approached.

"We must hurry," she said.

"Magistrate Woolsey thinks we should tarry here. What do you think?"

"It is a far walk on a hot day."

"He believes that women such as ourselves should let the men wearing armor go about their business."

"If you are ready for a walk," Phyllis replied, "I am as well."

"I cannot dissuade you, then?" Woolsey asked.

"No, I am afraid not," Catherine replied, and she and Phyllis started off at a steady pace toward the river road. After a short while, Phyllis's faster pace took her yards ahead of Catherine. She looked back at her mistress. Catherine waved her on and resumed her rolling gait that carried her with an easy motion belying her sixty years.

Massaquoit parted the covering to the entrance of the wigwam and made his way inside. Jane was asleep against the side of the wigwam, snoring lightly. Ninigret squatted, wide awake, a few feet from her.

"Let us take a walk," Massaquoit said.

Ninigret glanced at Jane, then nodded. It was late morning, but Niantic was quiet. Some people slept where they had collapsed the night before, after the dancing and feasting. They walked toward the meetinghouse where Willeweenaw still sat, her head cradled in her arms. Two young men stood on either side of the door. Willeweenaw lifted her head as they approached. She stood up, walked to Massaquoit, and handed him the paper he had taken out of Jonathan's mouth. Then she took Ninigret's arm and guided him a few feet away. She spoke to him, and then embraced him. Ninigret returned to Massaquoit while Willeweenaw resumed her place in front of the meetinghouse.

"She wants me to flee before the English come," Ninigret said.

"It is good advice."

Ninigret looked toward the meetinghouse. "I cannot. My brother is inside with the English priest. I must see what I can do. I do not think you would run if you were me."

"I do not know," Massaquoit said. "It has been a long time since I was as young as you, with such heat in my blood." He looked at the folded paper. "We must talk about this. And I am thirsty."

They retraced their steps to head toward the edge of the village, where a small stream provided water for bathing and drinking. As they passed Ninigret and Jane's wigwam, Massaquoit glanced through the thin reed cover. He could not see Jane, and so he was not surprised that she was at the stream's bank when they arrived there. She stood with hands on her hips as they approached.

"Ninigret," she said, "last night we slept together, and now in the morning I find you with a man I do not trust, and you should not either. He has lived too long with the English woman. I know, for I saw him with her."

Ninigret took her arm and held it against his own. "I did not wake up with white skin," he said.

She stepped back, a hard, scornful smile on her lips. She was wearing only a shift, and she pulled it over her head.

"Look at this white skin, then," she said. "If you want to get close to it again, you will heed what I say." She waited for him to respond, and when he didn't, she shrugged, turned, and slipped into the shallow water of the stream. She swam underwater to midstream, about fifteen yards from shore, and then she rose in a spray of water. The sun hitting the water gave her red hair a halo, and she opened her mouth in a laugh of pure joy. Then she swam toward the opposite shore. Ninigret squatted on his haunches, his eyes following her.

Massaquoit took his place beside him. "You must tell me what happened."

"What is in the paper?" Ninigret asked.

"That is not important."

"Not important? It is that paper that is the cause of everything."

"I know."

Ninigret picked up a stick and drew a figure in the soft dirt of the stream bank. The figure had a large brimmed hat, such as Roger wore. He drew a smaller figure next to it.

"I wanted only the paper," he said.

"Why?"

"I found it in a pouch on the beach. Then that priest stole it." He looked across the stream, where Jane now lay on her back in the shallow water. "She bade me get it back from her brother. I do not know how he got it."

"It was taken from the priest," Massaquoit said. "And sold to the brother."

Ninigret rubbed his eyes as though to clear away confusion. "She said it would make us rich."

"You believed her?"

Ninigret hunched his shoulders. "I did not believe or not believe. But when I saw how fiercely the English fought to keep it, I thought maybe it would." He rubbed out the first figure he had drawn and then redrew it, lying on the ground.

"You did not mean to kill him," Massaquoit said.

"No. I threatened him with my knife, and he seized my wrist. He was very strong. But I was quicker."

"I see."

"Do you think the English will believe me?"

Massaquoit hesitated. "No. But that is why we have the English priest still alive, missing only one finger. If you had killed him, my only counsel would be to flee. And I still think that a wise choice. But I know you will not. So we must trade."

"Will they?"

"Perhaps. Especially if Wequashcook leads them here, as I think he will."

"He is an excellent trader, I hear," Ninigret said.

"He is the very best." Massaquoit looked across the stream at Jane, who now stood up with water streaming off her naked body. The sunlight lit the drops of waters into many-colored jewels. "And her?" he asked.

"She is my woman."

"Her white skin, is that it?"

"She is my woman," Ninigret repeated.

"Then go to her."

Ninigret stood up. "That piece of paper is a danger to us," he said.

"It is."

"But you cannot give it to me?"

"No."

"I did not think so." Ninigret splashed into the shallow water for a few feet and then dived in. He swam with strong strokes until he reached Jane.

Willeweenaw was waiting for Massaquoit on the path that entered the village. She looked from the meetinghouse and then past Massaquoit in the direction of the stream.

"One son keeping company with an English priest, and the other with an English woman. What do you think?"

"I think it is the times."

"Not much of an answer."

"No."

"He will not flee?"

Massaquoit shook his head.

"And the other cannot."

"I promise . . . ," he began.

She put her hands to his lips, and he felt the strength in her fingers. "Don't," she said. "It is the times."

They stood in silence for a few moments. Massaquoit sought the words of assurance she would not let him say, and yet she seemed reluctant for him to leave her side. Then they heard the sound of drums approaching from the other side of the village.

"They are here," Massaquoit said.

"It is too late, then," Willeweenaw said.

Massaquoit held out the letter. "This might save Ninigret. Or condemn him."

"Use it as you think best," she said, and trotted toward the meetinghouse.

He looked across the stream, where a moment before Ninigret and Jane had been splashing each other with water like children, but they were gone. "As I think best," Massaquoit muttered to himself, and he followed Willeweenaw. He caught up to her as she positioned herself in front of the meetinghouse door. She stood with her arms across her chest, her legs spread in a stance suggesting that anyone wanting to gain entrance to the building would do so only by removing her body. Massaquoit held her gaze for a moment, then headed toward the entrance to the village, where the sound of drums was growing ever louder. He reached the field separating the path through the woods and the village, and saw the advancing column. He looked for the beaver hat and did not see it. He knew that Wequashcook must have led the English, and it took only a moment's reflection to understand why he was not now in front of the English soldiers, leading them into this village as he had done years before at Mystic. However, there was nothing Massaquoit could do to intercept Wequashcook, who must be in the woods, circling the village and heading toward the stream. More important, right now, was to make sure that Willeweenaw did not have to offer her body in defense of her other son, and incidentally sacrifice herself to protect Jonathan.

Several hundred yards behind the rear of the column, at a place on the path that was still working its way through the forest before it reached the clearing, Phyllis sat on the stump of a dead tree. Her face was red and covered with perspiration that dripped down her neck and pooled at the base of her spine. She breathed hard and shook her head from side to side. She watched as Catherine approached.

"Come along," Catherine said as she reached Phyllis. "Do you not hear how the drums are loud and have stopped advancing in front of us?"

"Yes," Phyllis said. "Surely I do, for that is why I am sitting here gathering my breath."

"Take your time, then," Catherine said over her shoulder. She continued at the same pace that had carried her the five miles from Newbury to Niantic. Phyllis, as though to demonstrate the superiority of her youthful energy, had walked faster until she was well ahead of her mistress, but then she had to recover her wind, as she was now again doing. She rose unhappily to her feet.

"I would not want you to go unattended," she said, and walked fast enough to catch up to Catherine. She was about to move ahead when Catherine seized her elbow.

"Let us walk in together," Catherine said.

They arrived at the village in time to see the soldiers milling about in front of the meetinghouse. Indians, old and young, men and women, strolled about, eyeing the soldiers. Some of the young Indian men held weapons—muskets and bows and arrows—tightly in their hands. Dogs sniffed at the feet of the soldiers, who tried to ignore them but continually shifted their glance from the dogs to the Indian warriors and their weapons, and then to Lieutenant Waters, who seemed to be in conversation with an old Indian man and an Indian woman of about thirty or forty who were positioned in front of the door. Massaquoit stood in front of the door and behind the Indian man and woman. He was not speaking.

Massaquoit was, in fact, listening to the negotiations between Rawandag and the lieutenant. He remembered Waters very well indeed, but he bore him no personal ill will. The English officer was a soldier doing what he had to do. Massaquoit recognized that, and he was glad that he was leading these troops rather than some younger, inexperienced, and likely hotheaded English. When Waters had arrived at the head of the column, he had exchanged a silent greeting with Massaquoit, two old soldiers who had seen too much blood spilled for too little reason. On each side of the meetinghouse stood a young brave with a lit torch.

"I must have Master Peters," the lieutenant said. "And the woman called Jane, who now lives with a brave named Ninigret."

Rawandag handed Waters a folded piece of cloth, stained red with blood.

"What is this?" the lieutenant asked.

"You want your priest?" Rawandag asked.

Waters opened the cloth and lifted the severed thumb from it.

Rawandag turned back to the door of the meetinghouse. "The rest of your priest is inside the building." He swept his arm to indicate the bundles of dried reeds pushed against the wooden planking of the building, and the torches held above them at each corner. "He will burn very well. The smoke will carry him to the nose of your god that you think lives in the sky."

Willeweenaw, her face set in a desperate anger, started to take a step forward, but Massaquoit took her arm and held her back. Her motion, however, was noticed by the lieutenant. He looked hard at her. "I take it Master Peters is not alone in that building."

Rawandag shrugged. "That is not important. The other is of no interest to us."

"The woman?" Waters asked.

"I know nothing of her. Or Ninigret. You can search the village. You will not find them."

"I did not think they would be waiting for us here, in truth," Waters said. He turned back to face his soldiers.

"Here, you two," he said to soldiers right in front of him, "search the village from that side." He pointed to the eastern edge. "You two," he continued, indicating another pair, resting on their pikes a few feet from the first pair, "you look from the other side. You seek the Englishwoman Jane, and the Indian Ninigret."

"How will we . . . ," one of the first soldiers began. He was a boy of no more than seventeen, and he scratched the beginning of a scruffy beard on his chin.

"I do not think there are too many Englishwomen hereabouts to confuse you," the lieutenant said, "and I am certain they will be together."

The two pairs of soldiers looked at each other for a moment and then separated in the directions indicated by Waters. They walked slowly and fearfully toward the wigwams. Mangy dogs sniffed at their heels, and the women sneered at them as they passed. They held their pikes and muskets more tightly. While others' eyes followed the soldiers, Massaquoit looked at those remaining. He noted a red-faced man of about forty, sweating beneath his helmet and cradling his heavy musket in his arms. It was an ancient matchlock, and the tip of its cord was glowing, ready to ignite the powder in the pan as soon as the man squeezed the leverlike trigger.

"You will not find them," Rawandag said.

"I do not expect to. But still I must be certain," Waters replied. "Tell those two to move away from the building."

Rawandag shook his head. The man with the musket shifted his position so that he was more at an angle that would permit him to lift his weapon and fire it.

"That would be foolish," Rawandag said.

"We are too many for you," Waters observed. He noted the direction of Massaquoit's gaze, and he turned. "Steady, Jones," he said. "There is no need for that." The soldier relaxed, but continued to perspire and to breathe heavily.

"Perhaps too many for us," Rawandag said, his glance also now directed at Jones. Then he looked back at the building. "But not for the fire."

By this time, Catherine and Phyllis had reached the group. Lieutenant Waters acknowledged their presence with an expression that hovered between disgust at their possible interference in a mission that was becoming increasingly difficult, and hope that

Catherine, whose gift for taking control of a situation he had witnessed, might provide help in finding a resolution. Phyllis stepped back to stand near the protection afforded by the soldiers while Catherine walked up to Waters.

"Lieutenant," Catherine said, "I do not think the governor would be pleased to receive his nephew back as a pile of ashes. Nor would he be happy to hear of the outbreak of hostilities."

"I know that, Mistress Williams," Waters replied. "But. . . ."

"But," Catherine continued for him, "you see no alternative to force."

"That is the case. I have my orders, and I must obey them."

"At any cost?"

"At the cost my judgment sees fit."

Massaquoit stepped forward. "I am pleased to hear that, for I respect your judgment, and know you to be a man of sense."

"Aye, and I know you, too," the lieutenant said.

"Walk aside for a moment." Massaquoit gestured toward the shade of a tall maple twenty feet to the side of the meetinghouse. "It will be cooler there."

Massaquoit squatted next to the trunk of the tree. Waters remained standing. He was wearing a corselet and a morion helmet, and a long sword hung from his waist. The sun glinted off the crest of the helmet as the lieutenant remained for a moment beyond the shade of the tree. He stepped beneath the branches and bent his knees as though contemplating lowering himself, but the sword and the steel of his armor made such a movement awkward. He contented himself with standing with his legs comfortably apart and his arms behind his back.

"If we fight," Massaquoit said, "nobody wins. Rawandag is an angry man. He has not forgotten how he lost the use of his arm to the English. And some of the young men seek vengeance on your English priest for attacking the girl. They will listen to him and are prepared to die. That meetinghouse will burn, and you will have nothing but burned bodies inside and bleeding and dying bodies outside."

"Not a pretty picture," Waters replied, "but I have seen worse."

Massaquoit stood up. He was a little taller than the lieutenant, who was broader of shoulder and thicker in the trunk. "I think you and I are evenly matched," he said. Waters nodded his assent. "And we have both heard the moans of dying men."

Waters shrugged. "I must have the priest. He is of the governor's blood."

"You can have him."

"And the woman."

Massaquoit paused. He did not care about Jane, but he had to respect Ninigret's relationship to her. "Perhaps."

"And her lover."

"No," Massaquoit said. "You cannot have him."

Lieutenant Waters scratched his chin. "The priest and the woman. For now."

Before Massaquoit could answer, they heard the barking of the dogs and then curses in English coming from the western flank of the village. A young Indian man, no more than seventeen or eighteen, came running toward the meetinghouse, accompanied by some of his companions and followed by the soldiers who had been sent to search the village for Ninigret and Jane. The soldiers were breathing hard and running awkwardly, weighed down by their armor and their weapons. The pack of dogs nipped at their feet and legs. The moiling group came to an abrupt stop near the lieutenant and Rawandag. One of the trailing soldiers, who had now caught up, urged the Indian teenager forward with the point of his pike. The Indian swiped at the blade of the weapon and then stumbled forward onto his knees as it pressed against his spine. His friends formed a tight semicircle around him and the soldiers. The opening of the circle was toward the space where Rawandag stood. Massaquoit and Waters arrived and closed the circle.

"Lieutenant," Massaquoit said, "your men have made a mistake. That is not Ninigret."

"I can see that," the lieutenant said, his voice tinged with disgust. "Let him go," he said to the soldiers. One of them was bleeding from the mouth.

"He struck me, lieutenant," this soldier said.

"Let him go, nonetheless."

A musket fired. Everyone turned in the direction of the shot. One of the Indians at the side of the meetinghouse clutched his arm and dropped his torch. A moment later there was the barely audible *pong* of a drawn bow being released, and then the whisper of an arrow in the air. A man groaned. Jones staggered a step or two forward, an arrow in his neck. He dropped onto his stomach and rolled onto his back, blood gushing from the wound. The torch lit the reeds against the meetinghouse, and in seconds that side of the building was ablaze.

A figure in a beaver hat came dashing toward the fire. Wequashcook hurled his hat onto the flame and stomped on it. Willeweenaw seized one of the logs jammed against the front door. She heaved against it, but it would not move. Massaquoit went to help her, but Rawandag stepped into his path. "Let it burn," he said.

"I cannot," Massaquoit replied.

Lieutenant Waters unsheathed his sword and put it to Rawandag's throat. Massaquoit grasped the flat of the blade and pushed it down. Waters let it drop to his waist, but then his arm stiffened.

"That is not necessary," Massaquoit said. "Is it, old man?" he asked Rawandag. When the old Indian did not respond, Massaquoit strode past him. Rawandag lifted his one good arm as though to attempt to stop him, but Waters pressed the blade against his chest and shook his head. Rawandag stepped back, muttering unintelligible words. Massaquoit rushed to Willeweenaw's side and helped her pull the log back. Together, they seized and removed the other log, then pulled the door open. Smoke billowed out, and then two figures followed, coughing and gasping for breath. Lieutenant Waters sheathed his sword and grabbed Jonathan, who was stumbling about, blinded by the smoke. Willeweenaw took Peter's arm and led him away, but they were stopped after a short distance by the soldiers.

Other Indians were attempting to beat out the fire with blankets. Wequashcook had picked up his hat and was now standing aside, catching his breath.

"Let the house to the white man's god burn," Rawandag said. The Indians, a couple of women and several young men, stopped their efforts and stepped back. Rawandag turned to Lieutenant Waters. "Do you have any objections?"

Waters shook his head. "It is your meetinghouse. I do not think the governor will raise money for another."

Peter stepped away from Willeweenaw. "We can build another, after our own fashion," he said.

Rawandag approached Waters and gestured to the armed young braves. They surrounded the lieutenant and Jonathan. "We have unfinished business," he said.

At the musket shot, Catherine had turned to see Jones watching where his ball hit, and then she had seen him collapse as the arrow pierced his neck. She now knelt next to him, her hands pressed against the punctured artery in his neck. The blood continued to spurt against and through her fingers. Then it stopped, and she knew the man was dead.

Smoke curled up from the ashes of the meetinghouse. The soldiers stood or knelt around the body of their dead comrade. Lieutenant Waters moved among them, offering words intended to console or to diffuse anger. An Indian woman bandaged the wounded brave, surrounded by his armed comrades, their expressions set hard in anger. Rawandag hovered stone-faced next to the woman as she worked. Jonathan and Peter stood between the two groups, each closer to his own. Waters walked to Jonathan and handed him the cloth containing his severed finger.

"Something to show your grandchildren, if you like," Waters said.

Jonathan turned pale and shook his head. The lieutenant closed his hand around the cloth and rejoined his soldiers.

Catherine, Massaquoit, and Wequashcook formed their own small circle some distance from everyone else.

"I could have brought them in," Wequashcook said. "But my heart argued against it."

"The governor will be happy to have his nephew back, almost whole," Catherine said. "But two Englishmen have died in his town, and he will want some satisfaction."

"I did not think he bore much love for the sailor or the Quaker," Massaquoit said.

"He did not," Catherine replied. "Nor for justice, in the abstract. But it is the show of it that he loves."

"We must give him something, then," Wequashcook said.

"Not Ninigret," Massaquoit said.

He handed the letter to Catherine. She read it, then nodded. "I thought as much. And I have been told more by a Quaker boy who saw Roger killed."

"Let us give the governor the woman," Wequashcook said. He looked at Massaquoit. "You will have to talk to our young friend. Convince him that there are other women but he has only one neck."

"We can both talk to him," Massaquoit said, "but first the lieutenant must be satisfied."

"I think he might listen to me," Catherine said. She strode over to the lieutenant, and Massaquoit watched their brief, but intense conversation. She came back slowly.

"The lieutenant approves the trade of Jonathan and

Jane for Ninigret. For now. He reserves his right to seek Ninigret again, if he is so ordered by the governor."

"Do you not think the governor will be satisfied?" Massaquoit asked.

Catherine looked at the smoldering building, the soldiers now preparing a litter to take away their dead comrade, and the angry expressions on the faces of Rawandag and his braves. "I will make him see the wisdom of leaving Niantic to recover itself, but still Ninigret may have to come forward with his tale. What the Quaker boy told me will offer him some security."

"Still, I do not know if I can allow that," Massaquoit said.

"He will be hunted down, else," Catherine replied. She looked at the ruined meetinghouse, the shabby wigwams, the angry people, and the pack of thin dogs. "There are those who will help the soldiers find him," she added.

Massaquoit followed her gaze, and in his mind he had to agree. "We will set the terms to protect him, then."

"And my friend Magistrate Woolsey will convince the governor to honor them."

Wequashcook took off his beaver hat, and waved it in front of him so that the odor of its burnt edges spread.

"I will need another hat," he said. He put it back on his head. "I must go where I have left them. They will not wait for me much longer, and the smoke from the building may have sent them further into the woods."

"What did you tell them to make them wait for you?" Catherine asked.

Wequashcook offered a quick smile. "Only that if they fled, the next time they saw me, I would be at the head of a company of English soldiers after their blood. Ninigret swelled up in pride for a moment, but the woman did not look as though she had any appetite for running. There was a weariness in her eyes, and she just sat down to wait."

"Go ahead, then," Massaquoit said. "I will follow soon." He had seen Willeweenaw out of the corner of his eye, and he now walked toward her.

"I have one son back," she said. "Will I have the other?"

"I think so."

"Then I have you to thank." She took both his hands in hers and pressed them hard.

TWELVE

❦

CATHERINE PAUSED IN the doorway of the jail as Jane was led out between two soldiers. Jailer Drake scratched at his stubble and opened his mouth in a crooked grin. "She was not much trouble, no trouble at all," he said.

Jane looked back at Drake and spat. The jailer shrugged, then stepped aside as Henry Jenkins walked out behind Minister Davis. The boy was moving his lips, perhaps in prayer. Another pair of soldiers followed the minister and the prisoner.

"I have seen many a jailhouse conversion," Drake said to Catherine.

"Do you not believe he found God?" Catherine asked.

"He might have," Drake said, "what with the help of the minister. But if he thinks it will keep him from the end of a rope, I believe he is mistaken."

Catherine handed a coin to the jailer. "Make sure she is well attended to when she comes back."

"If she comes back," Drake replied.

"If not, keep the coin as a token of good faith." Catherine looked at her town, which under the agreement negotiated by Massaquoit and Wequashcook on one side, and Waters and Magistrate Woolsey on the other, aided by her own efforts, had been transformed for the day from a quiet seaport village to an armed camp. On one side of the village common was Ninigret, well guarded by a phalanx of a dozen soldiers under the command of Lieutenant Waters. On the other was Jonathan, surrounded by an equal number of Indians, headed by Rawandag. Both groups were heavily armed and tense. Between them and in front of the meetinghouse stood the governor, towering above Magistrate Woolsey. A few feet away, each with arms crossed across his chest, were Massaquoit and Wequashcook. All watched in silence as Jane and Henry were led past them and into the meetinghouse. On the sides of the common, the citizens of Newbury had gathered, but they kept their distance, their eyes warily on the armed soldiers and Indians.

Catherine approached, and the four men stepped closer together and faced her.

"I must say, Mistress Williams," the governor declared, "that I am not at ease with this arrangement."

Catherine glanced at Jonathan. "There is your nephew."

"Yes, Mistress," the governor replied, then pointed toward Ninigret. "And there is a savage murderer."

"That is not yet proved," Catherine replied.

"It was not easy to restrain Rawandag," Wequash-cook said, "and so preserve your nephew's life."

"Or take Ninigret," Massaquoit replied. "Else he and the woman Jane would have fled where only I and Wequashcook could have found them."

"A murderer, still," the governor insisted.

"That is not yet proven," Woolsey said.

Governor Peters frowned, then relaxed his face into an expression of resignation. "Then, as we agreed," he said, "they wait on the verdict." He turned and walked into the meetinghouse, followed by Woolsey.

"We will wait here," Massaquoit said to Catherine, his eyes on the crowd entering the meetinghouse. "I do not think we will be welcome."

"No, I think not."

Massaquoit looked in the direction of Ninigret. "He will be ready," he said.

Inside the meetinghouse, Catherine saw Jane and Henry on two stools before a long table that had been placed in front of the pulpit. Behind the table sat the governor, Woolsey, young Magistrate Pendleton, and Will Best. Catherine walked to the edge of the table. In her hands were two letters, the one she had been given by Roger and Jane when they arrived, and the one recovered by Massaquoit. She studied the impassive face of the sailor and the energized expression of the woman she had come to know more fully not an hour before in the jail. Her mind since then had been processing Jane's confessions, revelations, and defenses. Now she would have to decide how to present her case, for as Jane's putative guardian it fell to her to present the evidence to the magistrates. She moved her eyes to the first bench, where Abigail King and her mother sat. Abigail held her sleeping babe at her shoulder. Across the aisle from them sat Minister Davis and his niece Grace. The young woman, recently recovered from her miscarriage, looked pale. She kept her eyes steadfastly on the empty pulpit.

There had been a steady stream of people coming through the front door and taking seats, their eyes fixed on the two defendants. The door, which had remained shut for the last ten minutes, now opened slowly. At first nobody appeared, and Catherine wondered for a moment if a sudden gust had blown it open, even though the summer air hung hot and still. Then a teenaged boy entered, and she recognized him as Jethro Martin. He was holding a wide-brimmed hat in his hands. He twisted the brim as he walked, and he kept his eyes on the floor in front of him. He moved to the rearmost bench in the meetinghouse and sat down. He looked as though he would gladly turn himself invisible if he only could find the potion that would perform that miracle. After a few moments, Rachel and Susan Martin, his mother and sister, hurried in. Each glanced at Catherine, then sat on one side of Jethro. The door stood open until Israel Martin walked in, his injured arm still in the splint that Catherine had fashioned. He stepped with careful tread and held his arm stiffly at his side, so as not to jar it or brush against anything. Still, at each step he grimaced in pain. He, too, made his way to the rear of the building and sat on the other side of his son.

Catherine did not know whether she should be

happy that the Martins had joined the proceedings or not. She did not doubt Jethro's veracity, but in light of what Jane had told her, she feared the damaging effect his words would surely have. She took a seat in the front row next to Abigail. The governor cleared his throat and looked out over the now filled meetinghouse, and then toward Will.

"I would have Henry Jenkins's confession read into the record of our proceedings." He motioned to Will, who stood up and placed a piece of paper in front of him on the table. At his full height, Will's chest was almost even with the top of the table.

"Though I cannot read it, I can say it again," Henry said.

Governor Peters cast a stern expression at Henry. "That will not do," he said. "You have made your mark on the statement that has been properly recorded and witnessed. Will Best, if you please."

The little man began reading: the formalities of name and place and circumstances of confession, and how it had not been coerced. Nevertheless, Catherine felt that Minister Davis's heavy hand was pressing on the young sailor as he offered his story.

"She, meaning the woman now called Jane, came to me and Billy Lockhart at the Sign of the Lion, a tavern on King's Street in Southampton, just before we shipped out on *The Good Hope*. She said she had no money but she must get aboard the ship and leave England. I thought it very bad luck to do such a thing, but I could see Billy was more than passing interested, and truth is, she was a comely woman, and that it is, I think, that caught Billy's eye. And I must confess I felt the devil stirring lust in me own blood.

"We took her aboard past midnight when nobody was on deck, and led her downstairs, where we found her a place in the hold. There she stayed when the ship left the harbor and for a week or so, until Master Whitcomb starts to come down to visit her. He did so because of Billy, you see, because Billy was serving meals to him and his sister in their cabin. He seen how the young lady was unwell from the beginning, and then she got a fever and died before we was more than a week out to sea.

"While she was sick, Billy started bringing the master down to the hold to have conversation with our stowaway. I don't know how that started, but I guess that Billy must have had something to do with it. Then there was a lot of talking down in that cargo hold, and Billy, he was always lurking about, and there was something about writing a letter. I heard that much myself.

"Then the sister dies. She never got out of her bed in the cabin. And one night, me and Billy, at the bidding of Master Whitcomb, we slid her into the water, I shudder to say so now. May the Lord forgive me my part in this and all that I relate. And then the woman down in the hold comes up to the cabin and there she stays until the ship reaches Newbury harbor.

"But things was not going so smooth with Billy and them two. He—that is, Billy—confided in me that he knew what they were about when they got ashore, how Master Whitcomb and the woman was going to say that she was his sister, and say nothing at all about the one we dumped into the water. And Billy says he did not care if Master Whitcomb called himself the king of England, and the woman his queen, but he would have some money to hold his tongue. Then one day, when Billy was otherwise tending to his duties, I was summoned to their cabin, and the woman seduced me, she did, like Eve giving Adam that fruit, so as to damn my soul to hell. I hope the Lord can forgive me. She says Billy has been a very bad boy and must be gotten rid of. She offered me her body if I would help her, and my flesh overwhelmed my head, and so I agreed. I got Billy to drinking his rum. That was an easy thing to do. And then she and Master Whitcomb come at him. We was on the aft deck. They got him to talking about the money he wanted from them, and while they was at it, I hit. He fell down, unconscious, and then we lifted him over the rail and into the water. As you know well.

"May the Lord forgive my part in this sordid affair.

"Signed, Henry Jenkins."

Will looked at the governor and then took his seat.

Catherine had kept her eyes steadily on Henry and Jane as Will read. Henry's face showed his concentration, as if he wanted very much to make sure that his words had been recorded correctly. At the more striking revelations, he cast his eyes up in supplication. However, at no time did a hint of a blush color his cheek, nor did any tremor or muscle twitch change the smooth surface of his complexion.

Jane, on the other hand, seemed uninterested in the account, perhaps regarding it as a description of events concerning somebody else. Catherine now understood that this impenetrable surface masked a mind riven and scarred by years of emotional trauma. Although she did not credit everything Jane had told her earlier in the day, she had seen into the woman's soul, and there found a deeply troubled past that explained, if it did not exonerate, her subsequent actions. Still, she wished that she could counsel the young woman to show a more repentant attitude as she sat before the stern faces of the magistrates and the equally unforgiving countenances of the citizens of Newbury, who looked at her with harsh censure from the benches of the meetinghouse.

"If it please you," Magistrate Woolsey said to the governor.

"By all means," the governor replied.

Woolsey waited a moment while he took Henry's measure. "There is the matter of Master Roger Whitcomb," he said.

"I know little of that," Henry replied, and his tone now had the saucy quality that Catherine remembered.

"Then tell what little you know," Woolsey urged.

"I was given a job to do by the savage what calls himself William, the one with the hat."

"And did you do this job?"

Henry shook his head. "Not for want of effort, mind you, because I take it as a personal point of honor to do what I say I am going to do. But that other savage"—he looked at Jane—"her savage got there first, and when I seen that, I decided better against it."

"And your honor?" the governor asked.

"My honor is one thing," Henry replied, "but my skin is another." He paused like a scholar remembering his lesson. "My skin, that is, which I now have given over to my Lord, asking Him for His forgiveness."

"Yes," Woolsey said in dry tones.

Henry pointed at Jane. "She would have you think I killed that man, but I did not. One killing is enough for my conscience. And I can only hang once, so what do I have to hide? I tell you I did not touch Master Whitcomb."

Governor Peters now looked toward Jane. "How say you to this confession?" he asked.

Jane shrugged, her whole body seeming to shrink into its exhaustion. "It is as he says."

"All of it?" Woolsey asked.

Jane seemed to stir herself. "Except who killed Roger. I saw him running away. I found Roger lying on the ground. I thought. . . ." She paused and bowed her head, as though to weary too continue.

"And the one they call Ninigret, although Nathaniel would be a better name?" Woolsey now inquired.

"You must question him yourself," Jane said. "You know well enough where to find him."

"That we do, and will," Governor Peters replied. He looked at Catherine. "Mistress Williams, can you shed further light?"

Catherine stood and glanced at the letters in her hand. "As you well know, this woman and Roger Whitcomb came to stay with me, presenting themselves as brother and sister." She walked to the table and put a letter in front of the governor. "That letter is the one Roger gave me. It is signed by his father." She waited while the governor read the paper and then passed it to Woolsey, who then slid it to Pendleton. After Pendleton signified that he, too, had read its contents, Catherine continued. "Do you gentlemen see anything amiss in that letter as regards the prisoner Jane?" The three men shook their heads after again skimming the contents and then staring at Jane.

"The bit about her red hair seems odd," Pendleton said in a soft voice, and then he cast a watchful eye at the governor and Woolsey.

The governor looked again at the letter. "It does," he said.

Pendleton relaxed, permitting himself a quick smile of relief.

"Magistrate Pendleton is observant, indeed," Catherine said, and she now placed the second letter on the table. Again she waited while it was read by the governor and the magistrates. She watched as their expressions changed when their eyes reached the end of the letter.

"Why, I see," the governor said.

"Extraordinary," Woolsey affirmed. Both now looked with stunned contempt at Jane.

"As I thought," added Pendleton, his voice now confident.

"Yes," Catherine replied. She retrieved the second letter.

"The loving father of Jane Whitcomb closes his letter by asking my especial solicitude in caring for his"—she looked down at the letter and read—" 'little daughter, frail from birth, having attained in adulthood a body no bigger than a child.' Not long ago, a crate arrived from Jane's mother, containing clothes for her daughter." Catherine looked toward the door, and on cue Phyllis and Edward came in, carrying the crate. They set it down before the table, and Catherine lifted the lid. She removed the bodice and gown and held them up.

"A fine sight I would be in that," Jane now said. "The poor little bird could not take the sea air and flew to heaven, I trow, leaving her brother for me to tend to."

"Oh!" The exclamation came from the front bench, where Grace sat with her uncle. The minister looked at his niece with a harsh expression, but then, as she began to sob, he held her to him.

"That one," Jane said. "She is the cause of much of this sadness, for she lured him to her bed, and he swore he would renounce me and return to his faith for her sake."

"He called you his Whore of Babylon," Grace said.

"Would you not want to know what he told me of you?" Jane replied.

"Quite enough," Governor Peters declared.

"Yes it is," Jane said. "But remember you how I played the part and bore your whip on my back. And then he was to leave me. For her."

"You must have wanted him dead," the governor prompted.

Jane shook her head vigorously. "I wanted only the letter. It was all about the letter."

Magistrate Woolsey now cleared his throat, announcing his intention to say something he had weighed in his mind and found of sufficient gravity to demand his most thoughtful utterance. "Know you the hand of those letters, Mistress Williams?"

Catherine shook her head.

"I cannot say. My correspondence with the Whitcombs was but occasional. They were my late husband's associates more than my own." She placed the two letters side by side on the table. "But anyone can see that they look very much the same."

"I heard her say," Henry interrupted, "that she could copy a hand as well as any man."

"Is that so?" the governor asked Jane.

"I say many things," Jane replied, "but I do not always mean what I say." She stroked the ends of her red hair that protruded from beneath the edge of her bonnet. "But the poor bird did not have such bright feathers as I."

"It seems to me," Catherine declared, "that I can put some of this story together."

"If you please," Woolsey requested, "for I fear my head begins to spin."

"This woman stowed away on my ship, for reasons she has only just revealed to me, and which I will tell you about later. While on board, she heard of the sickness and impending death of Jane Whitcomb, and she made herself"—Catherine paused, looking for the least derogatory term—"available to Roger, who in his grief and weakness, permitted himself to be seduced by her. In short, they became lovers. She must have told him her story, the one I will reveal to you, and he was sympathetic."

"Like Delilah, no doubt," Minister Davis intoned, unable to sit quiet in a building where he was used to presiding.

Catherine scanned the rear of the building and saw

Timothy there, as he had said he would be. She gestured, and Timothy stood up.

"Know you that man?" Catherine demanded.

Minister Davis looked over his shoulder. "I do not think I have seen him at meeting."

"Come now," Catherine replied, "do not force me to bring him forward to tell your relationship."

"I did talk with him once," the minister conceded. "I told him of my concerns that this Quaker, this Master Whitcomb, was a pollution among us, and that he had bewitched my niece."

"Did you seek him out?" Catherine asked. Out of the side of her eye she saw the governor's back stiffen, and she knew that she should not pursue this line of questioning much farther. Still, she wanted to take it one more step. "Did he not have your coin in his pocket when he assaulted Roger?"

"He did work for me," Minister Davis said, "and I paid him for his services, but I know nothing of any attack."

"Have you proof, mistress?" the governor asked.

"Only that I stitched his wounds, and heard his words."

"Uncle!" Grace exclaimed, and stood up. "You promised me!"

"I did only what was best," the minister replied.

"For you, no doubt," the young woman declared, and sat down, farther from her uncle.

"Return to your story, Mistress," the governor said, "and desist impugning our good minister's integrity."

Catherine bit her lip, realizing there might be satisfaction, but no advantage, in laying out how she had

contemplated the minister's possible responsibility
for Roger's death. She would, of course, have to explain how she abandoned that theory, but in the
process she could indicate how the minister's poiso-
nous contempt toward all Quakers, and Roger and
Jane in particular, made him guilty of creating an atmosphere in which Roger was fair game. Further, she
could present her belief that the minister was more
than willing to let Timothy perjure himself in his ac-
cusation of Henry. But she also recognized that attacking the man of the cloth would only harden the
governor, and probably Pendleton, against her, and
therefore Jane. She looked back at the Martins, and
saw in their faces that they, too, for different reasons,
would have her leave them out of this affair.

"As you please, governor," she said. "There is not
much more to tell. It is clear that the sailor Billy
asked that his silence be bought, and to protect himself, he stole the original letter. When he was killed to
make sure of his silence, his killers did not know that
he had stolen the letter, and kept it close about him in
a leather pouch. I have learned from Matthew that he
saw that very same pouch lifted by a seagull from the
dead body, and then dropped down the beach. It fell
into the hands of an Indian girl, and then passed to
Jonathan Peters." She again paused, and thought better, at least for now, of touching upon Jonathan's attempted rape. "It was stolen from Jonathan, and
whoever stole it, returned it to Roger, no doubt for a
price. Roger had it when he was killed, and it was because of it that he was slain." She watched the governor's and Woolsey's faces as she spun this tale. She

saw Woolsey struggle, and then lose the thread, but the governor stayed with her.

"And who, precisely, did kill him?" Peters asked.

"For that," Catherine said, "you must inquire of Ninigret. Perhaps he can tell you." She said this with one eye on Jethro Martin. He returned her glance with a nervous nod.

"Bring in the savage called Ninigret," the governor ordered.

Outside the meetinghouse, Lieutenant Waters conferred with Rawandag. Massaquoit stood between them as a buffer. Wequashcook had withdrawn a short distance away, well within earshot, to sit in the shade of a tree. He had his hat on his knees, and he was examining where the fire had singed it. The smell of burned animal hide was acrid in his nostrils. He appeared not to be paying attention to the transaction, but Massaquoit knew that the old Indian was following every word and gesture.

"I need to bring him in now," Lieutenant Waters said.

Rawandag pointed at Jonathan, still surrounded by half a dozen braves, variously armed with knives, bows and arrows, and one musket.

"I understand," the lieutenant said. "I will bring him back out in safety. If there are further negotiations, they are beyond my orders."

Rawandag scowled.

"The English want their priest back," Massaquoit interjected.

"I do not trust them," Rawandag replied.

"You do not have to," Massaquoit rejoined.

Waters gave the order, and four soldiers detached

themselves from the group and formed a square about Ninigret. Massaquoit walked to them.

"Are you ready?" he asked Ninigret.

"I will tell what happened," Ninigret answered.

Massaquoit nodded and took a position at the head of the group. Waters motioned them forward, and Massaquoit led them into the meetinghouse.

Inside, Catherine felt the tension sap the air from the building. The door swung open again, and she felt a moment's relief as she saw Massaquoit enter. Then the onlookers began an excited and hostile murmuring as Ninigret, surrounded by the soldiers, followed. She recalled how these same people enjoyed watching Roger's back laid open under the whip, and now directed anger at the man they wanted to believe had killed him. The soldiers led Ninigret to a position in front of the table and withdrew a few feet. Ninigret looked around, his expression proud and unyielding, until they backed a little farther away.

"We have heard various testimony that points at you as the man who took Roger Whitcomb's life," the governor said, without preamble. "What say you to that supposition?"

"I say it is true," Ninigret declared, and a hush fell over the audience on the benches.

"You confess, then, to the murder?" Magistrate Woolsey asked.

"No."

"Explain yourself," Governor Peters demanded.

"It is not murder, as you English use the word, when a man has a knife at his throat, and turns that knife against the one who holds it."

"I see," Woolsey said. "You say you acted to defend yourself."

"Yes."

"Why would Roger Whitcomb attack you?" the governor asked.

"He did not. I stopped him on the river road. I sought only the letter that was in his pouch. He would not give it to me. I said that my woman wanted it very much. He laughed at me. I reached for his pouch, and he pulled the knife I had in my belt. We struggled. He was a strong man, but I was quicker." He looked toward Henry. "I saw that one over there, and I ran."

"With the letter?" Woolsey asked.

"No."

Governor Peters whispered something to Woolsey, who nodded in agreement.

"Take him back out," the governor said. After Ninigret was marched out, Peters beckoned Catherine forward.

"Believe you him?" he asked.

"I do."

"What is to be done, then?" Woolsey asked.

"Nothing, until we hear from one more witness," Catherine declared.

"Indeed," Peters rejoined.

"Yes," Catherine replied, although, had she listened to her heart, she might have let Ninigret's testimony be the last heard.

"And who might that be?" Peters demanded.

Catherine looked toward the Martins.

"One of those Quakers?" Peters asked, his voice incredulous.

"Yes."

"They will offer nothing on oath," he said. "What good, then, is such testimony?"

"Only that it offers the truth," Catherine answered.

"Let us hear it, then," Woolsey said.

"Jethro Martin," Catherine called.

The boy, still clutching his hat, walked very slowly to the front and stood, eyes fixed on his feet, before the table. Catherine took the hat from him and examined it.

"I think I know this hat," she said.

"Thou shouldst," the young man replied in a voice that was barely audible.

"Speak up," the governor demanded.

"It is not your hat, is it?" Catherine coaxed.

"It is not," Jethro replied in a louder voice, keeping his eyes fixed on the floor.

"And where did you find it?" Catherine asked.

"Next to the body."

"Of Master Whitcomb?" Peters asked.

Jethro stiffened a little at the term and raised his eyes to look at the governor. "At the side of Roger Whitcomb, who was a member of our community. We know not masters."

"Let us not argue about his title," Woolsey soothed. "You say at the side of the body, which was dead, no doubt."

"He was dead, and the hat was lying there. I took it. Not to steal, but I cannot tell thee why. I was distraught by what I had seen."

Catherine hesitated, and then took the plunge. "Which was?"

Jethro turned slowly toward Henry and Jane.

"I saw her," he said. "Kneeling over the body. Putting something on his face."

"Was he moving? Did he struggle?" Peters asked.

"I saw no motion from him."

"He was dead," Jane declared, rising to her feet. "I wanted only to cover his face, for let the world know I did love him until he betrayed me."

"By your hand?" Governor Peters demanded.

Jane looked down, and when she lifted her face again, her eyes glistened. "His face," she said again, "only to cover his face."

"The rest of the story, Mistress," Governor Peters demanded. He and Woolsey were still in their seats. Will Best handed a sheaf of papers to the governor, bowed, and left. Abigail remained on the bench, suckling her baby. Jane and Henry had been led back to jail, and the rest of the meetinghouse was now empty, although Catherine fancied she still could hear the echoes of the shocked reactions to Jethro's testimony and Jane's statements.

"It is a simple tale," Catherine replied, "of a young girl forced by a desperate father into a marriage to an older man who beat her rather than loved her, starved her rather than fed her, and treated her no better than a servant."

Governor Peters frowned. "From what I have seen and heard, I have no doubt that the husband had just cause."

"I imagine you would," Catherine replied.

"There is no proof," Woolsey interjected.

"Only her word," Catherine conceded, "only what

she told me, knowing full well that the gallows might await her."

"A pretty story, then, no doubt," the governor responded, "to cheat the rope."

"I do not think so," Catherine rejoined. "I do not see such fear of death in her. Her life has hardened her."

"Proceed, then, if you must," Peters said.

"She fled him. That is all. And stowed away, as we have heard."

"She was not one of them, then, was she?" Woolsey asked.

"A Quaker? No, although perhaps with her rebellious spirit, she might have been comfortable in that community. She saw in Roger a wealthy young man and an opportunity to escape her plight. For what did she have to look forward to when the ship arrived in Newbury? The sailors who harbored her made it clear that they wanted payment from her body if she had no coin. Roger made no such demands. He fell in love, perhaps because he was distracted by his sister's death. They planned to stay in Newbury only long enough to establish themselves here to the satisfaction of Roger's parents, who would then settle the family business on this side of the ocean on him. They would move after a while. They talked of various places: New Amsterdam, or Charlestown in the Virginias. He talked of marriage. I do not know what she intended. But after some time, his ardor for her cooled, and he began to regret the fraud he was perpetrating. The whipping rekindled his faith, contrary to the intended effect. He turned to Grace, who seemed a more genuine lover. Jane despaired. She saw her life unraveling. She imagined being sent back to her husband. She chose a desperate plan to escape with the Indian Ninigret beyond where we could harm her."

"One man after another, it appears to me," the governor interjected. "She is no better than a harlot. Who should be hanged."

"On what evidence?" Woolsey asked. "The Quaker boy will not offer testimony under oath, as you yourself said. And it is unclear what he saw."

Catherine took a deep breath. "What he saw is uncertain. What she told me is that he was bleeding, perhaps mortally wounded, and she saw her opportunity to free herself. He was going to unmask their deceit. She could not have him do so. She took the knife, which still lay there, cut a piece of her gown off, and held it over his face until she was quite sure he would breathe no longer."

"But," Woolsey said slowly, "you say he might have died anyway."

"I was not there, of course," Catherine said, "but later I did see his wound. It was grievous."

"And she did not confess just now, and might not, given another opportunity," Woolsey declared.

"I doubt she would say to you," Catherine replied, her eyes on the governor, "what she has told to me."

"But still . . . ," Peters began.

"But still," Catherine continued, turning toward Abigail, "there is the matter of your nephew, still held by the Indians."

Governor Peters's face darkened to purple, but he struggled against his rage. "He is, Mistress. What do you propose?"

"A trade."

"And justice?" the governor demanded.

"Will be served well enough, under the circumstances," Catherine replied.

"Terms?" Peters asked, his voice resigned.

"She is banished. Ninigret is sent back to his people, and forbidden to appear in Newbury. Perhaps they will live together. Jonathan is released to you, but. . . ."

"Careful, Mistress Williams," the governor said.

"But," Catherine continued, "he acknowledges Abigail King's child as his own."

"He will not marry her," Peters said with emphasis.

"I would not have him do so," Catherine replied. "But he can pay for the child's keep."

"This acknowledgment . . . ," Peters said slowly.

Catherine understood. "Need not be public. He can avow his responsibility in private to Abigail herself, and then the necessary papers can be drawn up. Will Best can do so."

"I would serve that office," Woolsey said. Peters offered him a withering look, then sat back in his chair.

"Is that all, Mistress?"

"Yes."

"It is quite sufficient," Peters declared. He rose, and Catherine walked over to Abigail.

"Thank you," Abigail said. She turned her baby, now asleep, toward Catherine. "And young Jonathan thanks you as well."

•   •   •

From his position next to Jonathan, Massaquoit watched as Governor Peters and Magistrate Woolsey, followed by Pendleton, whose steps mimicked that of his elders, walked with stately gait out of the meetinghouse and joined Minister Davis. The four men stood between the English soldiers and Indian braves, each group keeping close watch on Ninigret and Jonathan. The citizens of Newbury now formed a long semicircle at the edge of the common.

The governor separated himself from his companions and spoke in a voice loud enough to reach every person on the common. "The magistrates, having heard the evidence presented, and having obtained the counsel of our minister, have reached several decisions.

"In the matter of the murder of William Lockhart, a member of the crew of *The Good Hope*, found dead in the shallows of Newbury harbor, we conclude that there is good cause to hold Henry Jenkins, also a crew member of that vessel, responsible for that death, and he is herewith charged with murder.

"In the matter of the murder of Roger Whitcomb. . . ." He paused as a rumble of voices lifted from the crowd of onlookers, and both soldiers and Indians reflected their tension in the stiffened attitudes of their bodies and in the tightened grips on their weapons. "In that matter," the governor continued, "we find suspicion does fall on the Indian Ninigret." He again stopped, this time in response to the absolute hush over the common. One Indian strung an arrow on his bow, and a soldier shouldered his musket. Governor Peters walked forward until he was abreast of these two, who faced one another. He

looked hard at each, and then at Lieutenant Waters
and Rawandag, each of whom had come to the side
of the man under his command. Massaquoit took the
arm of the Indian and pushed it down, and the soldier
lowered his musket. "We find suspicion does fall on
the Indian Ninigret," the governor repeated, "but not
sufficient or reliable evidence to reach a determination. He is henceforth banished from Newbury, but
we offer him no further harm."

Ninigret looked at his captors, and the governor
held up his hand.

"In time," he said, and looked across at Jonathan,
"in time for both. I have one more judgment to de-
liver, and that involves the woman we knew as Jane
Whitcomb, but who in truth we now know to be an
impostor whose real name we believe to be Mary
Norris of Southampton, England, wife of Samuel
Norris. Although the shadow of guilt for both
William Lockhart and Roger Whitcomb's deaths falls
heavily on this woman, we have failed to find sufficient evidence to try her for murder. Instead, she is
banished, and must leave Newbury by sundown tomorrow."

The citizens of Newbury had now heard their leaders' decisions, and turned to their neighbors to offer
their comments. Governor Peters waited until relative
quiet returned, and then, as though impatient to end
this business, he simply declared, "Release them!"

Lieutenant Waters urged Ninigret forward, and
then Rawandag pushed Jonathan toward him. The
two walked toward each other and paused when they
reached the middle ground between the two lines,

their eyes locked. They continued to their respective sides.

Massaquoit embraced Ninigret. The governor intercepted his nephew and led him across the common to the road that led to the harbor and his mansion overlooking the water.

Catherine, standing just in the front of the meetinghouse, had her arms around Grace and Abigail.

"It is done," she said, and squeezed the two young women against her.

"I think I understand Mary Norris," Abigail said, and shifted her baby, now awake and blinking in the sun.

"I do not know if I do," Grace said. "My thoughts are only of Roger"—she looked at the baby—"and what might have been."

THIRTEEN

THE PUNGENT AROMA of freshly sawn lumber floated on the warm morning air as Newbury citizens again gathered on the village common. This time they surrounded the newly constructed gallows, on the platform of which stood Minister Davis and the condemned man. The trial, based on his confession, had been swift. The Sunday before his execution, Henry had stood up in the meetinghouse and proclaimed his repentance. Two sturdy young men, serving as special constables for the occasion, had been stationed by the front door in case Henry had changed his mind and decided a dash for freedom suited him better than squaring his accounts with God. Catherine had listened to the young sailor beg God's forgiveness, but remained unconvinced of his sincerity, especially because Henry's eyes roamed to the door as he spoke and his expression seemed to indicate that he was still calculating his chances. Now, observing him on the gallows platform, his head bowed as Minister Davis offered the usual platitudes about God's love for a repentant sinner, laced with references to the parable of the prodigal son, the thought occurred to Catherine that if Henry's contrition was a ploy in search of mercy, it had failed, and he would soon have a chance to know God's disposition directly.

Off to the side of the gallows, on chairs put there especially for them, sat Governor Peters and Magistrates Woolsey and Pendleton. Catherine saw the grim expression on Woolsey's face, and knew that her old friend did not relish these occasions; it would take several days, or longer, for him to recover his equanimity. The governor, on the other hand, seemed if not joyful, at least content that justice, of a sort, was being served in his jurisdiction. Pendleton seemed unsure whether to reflect the governor's or Woolsey's attitude, and so succeeded only in appearing uncomfortable. Behind them, his hand still bandaged, was Jonathan Peters. He placed his good hand on his uncle's shoulder and whispered something to him. Catherine hoped he was talking about his arrangements to sail back to England on the next outward ship, for that was part of the agreement that had been reached with Abigail King, who would receive from the governor, as agent of his nephew, a decent stipend toward the support of her babe. An initial payment in the form of a lump sum to seal the deal had already been given directly to Abigail, who stood not far from Catherine. She was wearing a new gown and cap. Catherine saw, however, that she could not refrain from stealing glances at Jonathan, and she could only wonder at the girl's continuing to be drawn to the man who had used her so badly. Catherine took one more look at the gallows, where Minister Davis seemed to be winding up his remarks, then turned her back on the scene and started to make her way through the crowd.

"Are you not going to stay?" Phyllis asked.

"I think not. I do not take pleasure in seeing a young life so shortened."

"You do not mind if I do, then, do you?"

"Of course not," Catherine replied. "Stay here with Edward, if it please you both." It was not only her discomfort witnessing a man hang that was driving her away, but the piece of paper in her pocket. She wanted to reflect on it in the quiet of her own home. As she worked her way through the crowd, she saw all eyes looking past her toward the gallows, and just as she reached the edge, where the Martin family stood with other members of their sect, she heard a collective gasp, and she knew that Henry now swung at the rope's end. She stopped, unable to keep herself from looking at the eyes of the nearest witnesses. Some people shut their lids tight, but in those whose eyes remained open, Catherine could read the young man's end, and she envisioned his body jerking as the onlookers seemed to hold their breaths until he breathed his last. She started on her way again, only to find Jethro in her path. The young man's face was bruised. Israel Martin joined his son.

"How does your wrist mend?" Catherine asked.

"Well, and I thank thee." He looked toward his wife and daughter, whose eyes were still fastened on the gallows where Jailer Drake, who conducted the execution for a small fee, was now cutting the body down. It would be placed on a cart and taken to the side of the hill opposite Newbury cemetery, where it would be deposited in an unmarked, shallow grave. "We are thinking of finding a more hospitable place to live," Israel said. He looked toward his son. "Yesternight, he was accosted in the field by some who said we Friends are to blame for what has happened in Newbury, that God is punishing the village for permitting us to stay here. When he said what folly such an idea was, they were upon him."

"I regret that you feel you must leave Newbury," Catherine replied, "but I cannot argue with the wisdom of your choice."

"I just wanted to tell thee," Israel said.

In Niantic, too, the air was rich with the aroma of freshly cut wood. Massaquoit stopped near Peter, whose body glowed with perspiration, as did those of the half-dozen men of various ages who were working with him on the construction of a new building on the site of the old one.

"I thought you might be discouraged," Massaquoit said.

Peter shook his head. "It does not matter what I feel. The English are here to stay, and they have brought their God with them. If we learn to worship him, we can survive."

"Yes," Massaquoit replied, "but as what? English Indians?"

Peter offered a bemused smile. "As what we are. Perhaps you will join us for meeting here, instead of Newbury."

The thought struck Massaquoit as an alternative he had never before considered. He attended worship among the English in Newbury because he had to. Would it make more sense to do so on his own in Niantic? He would leave that decision for another day.

"It is possible," he said, then hurried on.

He found Ninigret and Mary Norris in front of the wigwam where they had been that night the English came. She offered an insincere smile as he approached, and he knew that she still blamed him for their misfortune. Ninigret motioned for her to pick up a bundle at her feet. She did so, with slow motions that showed she was being cooperative to avoid an unpleasant scene. She put her arms through straps on the bundle and positioned it on her back. She walked into the wigwam, and the bundle jangled. She was carrying cooking utensils, no doubt, but Massaquoit could not imagine that she would easily fit into the role of Ninigret's helpmate.

Ninigret looked after her. "Presents from my mother," he said. "She expects my woman to cook for me."

"Will she?"

Ninigret smiled, and then his expression turned serious. "I owe you my life," he said. "You and Mistress Williams."

"Your woman does not think so."

"I am sorry for that."

"I would like to visit you, after a while," Massaquoit said.

"That would be good," a voice behind him said.

He turned to see Willeweenaw. "My son could

benefit from your wisdom," she said. Something in her eyes suggested that she intended more.

He took a step toward her. "And his mother?"

Willeweenaw frowned, although her lips snapped back into a half-smile. "She would not be unhappy to see you again."

Ninigret embraced Massaquoit and disappeared into the wigwam.

"That woman," Willeweenaw said, "I do not care for her."

"But your son does."

"I have lost one to the English god, and another to an English woman."

Massaquoit took her in his arms and held her for a moment. He looked past her at the sad village, and heard the clang of hammers against iron nails from the site of the new meetinghouse. "I do not know where I should live," he said. He hoped she would tell him to stay with her in Niantic. Instead, she stepped back. "I cannot answer that for you," she said. "But I am going to try to convince Ninigret that he and his English woman should leave with me."

Massaquoit felt the disappointment like a physical blow. "Leave?"

She smiled at his distress. "Yes," she replied, "but I will be sure to tell you where we might go."

She took his hand for a moment, then dropped it. She went into the wigwam, leaving Massaquoit with the realization that in all likelihood she was slipping through his fingers before he had even extended his hand to hold her. And if that were so, it was so because they both had already lost so much that it was not possible to rebuild their lives together. He turned his back on the wigwam, and on Niantic, and directed his steps back toward Newbury.

Catherine sat in her kitchen, three letters spread out before her on the table. She had stirred the fire so that it now crackled. The papers would burn quickly. The memory of what they said, however, would stay in her mind, perhaps forever. Two of the letters were the original and the forgery from Roger and Jane's father. The new one was addressed to Magistrate Woolsey, who had given it to her that morning. It was signed by Samuel Norris. It sought news about his young wife, Mary, who, he had recently learned, had been seen boarding *The Good Hope* as it sailed from Southampton to Newbury. The husband professed his deep and abiding affection for his wife, and claimed to have no idea why she might have fled from him. He noted how distressed he was to hear from the owner of the Sign of the Lion that his wife had been entertaining sailors like a common prostitute. Still, the husband declared, he would welcome her back to his hearth and home.

Catherine read over the words, as she had already done several times, and stopped where she had before. To this point, she could almost believe that Samuel Norris was an aggrieved husband dealing with a rebellious young wife. It was even likely that he was a widower marrying again—after his wife died in childbirth, or of simple exhaustion from too many children—looking for a new companion, and perhaps more children. More power to him, Catherine supposed, if he had the means to support them and a disposition to treat them well.

But the end of the letter gave her serious pause. In it, he offered a money reward for the return of his wife, in terms that one would use to recover an escaped servant. And then Catherine remembered that morning in the jailhouse when Mary had lifted her gown and shift to reveal the deep scars on the backs of her legs and across her buttocks, where, she said, her husband's leather strap had taken off her skin. Those old scars, Catherine thought with a bitter frown, balanced the fresher ones opened on Mary's back by Constable Larkins's whip.

Catherine took all three letters to the fire and watched them curl into ash in the flame. Then she sat down again at the table, took out a piece of paper, and quill and ink, and prepared to write to the senior Whitcombs to explain to them how and why they were now childless.